THEY SAY IT'S A MYTH

Also by Kim Malaj

Ember in Time Series
Castle of Teskom
Recover or Yield
Protectors of Time
Guide Time Inside

Who Is Maggie
Twisting Hercules

My Mom is an Alien
Magic with Every Adventure
Figgy Meets Ernie

The Old Untold
Travel & Bird Journal

One Billion Million Trillion (Coming 2025)

Failed Book Cover Journals A-Z

Kim Malaj

They Say It's a Myth

They Say It's a Myth

ISBN: 9781958502181 Paperback
9781958502273 Paperback
9781958502280 Hardcover

Kim Malaj
Haxhaj Nd. 19
Bajze, Albania 4306
www.kimmalaj.com

This is a work of fiction. Names, characters, places, and incidents are either the product of the author's imagination or are used fictitiously, and any resemblance to actual business establishments, events, locations, or persons, living or dead, is entirely coincidental.

First Edition: November 26, 2024

Finding out there is more—is enlightening.

Prologue

"We've got company," Eli says, tapping on a screen near the door to the white chamber.

"How many?" Captain Wilson asks.

"Four, three guys and a woman. All appear to be under thirty."

Charlotte rushes over to the monitor. "Uniforms?"

"No," Eli says. "Best guess is the cryptic text Silvey sent was enough to tip her friend off."

"And the tall one there with the curly hair," Charlotte says. "Is that Baxton Auburn?"

Eli squints at the screen. "Um, I only met him once, but it could be."

"Captain," Charlotte says. "Is it safe to let them in?"

Captain Wilson nods. "It's probably better than letting them leave and grab the uniforms on the other side of the base."

"And Silvey?" Charlotte asks.

"Submerged," Captain Wilson says.

"Ok," Charlotte says. "Let's go, Eli."

Eli nods and opens the door to the white chamber for Charlotte. She takes his hand, and they walk towards the door to the hallway.

Charlotte hesitates when they reach the door. "What do we tell them?"

"Start with what we witnessed this morning," Eli says, pressing a red button parallel to the door. It clicks, and he pulls it open.

A woman charges in. "Where's Silvey? We know you have her!"

Charlotte steps back and holds up both hands. "Whoa, and you are?"

"Andrea Meyer." She points to her husband. "Scott Meyer." She gestures to the other men. "Bax and Gage Auburn, and you?"

"Charlotte and Eli," Charlotte says. "We own Greening Up."

"And Silvey?" Bax asks, stepping forward and towering over the pair. "Where is she?"

"Here and safe," Eli says. "Can we tell you how?"

"After you take us to Silvey," Andrea says, looking around the room.

"She's resting," Charlotte says. "It was an eventful morning, and I really want you to understand why she's here more than anything."

"Talk fast," Andrea says.

Eli nods. "We intercepted the FBI's attempt to take Silvey."

"How?" Andrea asks.

"Long story short," Charlotte says. "We watched two FBI agents, Michelle Vickers and Neil Carlton, handover a wad of cash to a hospital security officer. We followed the security officer and overheard him recruiting the others."

"Why were you at the hospital?" Bax asks.

"We wanted to speak with Silvey," Charlotte says. "We have a mutual friend."

"You mean Captain Wilson," Andrea says. "The message said she was with the captain. I presume neither of you are that rank nor any at all."

2

"Correct," Eli says. "We reached out to Captain Wilson because we found him down here before the tornado."

"Here, in this white abyss?" Scott asks.

"No," Eli says. "In the next room."

"With the reactor?" Bax asks.

"You know about the reactor?" Eli asks.

"Yes," Bax says.

"Well, this next part might not seem so farfetched," Charlotte says, pointing to the wall behind Andrea and Scott. "When we purchased the property, we received the original deed, but when clearing the land north of the silo, we found an entrance that we didn't find on the original plans." She waves her hand around. "And discovered the ramp leading down to this room and the attached spaces. One, the fusion reactor and the other a suspension chamber with the captain."

"What is a suspension chamber?" Andrea asks.

"A stasis device that literally looks like a glass coffin," Charlotte says. "I was very startled upon first sight. We found Captain Wilson inside. He appeared to be sleeping. We searched the room high and low for instructions on how to free him beyond the note stuck to the lid. We were at a loss."

"Then the tornado," Eli says. "And we saw the captain in the viral video and rushed back. The device was open."

"Let me get this straight," Andrea says. "You found a man stuck in a coffin and didn't call the authorities?"

Eli nods. "The note attached to the suspension chamber stated that the project was classified and to trust no one."

"You leave a man trapped and kidnapped my best friend," Andrea says. "I'm not trusting you with Silvey a minute longer." She turns and marches towards the wall, finds her reflection and goes around until she finds a doorway. "Silvey!"

"Wait," Charlotte says, racing after her.

Gage steps in front of Charlotte.

Scott and Bax go after Andrea.

Andrea skids to a stop when she enters the room and spots Silvey's hair inside the glass coffin. "What the hell!"

Captain Wilson stands, extending his arms out. "She's safe."

"Silvey!" Andrea cries out and rushes towards the suspension chamber. "What have you done!" She bangs on the glass cover. "Release her at once!"

Scott points to the chamber. "What is going on?"

"She's perfectly safe," Captain Wilson says.

"Explain!" Bax says, poking Captain Wilson hard in the chest.

"The white particles surrounding Silvey are nano particles. They're working to repair her cell by cell. We can't interrupt the process."

Bax points to the chamber. "She's alive?"

"Oh yes," Captain Wilson says. "The door will automatically open once the process is complete."

"And you know this how?" Andrea asks, turning towards the captain. She doesn't bother to wipe her tears streaming down her face.

"I spent sixty years in a perfect state of stasis," Captain Wilson says, waving a hand from his head down to his feet. "It's perfectly safe."

"She's stuck for sixty years?" Scott asks.

"Oh, heavens no," Captain Wilson says, walking to the side of the chamber. "She's only in for repair." He points to the screen. "And the process started thirty minutes ago. If her injuries were severe, it could take a few hours, but I promise she's perfectly safe."

"And Silvey did consent to the chamber before we placed her inside," Charlotte says from the door. "Eli and I have both tested the chamber under the supervision of Captain Wilson, and it is remarkable. I had a chronic condition that was healed with zero side effects and Eli had a bum shoulder for years that was repaired."

"Also, a minor heart arrythmia and some acne scarring all disappeared after my time inside the chamber," Eli says, stepping beside Charlotte. "That's what we wanted to talk to Silvey about this morning at the hospital."

"We read the article," Charlotte says.

"What article?" Andrea asks. "Silvey's not had any reporters at her bedside."

"A medic stated that he found a woman that was working at the base in a field a mile away and that her injuries were severe," Charlotte says. "We put it together that it was Silvey. And we really were just going to start the conversation today."

Andrea shakes her head. "The FBI. Do they know that this exists?"

"We don't know for sure if that's what they are after," Captain Wilson says. "Or if it's the time mechanism tied to the fusion reactor."

"Whatever it is they've been after Silvey and I," Bax says, "because of something you shared with them!"

"I was very confused when the chamber opened," Captain Wilson says. "Agent Carlton found me inside the Red Cross shelter and cornered me about the last thing I remembered and all I could say was Silvey Rhoades."

The chamber hisses and the cover pops open.

Captain Wilson rushes to the control panel. "Stasis complete."

Andrea steps away and watches Silvey's body float to the top of the white particles.

Charlotte rushes forward holding a hoodie and a pair of shorts.

Bax and Scott advert their eyes as her pale, naked body appears.

"What's happening?" Gage asks, stepping forward.

Bax holds up his hand. "Stop, she's naked."

Gage abruptly turns his back to the chamber and makes eye contact with Eli.

Eli holds up his hands. "I stepped out of the room when she was placed inside to send Andrea the message. I didn't see anything."

Bax glares at Eli.

"Seriously, man!" Eli says. "I have manners."

"Silvey!" Andrea says.

Silvey's eyes fly open. "Dre?" She leans over the edge of the chamber.

"Oh thank goodness," Andrea says, rushing towards Silvey.

"Hey," Silvey says. "Glad you got my message, but can I get some clothes."

Charlotte hands over the borrowed hoodie and shorts.

Silvey looks beyond her to the men with their backs turned. "You brought the calvary?" She slides on the hoodie and shimmies her way into the shorts, trying to keep the white particles from flying out but fails. "Alright, let's see if this thing actually worked." She swings her legs over the edge and reaches for Andrea's hand. "Dre?"

"You have a broken femur and fractured hip," Andrea says, taking Silvey's hand. "How?"

Silvey hops down and wobbles a bit.

Captain Wilson stands and claps.

The men turn around and gawk as Silvey makes a dramatic bow.

"Be careful, Silvey," Andrea says.

Charlotte smiles. "How do you feel?"

Silvey wiggles her toes, bends her knees, shakes her hips and rolls her shoulders. "Ready to go to work."

Bax walks over until he is standing in front of her. "You're actually healed?"

"Yeah," Silvey says. "You should take it for a spin. It may help your ribs and stitches heal up faster."

"Can I do that?" Bax asks.

"Whoa," Andrea says, stepping between Silvey and Bax. "Let's take a breath and process what the hell just happened."

Silvey rolls to her toes and taps her finger on Andrea's nose. "Bibbidi-Bobbidi-Boo, I am as good as new."

Andrea shakes her head. "Silvey."

"Andrea, relax," Silvey says, lifting the hoodie exposing her abdomen. "Do you see a single stitch or scar?" She turns giving her and the group a three-hundred-and-sixty-degree view of her flawless skin.

"No," Andrea says. "But how?"

Silvey takes a handful of the white particles. "Science, or maybe magic, but who cares! I've just skipped months of painful rehab and feel amazing. Please be happy!"

"I'm not mad," Andrea says, "just utterly shocked it worked."

"Same," Scott says, raising his hand.

"Me too," Gage says.

Silvey tilts her head to the side. "I'm sorry, but I don't believe I know who you are."

6

"Silvey," Bax says, "this is my cousin Gage."

"Ah yes," Silvey says, pointing at Gage. "Auburn Automotive, right?"

Gage nods. "It's nice to meet you."

"Does that kid Dusty still work for you?" Silvey asks.

Bax frowns.

Andrea smirks.

"He does," Gage says. "I understand he met you at the Job Corps program."

"Yep," Silvey says. "He never did work up the nerve to ask me out."

Gage laughs. "Did he stand a chance?"

Bax glares at Gage.

"He'll never know," Silvey says, stepping closer to Bax. He locks eyes with her. "Will he?"

Bax smiles ear to ear. "Not in my lifetime."

"Gross, kiss already!" Andrea says, shaking her head.

Silvey loops her hands around Bax's neck, and he leans his lips towards hers, but winces. She lets go.

"What's wrong?" Silvey asks.

Bax shakes his head. "I blew a few stitches." He lifts the edge of his shirt and green puss oozes out of the incision.

"Oh yeah, you're definitely going in," Silvey says, pointing to the captain. "Get it ready."

Captain Wilson smirks. "Aye captain Silvey."

"And thanks, by the way," Silvey says, gesturing to the chamber. "I really appreciate it."

Captain Wilson nods. "I'm happy to help."

Gage steps close to Bax. "You sure, dude?"

"It can't hurt, right?" Bax asks.

Silvey turns and smiles. "It tingles, and then you submerge into a dreamlike state."

"Got it."

1

Agent Neil Carlton taps on the steel door. "It looks old, minus the new tech." He inspects the newer small camera and card reading pad, both in stark contrast to the dark tunnel with cracked, faded concrete floors. "What do you think they are hiding?"

"Nothing good," Agent Michelle Vickers says, dusting off the knees of her white hazmat suit. "I can see a line of light under the door, but nothing else." She looks back down the dark hall at the other agents gearing up. "I believe we may be on thin ice."

"You saw them whispering too?" Agent Carlton asks.

"Yes," Agent Vickers says, "but I don't see why? We were given the 'by all means necessary' long leash to find and locate Captain Wilson."

Agent Carlton frowns. "Not our finest or cleanest operation by a long shot."

"You think that we were too aggressive?" Agent Vickers asks.

"Pretty sure that line was crossed when we became accessories to kidnapping a witness from an ICU."

Agent Vickers glares at him. "Keep your voice down." She glances at the other agents walking towards them. "We had to get something, and she was our only lead left."

Agent Carlton checks his phone as the other agents surround them. "I've got zero signal down here. Let's hope the command van has some signal up there."

Agent Vickers nods and turns to the waiting agents. "No weapons will be discharged. Is that clear?"

"Yes, ma'am," they answer in unison.

"Hoods and masks on, seals tight, and do not touch a thing," Agent Carlton says. "If there is any detection of radiation, evacuate immediately." He points to the gauge fastened on his chest before he zips up the remaining suit. He pulls the hood up and the mask over his face. He double checks the seal.

Agent Vickers nods to Agent Carlton. "You good?"

"Ready," Agent Carlton says, fastening his gloves on with a click.

Agent Vickers pulls up her hood and seals her suit. "In and out." She taps her radio. "In position. On your command."

"Command to Agent Vickers," Captain Denver says. "We've been granted permission to breech and clear."

Agent Vickers nods to the four agents holding the battering ram. "Let's go!" She turns on her body camera and motions them forward.

The agents ram the door four times before the damaged hinges give way and the door cracks open. They file in and spread out in formation.

A gaping hole in the rounded ceiling lets in an ominous ring of light inside the white-on-white expansive space.

"Clear," the lead agent says, disappearing behind a mirror in the corner of the room.

Agent Carlton slows and turns back to Agent Vickers.

She points up at the hole. "Escape hatch?"

"Or tornado damage," Agent Carlton says, shining his flashlight around the opening. "I don't see any scuff marks."

Agent Vickers nods and follows the agents into the next room. She stops short of entering, blocking Agent Carlton.

"What's wrong?" Agent Carlton asks, nudging her to the side.

"It's nuclear," she says, pointing to the coiled reactor in the middle of the lab. "And ancient." She surveys the dust covered equipment with hundreds of gauges and dials.

Agent Carlton checks the meter on his suit. "The needle hasn't moved. It's contained."

"Somehow that is not comforting," Agent Vickers mumbles.

"Clear," an agent says.

"Someone was here recently," Agent Carlton says, pointing to the shuffled papers on a desk. "No dust on the top paper, but definitely some on the papers below."

Agent Vickers leans over the table and aims the lens of her body camera down at the paper on top. "Command, are you seeing this?"

"Affirmative," Captain Denver answers. "Can you zoom in on the date in the corner?"

Agent Vickers taps the plus on the camera. "1961, sir."

A crackle of static answers her reply. She looks over at Agent Carlton. "Did you get a response?"

"Nothing, just static." Agent Carlton signals the four agents back towards the white room.

Agent Vickers follows the agents out of the lab and through a second door, also concealed by a second mirror.

"Clear," an agent says.

"Command, do you copy?" Agent Vickers asks, hesitantly walking towards a coffin shaped glass filled with tiny white particles in the center of the room. She stops when a squawk of static blares through her earpiece.

"Re—*chh*—turn—*chh*—to—*chh*—com—*chh*—mand—*chh*——copy, over."

"Copy," Agent Vickers says. "We're returning to command."

"Yes, ma'am," the agents say in unison.

"What do you make of that coffin?" Agent Carlton asks, falling in step with Agent Vickers.

"Bizarre," Agent Vickers says, pausing at the threshold to the white room. "Do you think Captain Wilson was telling the truth about time travel?"

"Maybe," Agent Carlton says, taking another look at the bare room.

"Hopefully, the team can collect enough evidence on the next sweep," Agent Vickers says, nudging him towards the retreating agents. "We better see what's going on up top."

They catch up with the others at the end of the tunnel.

Agent Vickers holds up her hand shielding her eyes as they climb up the ramp. "What is the wattage on those field lights? I can't see a thing!"

Agent Carlton stumbles. "Same!"

"Stop!" a man shouts.

Agent Vickers drops her hand and halts. "What's happening?"

A man dressed in a white hazmat suit points towards a zipped white tent. "Step inside."

"Why are you dressed in a hazmat suit?" Agent Carlton asks, walking towards the white tent. "Our meters never went off."

"We don't want to take any chances," the man says. "We'll spray you down here and then you can take off your suits on the next side."

Agent Vickers leans close to Agent Carlton. "Do you see the command van?" She rolls to her toes and stretches her neck. "Everyone here when we went down—are gone."

Agent Carlton turns away from the tent and scans the tall grass beyond the perimeter of the lights. "The hazmat team was in route when we headed down." He points. "Do you see something moving just there? There!"

"You're next," the man says, gesturing to Agent Carlton.

"Dude, there is a man in the shadows!" Agent Carlton yells, lunging towards the darkness.

The hazmat man steps in front of the agent with his arms out.

"Get out of the way!" he yells, pushing the man in the chest.

"Sir! You need to go through decontamination."

Agent Carlton points over the man's shoulder. "He's running away!"

"We have agents set up around the perimeter," the man says, blocking the agents every step. "Whoever that may be, they can't go far."

Agent Carlton raises both hands. "That's your head on a platter if it was Captain Wilson and you just let him slink away into the night!"

"Noted," the man says.

"Are you done throwing a tantrum?" Agent Vickers asks.

Agent Carlton snarls at her.

"You could melt the plastic covering my face with a look like that," she says, shaking her head. "After you."

He trudges into the tent without saying a word or looking back.

Thirty minutes later the two agents are escorted from the tent to a white van. They climb inside the empty van with an opaque divider covering the front seats from the bench row. The door slides shut and locks behind them.

"What the hell is the meaning of this?" Agent Vickers asks, yanking on the door handle.

The van rolls forward.

"Where are you taking us?" Agent Carlton asks, pounding his fists on the divider.

"My orders are to take you to the airport," the driver says. "Buckle up. The road between here and the airport can get a little bumpy."

"And where is Captain Denver?" Agent Vickers asks.

"You'll be briefed upon arrival," the driver says, turning the van out of the field and onto a gravel road.

The van rocks side to side.

Agent Vickers braces her weight against the divider and the door. "It's only a paved road to the highway between here and the airport."

"Unless we are heading to the small airport in Excelsior Springs," Agent Carlton says. "It has a single landing strip."

The van brakes hard, throwing them forward. They smack the divider and scramble back.

"Sorry folks," the driver says. "A deer just jumped out of nowhere. You guys, ok?"

Vickers points at Carlton's face. "You've got a bloody nose."

Agent Carlton tilts his head back. "Deer?"

"Yes, sir," the driver says. "A six-point buck, to be exact. Damn thing stopped in the middle of the road and stared me down."

Agent Vickers reaches for the seat belt, pulls it across her and clicks it in place. "When you see one, there is usually a few more."

"Yes, ma'am," the driver says, releasing the brake. "My head's on a swivel."

"Could this day get any worse?" Agent Carlton asks, leaning his head back further.

"I'm guessing they already know what we found and are taking us back to debrief," Agent Vickers says. "And if I'm right we've been reassigned."

Agent Carlton whips his head towards her. "Why do you think that?"

"The team on the ground is not our own," Agent Vickers says, pointing towards the driver. "And we're blind to our own escort. This is classic agency swap tactics."

"What the f…" Agent Carlton mumbles, pinching his nose and leaning his head back again. "And they let our only real lead vanish into the darkness."

"You really think it was Captain Wilson?" Agent Vickers asks, leaning closer to him.

"I would bet a grand on that!"

"And the civilians we were tracking are probably out there with everything we need to close this case," Agent Vickers says.

"They're kids," Agent Carlton says.

"They're all adults," Agent Vickers says.

"Barely," Agent Carlton says, bracing against the side of the van as it rocks side to side again.

"We've arrived," the driver says, slowing the van to a stop. The side door rolls open and two men motion the agents out.

Agent Vickers steps out and looks back over her shoulder at Agent Carlton's wide eyes locked on the small, sleek, black jet.

"I bet that grand," Agent Vickers mumbles. "I was right on the reassignment."

"Follow me," a man says, walking towards the jet.

The second man tails them.

The headlights of the van circle around the agents.

Agent Vicker's raises her hand to shield her eyes. She strains to see the driver, but it's too dark. She glances at Agent Carlton. "Did you catch a glimpse of the driver?"

"Negative," Agent Carlton says. "I don't see anything that would identify these guys, either."

The man stops at the steps to the open door. "You'll find your go bags from your issued car on board."

"And the commanding officer?" Agent Vickers asks.

"Also on board, ma'am."

Agent Vickers nods and steps up, but she hesitates. "Who are you with?"

"Ma'am, you'll be briefed inside," the man says with a wink.

"Right," Agent Carlton says. "Wink again and that eye will go suddenly black."

The man glances at Agent Vickers white-knuckled fist. "Ma'am, I meant no disrespect. I have a nervous tick in my left eye."

Agent Carlton laughs and pats the man on the shoulder. "Come on, let's go get this over with." He follows Agent Vickers up the steps.

Agent Vickers ducks at the entrance. The cockpit door is closed, and the galley is vacant. She steps toward the rear of the craft. Her eyes fall on a bald man with his back towards her seated in a tan leather seat. She pauses and looks back at Agent Carlton.

He shrugs and points towards the galley. "Never seen an agency jet with a fancy espresso set up or plush leather seats." He points to the eight seats.

Agent Vickers slowly walks to the seats across from the lone man. "Sir." She inspects his casual blue t-shirt, jeans, and loafers.

"Have a seat," he says, gesturing to the two vacant seats across from him.

"And you are?" Agent Carlton asks.

"My name is irrelevant." He grins and leans forward. "My rank may interest you, though." He points to the orange folders on the table.

"Shit," Agent Vickers whispers, scooting over to the window seat.

Agent Carlton slumps in the aisle seat.

The man slides the folders towards the agents. "You'll find a contract inside."

"A contract for what?" Agent Vickers asks, glancing down at the paper sticking out.

"Punishment or reassignment," the man says. "Depends on your actions."

"Excuse me!" Agent Carlton yells.

"Let me list the reasons why, Agent Carlton." The man leans back and shakes his head. "First. Your sloppy attempts to question, harass, kidnap, and assault civilians without any reasonable cause."

Agent Carlton wags his finger. "Now wait a minute…"

"No, sir," the man says. "Second. Your directive was to locate Captain Darryl Wilson and bring him back to headquarters for a few questions. And all you did was let him go and interview for a national news channel stirring up every conspiracy theory under the sun regarding the fountain of youth and time travel."

"He was taken by the owners of Greening Up," Agent Vickers says.

"So, they could locate him, but you two could not?" the man asks. "And third, disobeying a direct order to leave the kids injured in the damn tornado alone."

"We never received that order, sir," Agent Vickers says.

"Agent Carlton, would you like to share the order you received five days ago?" the man asks.

"What order?" Agent Carlton asks, looking at Agent Vickers pencil straight lips and her flared nostrils. "I never received anything but an all clear to get any lead by any means."

"Sure," the man says, reaching into his pocket and pulling out his phone. "Let's listen together, shall we?"

Agent Vickers elbows Agent Carlton in the arm. "Seriously, Neil, what is he talking about?"

The man clicks play.

"How in the hell could they help you locate a man they've never met?" a man yells.

"Sir," Agent Carlton says. "I believe they've met him more than once and I have a witness that has overheard Ms. Rhoades reference Captain Wilson in the present tense."

"The same Ms. Rhoades that just woke up from a coma?"

"Yes, but, sir."

"No buts. Follow the directive. Find and secure Captain Wilson. That's it. Leave the kids alone!"

The man clicks stop.

Agent Vickers vigorously shakes her head. "I had no knowledge of this conversation, and I believe that my partner here gave me a new set of orders on purpose."

"Agent Carlton," the man says.

Agent Carlton sighs and closes his eyes. "No comment."

"You coward!" Agent Vickers says.

The man nods. "If you speak of this investigation to anyone inside or outside the agency, you will be terminated and prosecuted."

Agent Vickers folds her arms across her chest. "You want us to sign a hush contract?"

"Want, no," the man says. "I wasn't asking. I am telling you."

"We don't take orders from a nameless nobody," Agent Carlton says.

The man smirks. "You'll only know me as General Hall." He points towards the cockpit. "They will take you to headquarters. The director would like a word." He hands them each a pen. "Sign."

Agent Vickers takes the pen and picks up the folder.

Agent Carlton stands and leans over General Hall. "I'm not walking away from this."

Agent Vickers yells, "Neil! Sit down!"

Agent Carlton straightens and turns toward Agent Vickers.

She holds up the contract and points to the seal at the top with the tip of her pen. "We need to sign." She clicks the pen and signs the contract.

Agent Carlton opens the folder and examines the embossed flaming torch on top of a world with two red atomic ellipses and thirteen stars seal at the top of the contract. "Is this real?"

General Hall stands. "Sign."

Agent Carlton reads over the three lines below the seal.

> *I, Neil Franklin Carlton, will return all the evidence, witness contacts, and findings to the agency director during the emergent brief.*
>
> *All communication about this investigation will cease post brief.*
>
> *Breaching the above orders will result in your termination, forfeiting all retirement and benefits.*

Agent Carlton clicks the pen and signs the contract.

General Hall extends his hand, palm up. "Thanks for your service."

Agent Vickers hands over her folder. "I'm keeping the pen."

General Hall nods. "Sure."

"I believe that I'll never see you again," Agent Carlton says, handing over his folder and pocketing the pen. "So, thanks for being a dodgy dick."

Agent Vickers elbows him in the ribs. "Seriously Neil!"

"Noted," General Hall says, examining the signatures on both contracts. "Wheels down in two hours." He turns and walks away. He taps on the cockpit door. "Wheels up." The engines fire up, and General Hall exits the jet without a look back.

They sit motionless as the cabin door is sealed and the jet starts its taxi.

"What the hell just happened?" Agent Vickers asks.

"This is all my fault," Agent Carlton says.

2

Silvey leans back in the booth. "I'm stuffed!"

"Breakfast of champions," Andrea says, picking the last piece of bacon off Scott's plate.

"Hey now," Scott says.

Andrea winks at him and takes a bite.

"Wow," Silvey says.

Andrea grins and swallows. "What are the chances we make it out of here without a single question from the table of men watching us?"

Silvey nods at the door swinging open and the bells jingle. "I think our buffer has arrived." Her dad walks over to their booth and leans over to kiss the top of her head.

"I see you didn't save me any scraps," Buzz says, chuckling.

"Never," Silvey says, patting her waist.

"Have they started their twenty questions?" Buzz asks, glancing at the old men looking towards their booth.

"Not yet," Silvey says.

"Go on," Buzz says. "I'll settle the check with Tiff."

"Already paid, but thanks dad." Silvey scoots out of the booth and gives him a hug. "And I covered their breakfast for the week." She glances towards the men.

Buzz chuckles. "Is that right?"

Silvey grins. "Yes, sir."

"Oh, now they are really going to drill me," Buzz says.

"Mom said to remind you about your heart appointment," Silvey says, tapping his chest.

Buzz rolls his eyes. "Yeah, yeah." He taps his temple. "My noggin works just fine."

Scott laughs.

"Do you guys still have reporters on your side of town?" Buzz asks.

"A few," Scott says, sliding out of the booth and offering his hand to Andrea. "But a few followed me here. I made a series of left hand turns around the town square until they got bored and retreated."

Andrea taps Scott's temple. "His noggin ain't so bad either."

Buzz laughs. "Go on, get out of here and do something that won't stress this old man out today."

"Good luck with them," Silvey says, glancing at the table of old timers huddling over their coffee mugs.

Buzz tips his forehead to hers. "They can talk, but you can walk, and I am thankful for that."

Silvey laughs. "You act like I was sucked up in a tornado or something."

"Silvey!" Buzz winks and walks towards the awaiting table.

Silvey flashes a wide smile and waves at the old men. She follows Scott and Andrea outside.

"Any chance you want to come over and start on an estimate for the electrical later today?" Scott asks, unlocking the car.

Andrea slaps Scott's shoulder.

"Hey," Scott says, holding his shoulder.

Silvey laughs. "I thought you had chosen the crew from Stanberry."

"Yeah, but we could always use a friend and family discount," Scott says. "From the best electrical contractor, we know."

"Unbelievable," Andrea says, rolling her eyes.

"I believe you'll be in good hands with their crew," Silvey says. "And I have other work to consider."

Andrea raises an eyebrow. "Silvey Lynn, what is going on inside that little blonde head of yours?"

"To be determined," Silvey says. "Next stop, please, I need to replace my phone."

"Absolutely," Andrea says, opening the back door. "Get in."

Silvey smirks and slides onto the back seat.

3

"Please secure your seat belts," the pilot says over the intercom. "We are landing."

Agent Carlton wakes and looks over at Agent Vickers. "Was I snoring?"

Agent Vickers points to the dark bags under her eyes. "Yes! Every time I was nearly asleep you would saw down an entire forest."

"My bad," Agent Carlton says, rubbing his face.

Agent Vickers braces as the wheels touch down and the jet brakes.

"Good morning," the pilot says over the intercom. "We've arrived and your escort is about five minutes out. Sit tight as we taxi towards the pickup."

Agent Carlton leans over Agent Vickers and raises the window cover. "Great, it's absolutely pouring."

"You're worried about the weather?" Agent Vickers asks, pushing Carlton's arm away from her.

"It's just icing on the cake," Agent Carlton says, unbuckling his seat belt.

The jet turns left, and a small aircraft hangar comes into view.

"Where are we?" Agent Vickers whispers.

"I'm guessing the small private airstrip north of headquarters," Agent Carlton says and stands. He stretches his arms over his head.

"I don't think so," Agent Vickers says. "Unless Virginia suddenly turned into a desert with cactus trees."

Agent Carlton races to the window opposite of their seats. "Son of a…" He slumps in the vacant seat. "We're in New Mexico. Look at the foothills to the east."

"It wasn't raining," Agent Vickers says. "It's a cloak rescinding. No, no, no! We are so screwed. There is no briefing."

"What do you mean?" Agent Carlton asks, pressing his face against the window.

The cloak clears revealing two black sleek sedans approaching the plane.

Agent Carlton squints and shakes his head. "The cars are tinted out and appear to be armored."

Agent Vickers releases her seat belt and stands. "We are officially at a black site. Hope you don't have any plans for the next three months."

Agent Carlton turns and looks up at her. "I've heard of this— never thought it was real."

"Rumors have honest origins," Agent Vickers says. "Remember the paper we signed."

He stands and nods. "You mean the gag order."

The cabin door hisses, opens and the steps lower. Cool dry air wafts into the cabin.

Agent Vickers wraps her arms across her middle.

Two armed men approach the jet.

"Ladies first," Agent Carlton says, extending his hand towards the open door.

16

Agent Vickers frowns. "Ha, then by all means." She waves him forward.

"Hilarious," Agent Carlton says, walking past her towards the door. He ducks his head and steps down.

Agent Vickers follows him to the tarmac. "Gentlemen." She nods to the two men. "Let's get this over with."

The back door to the first car opens and a thin, tall woman wearing a neon yellow hoodie and jeans steps out. "Search them."

The two-armed men step close. The agents comply extending their arms out and wait as they are patted down.

"Clean," the men say in unison.

"Agent Vickers with me," the woman commands.

Agent Carlton glances over at Agent Vickers. She shrugs, shakes her head, and walks to the awaiting car.

A black van arrives and two people are escorted to the awaiting jet with black hoods secured over their heads.

Agent Vickers pauses and looks them over as they are loaded on the jet with less grace than luggage.

The woman from the car shouts, "Agent Vickers, let's go!"

Agent Vickers takes one last look at Agent Carlton, and he mouths two words. *"The owners!"*

Agent Vickers nods once.

"Vickers!" the woman shouts again.

"Coming," Agent Vickers says, walking towards the car again.

The woman moves away from the open door and nods to her men.

Agent Vickers risks one glance back at the jet. The windows are dark. She folds into the car and the woman gets in beside her.

"Who are you and where are we?" Agent Vickers asks, glaring at the woman.

"My name is Director Gia," she says. "And our location is classified."

"The owners of Greening Up are civilians," Agent Vickers says, pointing to the jet. "Why were they here?"

Director Gia smirks. "That's also classified." She taps a switch on the door, and a tinted divider slides up between them and the driver. "You can ask all the questions you want after you've answered ours."

Agent Vickers looks out the window and watches the other car with Agent Carlton pull away. "I believe I don't have any answers."

"We'll see," Director Gia says as the car takes off.

"What the…" Agent Vickers says, looking down at a small needle retracting from her wrist. "What the hell!" She yanks her arm away, but her hand falls limp in her lap. Her head slumps forward, and her chin rests on her chest.

"Check with the other car," Director Gia says.

"Yes ma'am," the driver says.

Director Gia caps the syringe and presses two fingers on Agent Vicker's wrist. "Pulse slow but steady."

"Ma'am," the driver says. "The second agent is out."

"Proceed to the base," Director Gia says, releasing her fingers. "Let's hope they can provide more insight than the owners."

4

An hour later, Silvey returns to Andrea and Scott's car.

"Anyone feel the need for ice cream?" Silvey asks, silencing her phone's notifications.

"It's not even noon," Andrea says.

"And?" Silvey asks, glancing up from her phone.

Scott grins. "I'm game."

Andrea shakes her head. "You're driving."

Scott glances back at Silvey. "Do you need anything else from uptown before we head downtown?"

Silvey holds up a finger. "A new truck…but that can wait." She glances down at the phone flashing another dozen notifications. "Maybe I should have changed my number. This is crazy. There's over two hundred messages and I don't have that many contacts saved in my phone."

"Your name and number are listed on your service advertisements," Andrea says. "It's made it really easy for a bunch of reporters and I am sure a few random weirdos to reach out."

"Reporters?" Silvey asks.

"You survived a natural disaster," Andrea says, rolling her eyes. "And you time traveled to the sixties and back. Oh, and you were assaulted and kidnapped from the damn hospital yesterday. And now out here walking around because you were healed by some stolen tech."

"Yeah," Silvey says. "When you put it like that." She turns her phone over on the seat and glances out the window. "Was there any storm damage here?"

"Hail and rain," Scott says, pointing to a car lot as they pass. "They may have a hail sale at the lots here."

Silvey chuckles. "We'll see what insurance will give me for my old truck."

Andrea laughs. "It's going to be hard to replace old Rambo."

Silvey frowns. "Do you know if they found my truck in the field near the base?"

"They've started vehicle recovery from the pastures out near Vibbard," Scott says, "but the base is still blocked off." He winds the car downhill towards their favorite ice cream shop.

"We found Micah's truck near you," Andrea says, looking back at Silvey.

Silvey raises an eyebrow.

"You know—in the field," Andrea says.

"And that was where again?" Silvey asks.

Andrea turns toward the front as Scott slows to park. "About a mile from the base near the old Wright farm."

"Oh, the bonfire field," Silvey says, grinning.

Andrea laughs. "One and the same."

They pile out of the car and wait in line to order. Silvey glances around at the old brick flea market and the carwash behind the white ice cream shop with an old school cursive letter neon sign.

"It feels surreal doing something normal after everything," Silvey says.

20

"The usual?" Scott asks Andrea. She nods. He turns towards Silvey. "And you?"

"A caramel shake with mint chocolate chip ice cream," Silvey says, tapping her thin waist. "I think I need to put on a few pounds."

Andrea grins. "Let the record show…a woman says she needs to gain weight."

Scott laughs, walks to the window, and places their order.

"Do you think they'll find Captain Wilson?" Silvey asks Andrea.

Andrea shakes her head. "I hope not."

"Uh Silvey," Scott says, pointing over their shoulders. "We've got company."

A tall wiry man is approaching them with their phone out and the camera lens centered on Silvey's face.

Andrea steps between Silvey and the man. "What are you doing?"

"That's Silvey Rhoades," the man says, attempting to sidestep Andrea, but Scott blocks his path.

"And you are?" Andrea asks.

"Gray Turner." He taps his phone and thrusts it towards Silvey face. "Silvey, may I…"

"No, you may not," Andrea says, nodding her head towards the car. "Silvey's not taking any questions. Please respect her privacy and leave her the hell alone."

Silvey backs towards the car.

Scott's order is called from the window. He unlocks the car and waits for Silvey and Andrea to get in before retrieving their order. He returns with three shakes and slams the car door shut.

"The nerve of some idiots," Scott says, passing a cup and straw back to Silvey.

Silvey tilts her cup to Scott and Andrea. "Thanks for this and blocking his path."

Andrea ignores Silvey and is feverishly typing on her phone. "He's some conspiracy tiktoker."

Scott laughs. "The first of many that will come knocking. Sorry Silvey."

Silvey rolls her eyes. "Fun times." She chews on the straw. "Let's head back to town."

They ride in silence for several minutes as Scott weaves through downtown towards Salem Road.

"Scott, can you show Silvey the path of the tornado on our way back?" Andrea asks.

Scott looks in the rearview mirror. "If you're ready for it?"

"Is it worse than your street?" Silvey asks.

"In some areas, yes," Scott says.

Silvey slurps in a bit more of her shake and taps her temple. She swallows and sighs. "Mentally prepared."

Scott slows and points out the greenway repairs on the hole closes to the road. "They think it touched down somewhere between the old Shepherd machine shed and the golf course. And then again, near our neighborhood."

"It skipped most of the neighborhood behind the grade school," Andrea says, pointing back towards town. "Most homes between the golf course and our neighborhood will need new roofs or siding. Only a few homes in that area were destroyed."

Silvey nods and blinks her watery eyes allowing a few tears to fall. "But the patio homes that were under construction are gone?"

Scott stops in the middle of the road. "I completely forgot they were built here."

Andrea leans across Scott to look. "Damn, all that's left are the foundations."

Silvey nods. "One of my mom's clients was moving in next week."

Scott heads back towards town, crosses the train tracks, and takes a right down Silvey Road. "Does this road sign make you cringe or chuckle?"

"Neither," Silvey says. "I've heard it all. Were you conceived on Silvey Road, Silvey Rhoades? Your parents are so dumb they named you after a road. Let's ride down Silvey Rhoades, etc."

"Dang," Scott says. "Did you ever consider going by your middle name?"

22

"Ha, nope, Lynn is way too close to Evelyn," Silvey says, cringing. "Mom, can have it."

Scott slows and turns left down the first street. "Gotcha." He rolls past the first few homes and then slows again. "Wow, they've already got roofers working." He points to a house on the right.

"That's quick," Andrea says.

"Not really," Silvey says. "He's a roofer by trade. I've worked with him on a few projects."

"Is there anyone in the construction industry you don't know?" Scott asks, speeding back up.

"If they've worked in the Kansas City area in the last eight years," Silvey says. "Nine times out of ten I've crossed their path once or twice. The trade circle is rather small in scale to most jobs, considering it's a dying profession these days."

"Sad, but true," Scott says, turning right.

"Oh!" Silvey yelps.

Household belongings are stacked in haphazard piles in what used to be front yards of a few homes leveled to their foundations.

"Sorry," Andrea says, turning around to look at Silvey. "I should have prepared you before we turned."

"They're gone," Silvey whispers.

Andrea frowns. "Four of the six homes were flattened."

"Did they survive?" Silvey whispers.

"Only a few were home that morning," Andrea says. "Two walked away, but the others were found—after."

Silvey sniffles. "Devastating."

"I think that's enough for today," Andrea says, patting Scott's arm.

Scott nods and checks the rearview mirror.

Silvey's wiping away fast falling tears. She meets his eyes.

"Sorry," Scott says.

"This is the reality you two have had to endure the entire week," Silvey says. "I'm just catching up."

"True," Andrea says, checking the side mirror. "I believe we may have a tail, by the way."

Scott speeds up and turns right on Country Drive. "Son of a…"

"It's fine," Silvey says, rolling down the window and flipping the van off. "I've got this!"

"Silvey Lynn!" Andrea shouts. "Stop!"

Scott laughs. "It's not the first middle finger they've seen today."

"You didn't?" Andrea asks, glaring at Scott.

He smirks. "It was when we were playing ring around the town square. I got bored before they did."

"I swear," Andrea says, shaking her head. "You two need to grow up."

"Good news," Silvey says. "I'm no longer crying."

Andrea rolls her eyes and checks the mirror. "Well, it's not just the news van rolling behind us, but also the black tinted government plated vehicle."

Silvey yanks her hand back in the car. "F…"

Scott brakes and slows behind a car at the stop sign. "Still want to go back to your mom's house?"

"Drop me off on Fourth Street," Silvey says. "I'll cut through the alley and go in through the backyard."

"You sure?" Andrea asks, checking the mirrors. "If they catch up and snatch you again, your parents will absolutely kill me."

"And me," Scott says, speeding up. "I'm pulling down the alley."

"You may get blocked in," Silvey says. "The neighbor had his lawn mower out in the alley in a few hundred pieces last week. I'm not sure if it's clear for through traffic."

"A chance we'll take," Andrea says.

Scott nods and takes the last left off Moss Street. "Just be ready to bail when we stop." He slows and pauses at the stop sign, but runs the last one as the van behind them catches up.

"Scott!" Andrea yells.

"I looked both ways!" Scott says, turning right down the alley.

"Crap, it's blocked!" Andrea says, turning towards Silvey. "Go inside and lock the door. Wake your mom up and don't go anywhere alone!"

Silvey salutes and opens the door. She grabs her shake, phone, and the box it came in before shutting the door. She taps the top of the car twice and slides open the gate to her mom's house.

Scott throws the car in reverse and punches the gas as the van turns down the alley.

Silvey watches the van driver's face pale as they try to back out of Scott's way. Her eyes fall on Andrea, who is waving at her and mouthing *'GO INSIDE'*. She steps inside the gate and latches it.

"Could my week get any weirder?" Silvey mumbles, walking up to the back door. She slides it open and steps inside. "Mom, are you up?"

"Silvey?" Evelyn calls from upstairs.

"Yep, just me," Silvey says, locking the back door and drawing the blinds across it.

The front door rattles.

"Seriously?" Silvey runs to the front door and checks the dead bolt. *Thank goodness it's locked.* She peeks out of the long window and is met with the furry face of the neighbor's chow, Chewy. His long-wet tongue drags across the windowpane leaving a streak of saliva and possibly some crumbs behind.

"Mom!" Silvey yells.

"Why are you yelling?" Evelyn asks, walking down the steps towards the front door.

"Chewy is loose and trying to break in," Silvey says, pointing to the nose pressed against the window.

Evelyn rolls her eyes. "So, take him back over to the neighbors. You know he's harmless."

"I can't leave the house," Silvey says.

Evelyn stiffens. "Why?"

"I was followed home by at least one media van, and another tinted out ride with government plates," Silvey says, pointing towards the kitchen. "I came in from the alley."

"I'm calling the cops," Evelyn says, holding up her phone. "This is harassment, and something needs to be done!"

Silvey shakes her head. "I'm pretty sure they have bigger problems with securing the damaged homes and the cleanup from the tornado. Just call Mendy. She'll come and get Chewy."

Evelyn steps closer to the window. "Her car is gone. Pretty sure they go out to lunch after church." She slides on her shoes and opens the front door. "I'll go. Just lock the door behind me."

Silvey nods and watches her tiny blonde mom talk the huge chow into submission.

"At least someone obeys her commands," Silvey whispers, watching Chewy's fluffy tail wagging back and forth as they pause to look both ways before crossing the street.

Silvey closes the door and secures the dead bolt. She leans against the door and checks her phone. A new message from Andrea pops up. *Home safe and sound. You?*

Silvey types out her response. *All good.*

Andrea replies with a link.

Silvey clicks the link, and a video starts to play. The caption below the tan uniformed man says now live with the Pentagon Press Secretary.

"In light of the tragic tornado that touched down in Lawson, Missouri last week. The US Army and Air Force will have boots on the ground inspecting the former Nike Air Base. Please advise, all local traffic will be redirected at this time. And if you or anyone you know have had contact with Captain Darryl Wilson. Please contact your local police immediately. We believe that he could be a danger to himself and others." A picture of the Captain's face appears next to the man speaking. *"His last known contact was with Charlotte and Eli Montgomery. They are the owners of Greening Up and were apprehended early this morning and charged with two counts of assault and one count of larceny."*

The door handle jiggles against Silvey's back. She jumps away from the door.

"It's just me," Evelyn says, tapping on the window.

Silvey opens the door and stands back, allowing just enough room for her mom to enter. "Sorry I was distracted." She rewinds the video and hands the phone to Evelyn. She secures the dead bolt and marches towards the kitchen. "I need chips. Do we have chips?"

"Are you stress snacking?" Evelyn asks, following her to the kitchen.

26

"Yes. No. Well maybe. But I did suck down a giant milkshake and need something salty to even it out."

Evelyn doesn't look up from the phone. "I believe there are still crackers in the pantry. Chips may be a long shot."

Silvey opens the pantry. "Better than chips!" She pulls out the red box and tears it open.

"Can you please open boxes so they can be closed again?" Evelyn asks, shaking her head.

"Like father, like daughter," Silvey says, sliding out the plastic bag. "There won't be a need for the box. I'll put these on the list." She takes the pin from the wall mounted paper and jots down the cheesy crackers.

Evelyn clears her throat.

Silvey returns the pen and turns with the open bag. "Would you like some?"

"No," Evelyn says, holding up the phone. "What do you make of this?"

"I believe that they are all sorts of twisted about Captain Wilson," Silvey says, taking a handful of crackers. "But there isn't any information I can give them as to where he is now or where he could go." She tosses a handful of the cheesy crackers in her mouth and grins at her mother's gaping mouth.

"You really are Buzz junior," Evelyn says, handing Silvey her phone back. "I know you gave a statement to the press yesterday. But do you want to do any live interviews just to clear your name and get the media off our front stoop?"

"And tell them what?" Silvey asks over a full mouth.

"I don't know," Evelyn says. "You made a full recovery and are walking around town like you weren't just tossed a mile by the largest tornado ever to touch down here. People will start to talk and ask a billion questions…"

Silvey waves her hand. "And you want me to share the miracle that healed my body that was locked inside a secret chamber for over sixty years with the press and the fine citizens of this town to do what mom—stop the gossip about me and our family?"

Evelyn throws up her hands. "Ugh! No. I just don't want the center of my world to be crushed by a media van in the alley!"

5

Baxton paces the length of the porch rewatching the drone footage Scott sent him from the base. He pauses the footage over a grainy blur. He rolls it back frame by frame. "He got away."

"Who did?" Gage asks.

Bax whirls. "Dude!"

Gage smiles. "Morning, or should I say afternoon?"

"I thought you two left this morning," Bax says.

"We just went for a walk down to the creek," Rozanne says, walking up onto the porch. "Are you okay?"

Bax nods. "Scott sent over drone footage of the base."

"New footage?" Gage asks.

"Yes," Baxton says. "The guy who loaned us his jeep to find Silvey took this late last night." He turns the phone towards Gage and Rozanne.

They watch the aerial footage pan over a building and a lean-to. It pauses over the metal cover flush with the ground illuminated by several field lights.

"They found it," Gage says. He studies the footage as the camera rolls left, then right and pauses on a head poking up above the tall grass.

Rozanne hits pause and rolls back the footage. "Is that Captain Wilson?"

Baxton nods and takes the phone back. "I think he made it out."

"And you are going to go look for him?" Gage asks, raising an eyebrow.

"Um," Baxton says. "I don't know what I should do to be honest. He did heal Silvey and I."

"He didn't heal you," Gage says. "The white particles did."

Baxton smirks. "True…but he knows how it works, and it might be possible to recreate it."

"How?" Gage and Rozanne ask in unison.

"We have the schematics and a particle," Baxton says.

"What!" Gage and Rozanne shout.

"Silvey found a few particles in the clothes she was given after her session inside the chamber," Baxton says. "Plus, an encrypted link to the schematics to the whole setup."

"An instruction manual for the healing chamber?" Rozanne asks.

Baxton nods.

"Oh, hell," Rozanne says. "If they know that this stolen tech is real and that two civilians hold the keys to how to recreate it…they won't stop. They already have official boots on the ground."

"What do you mean by official boots?" Baxton asks.

"They made an announcement." She taps her phone and pulls up the broadcast clip.

Baxton shakes his head as the clip plays from the Pentagon Press Secretary. "They've just named Captain Wilson public enemy number one! Do you think Silvey knows?"

Rozanne nods. "I got the link from Andrea."

Baxton yanks his hairband out. Auburn curls spring out and down to his chin. He rubs the crown of his head. "This is giving me a headache."

"You don't have to run off or make any hasty decisions," Rozanne says. "I saved a plate for you. It's in the microwave. Eat and relax."

"Thanks," Baxton says, walking towards the front door.

"Plus, you have a date to get ready for," Gage says.

Baxton freezes.

"Dude, did you forget?" Gage asks.

"No," Baxton says, half smirking at Gage. "I made reservations on the way home last night and I promise this is the very last first date I will ever go on."

"Wow, cousin," Gage says, nodding. "Is that so?"

Rozanne pokes Gage's ribs. "Leave him alone. I've seen the way they look at each other."

Gage laughs.

Baxton rolls his eyes and walks inside.

"You were that lovesick once," Rozanne says, wrapping her arms around Gage's waist.

Gage leans away from her. "Hmm?"

Rozanne taps his chest. "And I believe you still are!"

He leans closer and nuzzles his nose against her. "Damn right."

"Hey guys," Baxton calls from inside.

"Killing the mood," Gage mumbles. "What is it?"

"We've got eyes on us," Baxton says. "And I think they mean business."

Gage and Rozanne look around at the empty yard beyond their cars.

"What are you talking about?" Gage asks, opening the door for Rozanne. They walk into the kitchen.

Baxton points at the window over the kitchen sink. "There is a drone on the edge of the property and it's not recreational."

Gage opens the back door and spots the hovering craft near the pond. He raises his hand and waves.

"What are you doing?" Rozanne whispers.

"Letting them know they are on private property," Gage says.

The microwave timer dings.

Rozanne jumps.

"And now they are threatening the safety and well-being of my family," Gage says. "Bax, keep your eyes on that."

Bax nods as Gage marches inside and walks to the spare bedroom.

Rozanne stands in the hallway just outside the room. "Are you going to shoot it down?"

"Free target practice," Gage says, swinging open the safe and loading his hunting rifle.

"Do you think that is the smartest move?" Rozanne asks.

"It's disrupting a beautiful Sunday afternoon," Gage says. He pecks her cheek and walks towards the kitchen. "Bax, has it moved?"

"Not an inch," Bax says.

"Great," Gage says, exiting the front door and scanning the tree line towards the drive. "Roz, turn on your favorite song and blare it on the porch speakers."

Roz laughs and taps her phone. The staccato guitar riff of *I Knew You Were Trouble* starts as Gage takes his position between the carport and the house. He levels the rifle and adjusts the scope until the drone is centered. He waits for the crescendo of the chorus, releases the safety, and fires on the word 'trouble'.

The drone falls into the pond with a small splash.

"Whoop!" Bax yells, throwing open the back door. "Great shot and timing."

Roz joins Bax on the porch and lowers the volume. "That may be a new reason to love that song."

Gage laughs and disarms the rifle. "Bax, eat and then we are going fishing."

6

Agent Carlton's eyes flutter open.

"What's going on?" he croaks.

He massages his throat and blinks until his vision clears. Slowly standing, he makes out a chair and a table in the center of the dim room. He braces his weight against the rough concrete wall until he steadies his balance.

"Hello?" He pushes off the wall and staggers towards the chair. "What do you want?" He clears his throat and smacks his lips. "I've done nothing to warrant this kind of treatment."

The single light overhead brightens.

"Have a seat," a woman says.

Agent Carlton whips around. *I'm still alone.*

"No, thanks." He straightens his posture and mentally shakes off the wooziness. "I'll stand."

The wall to his right slides open and the tall thin woman wearing the neon yellow hoodie from the tarmac saunters in.

"Agent Carlton. My name is Director Gia."

"Director Gia?"

She pulls down her hood revealing dark wavy hair past her shoulders. "Yes."

His bushy eyebrows bunch in the middle. "Just tell me what the hell I am doing here and why I was drugged!"

She pulls her phone out and turns the screen towards him. "Because you and your partner have managed to make a mess." She taps the screen. A reel of still photos plays out, showing Agent Vickers and him with the civilians they were questioning over the last five days. "I can say I am not impressed and slightly appalled at your tactics."

"Who took these photos?" Agent Carlton asks.

"Most were taken from CCTV," Director Gia says. "You two weren't very careful, and you made quite a scene at the hospital."

"He was a witness and we needed answers," Agent Carlton says, rapping a knuckle against the chair.

Director Gia nods. "And you thought drugging a witness and hauling him off in public would go unnoticed?"

"Like you!" Agent Carlton says, pointing a finger at her face.

"Did you see any witnesses on the tarmac?"

Agent Carlton picks up the chair and slams it down. "You have no right to question our investigation or me. I'm leaving!"

"You can try," Director Gia says, glancing at the opening.

Agent Carlton strides towards the opening, walking straight into an invisible barrier. "What the…" He turns holding his bloody nose and glares at her. "How did you manage that?"

"I wish I could tell you," she says. "Can we please get back to business?"

Agent Carlton pinches the bridge of his nose. "What do you want?"

"Start with Captain Wilson," Director Gia says.

"What about him?" Agent Carlton asks.

"According to the report, Captain Darryl Wilson was reported missing in 1962," Director Gia says. "But by his wife, not by his superiors at the Army Air Defense base. And then magically appears after a massive tornado hit said base after it was shuttered in the seventies?"

"Yep," Agent Carlton says, releasing his nose. He uses the back of his hand to dab under his nostrils and examines the blood on his hand. *Second bloody nose in less than a day.*

"And his whereabouts for sixty years?" Director Gia asks, lifting a single eyebrow.

"Classified," Agent Carlton says, leveling his eyes to hers.

"Hmm," Director Gia says. "Did you believe his story?"

"Again, that's classified," Agent Carlton says.

She leans towards him. "His story about being locked inside a chamber that kept him looking not a day older for the last sixty years."

Agent Carlton stares her down.

Director Gia meets his eyes and smiles. "And this didn't spark some kind of curiosity?"

Agent Carlton flattens his lips to prevent a smirk. "I don't know what you're talking about."

"It sounds like something in a science fiction or superhero movie, right?" she asks, winking.

He smiles. "I don't know what you mean."

"You know, we know. Why be coy about it?" She leans away from him. "Or is this resistance about the contract you signed?"

He raises his chin and shakes his head. "It's classified."

"Right," she says, tapping the table. "I'll leave you with this little nugget of classified information. Captain Darryl Wilson told you the truth."

"Don't react!" Agent Carlton thinks, schooling his face and relaxing his jaw.

She smirks. "Nice try, but your pupil dilation tells me everything I need to know." She walks through the opening.

He rushes towards her, but he crashes against the surface again. "Are you kidding me!"

Director Gia turns to face him, winks, and pulls up her hood.

"What is this place?" Agent Carlton asks, stepping back as the wall slides shut.

"Agent Vickers," Director Gia says, nudging her shoulder.

Agent Vickers groans.

"It's time to wake up." Director Gia circles the table and takes a seat across from the agent.

"Why can't I open my eyes?" Agent Vickers asks, trying to steady the weight of her head.

"The sedative should be wearing off."

Agent Vickers stands and wobbles. She crashes onto the table. "Ugh."

Director Gia leans forward and close to the agent. "Easy there. It may take longer to wear off than we expected."

Agent Vickers slumps into the chair. "Why did you drug me?"

"Protocol," Director Gia says, leaning back. "We have a few questions, and our location is undisclosed for many reasons."

"Undisclosed," Agent Vickers says and snorts. "Sounds like code for classified."

"Your partner loved that word," Director Gia says, smiling. "Are you going to be more transparent?"

Agent Vickers eyes flutter open, and she focuses on Gia's face. "You answer. I answer. Deal?"

Director Gia nods and points to her. "First question."

"Why were we lied to about our destination?" Agent Vickers asks.

"I believe that you were told the truth," Director Gia says.

"Wrong."

"What exactly did they tell you?" Director Gia asks.

Agent Vickers taps her chin. "I believe the phrase was they, meaning the pilots, will take you to headquarters. The director would like a word."

Director Gia nods. "General Hall told you the truth."

Agent Vickers looks around the room for the first time. The rough cement slab walls meet the glossy finished cement floors. *Only one exit, not even a visible air duct.* She levels her glare at Gia.

"You're wrong," Agent Vickers says. "I've been to headquarters several times. This is not…standard."

"You assumed to know which headquarters he was referencing." Director Gia smiles. "My turn. Did you know that Captain Wilson was part of a shelved experimental program?"

"I can't talk about the case," Agent Vickers says, keeping her eyes locked on hers. "You know that it's…"

"Classified," Director Gia says, finishing her sentence. "Yes, yes. We're aware of what you signed." She waves towards the entrance. A man enters and hands her a green folder. She turns it towards Agent Vickers. "Inside you will find that upon entering the jet you and your partner Agent Carlton were assigned to a new director."

Agent Vickers glances down at the black-lined document. "It appears redacted…or at least ninety percent of it." She shoves it back towards Gia. "Nice try, but I am not a newbie. I believe this parlor trick got you nowhere with Agent Carlton."

"I've just received the orders to pass along," Director Gia says, turning the top page over and sliding the open folder back towards Agent Vickers.

Agent Vickers picks up the second page and examines her signature on the contract. "How do you have the original?"

"Easy," Director Gia says, nodding towards a second man sauntering into the room. "General Hall returned an hour ago."

Agent Vickers looks him over. "Oh, what did Agent Carlton call you?" She snaps. "A dodgy dick."

General Hall frowns. "Unnecessary, but yes, I believe that was his term of endearment. Welcome to Project Q."

"Explain," Agent Vickers says, watching Director Gia and the first man retreat.

"We are a specialized division."

Agent Vickers folds her arms across her chest. "Special division of what?"

He flips the folder over and points to the black and white eagle emblem.

Agent Vickers leans forward and narrows her eyes on the small text circling the eagle. "Department of Science and

Technology." She looks up at his bemused grin. "Seriously, we've been demoted to a state department."

General Hall shakes his head. "We could've fired you two without your pensions." He checks his watch. "You and Agent Carlton will have thirty minutes to shower, change, and eat before you begin to question Mr. Baxton Auburn."

"He's here?" Agent Vickers asks.

"Yes," General Hall says.

Agent Vickers stands. "But you said they didn't know anything?"

"We believe that he doesn't know anything about Captain Wilson," he says. "But they were spotted at the base."

"They?"

"His cousin Gage," General Hall says.

"How did this go down?" Agent Vickers asks.

"We have a team," General Hall says. "We are working to draw Miss Rhoades out as we speak. And hopefully, gain a lead to what they were doing at the base."

Agent Vickers narrows her eyes. "You said we were sloppy and couldn't get the job done. Why us?"

"You two established first contact with them," General Hall says, tapping the folder. "And frankly, your presence will further agitate the situation. We are counting on that adrenaline rush and crash to get what we need."

"Let me get this straight," Agent Vickers says, pointing at General Hall. "You want us to be pawns."

General Hall smirks. "Yes, ma'am."

7

"Ugh!" Silvey tosses a dress on the pile of clothes mounted on her bed. "Why!"

Andrea laughs.

Silvey picks up her phone and glares at Andrea. "It's not funny. I don't understand why I can't figure out what to wear." She plops in the center of the pile. "It's not like it's my first date ever."

"Silvey Lynn," Andrea says, shaking her head. "You think it might be because you actually really like Bax?"

Silvey rolls her eyes. "What did you call it? Trauma bond?"

Andrea laughs again. "Maybe, but he really seems to be smitten."

Silvey shakes her head. "It's mutual." Her cheeks flush.

"Are you blushing?" Andrea asks.

"No!" Silvey turns the phone away from her face, showing Andrea the pile. "Pick please. Blue, teal, or black?"

"Teal," Andrea says. "And the wedge sandals that I know are buried somewhere in your closet."

"Fine," Silvey says. "Hair up or down?"

"Half up."

Silvey holds up the teal dress and turns with the phone towards the mirror. "It's not too much?"

"It's a t-shirt dress," Andrea says. "Would you rather wear a potato sack?"

Silvey laughs. "It's fitted, Dre."

"And Bax will love it."

Silvey grins. "Alright, fine. Are you and Scott staying in tonight?"

"Yes," Andrea says. "Be careful out there. You know the press are still patrolling and with Captain Wilson still out there, they will be after any new leads."

Silvey nods. "I know. I just hope he is hiding somewhere safe."

"Silvey!" Evelyn yells.

"Mom's yelling," Silvey says, opening her bedroom door. "On the phone with Dre."

"We just got a package," Evelyn says. "It looks suspicious."

"Got to go Dre," Silvey says.

"Did she say something suspicious?" Andrea asks.

"I'll call you back," Silvey says.

Andrea nods.

Silvey ends the call and walks downstairs. She stops next to her mom at the front door. "Did you see who dropped it off?"

Evelyn taps the long window. "I saw a blacked-out SUV pull away from the curb when I moved the curtain to see who knocked."

Silvey pulls back the curtain. She cranes her neck to look up and down the street. Her eyes land on her full name, neatly printed in all caps in red, across the center of an envelope on the bright blue welcome mat.

"Um," Silvey says, stepping away from the window. "You're right, that looks very suspicious."

Evelyn unlocks the front door.

"Wait!" Silvey says, holding her hand up, palm out.

Evelyn pauses with her hand on the knob.

"Do you still have gloves in your salon bag?" Silvey asks.

Evelyn nods and walks to the hall closet. She pulls out a large pink tote and rummages through the contents. "Bingo." She holds up a box of disposable gloves.

"Great," Silvey says. "I'll open it outside just in case."

Evelyn pulls on a pair of black gloves and shakes her head. "No. I'll do this, but keep your phone dialed to 911."

"Mom," Silvey says.

"Just in case," Evelyn says. "I can't risk anything happening to you…or your father will have another heart attack because something else happened to you on my watch."

Silvey frowns and cautiously opens the front door.

Evelyn steps out and looks around before she bends to pick up the thin envelope. She turns it over and unclasps the gold metal tee. The folded lip pops open. "It wasn't sealed shut." She tips the contents out away from her. A single large paper floats down to the ground. She bends over and straightens immediately.

"What is it?" Silvey asks, stepping close to Evelyn. "No!"

Baxton's chiseled face, auburn curly hair, and his hazel-green eyes are staring directly up at Silvey.

"That's the boy that worked for Micah, right?" Evelyn asks.

Silvey nods. "Can you flip it over?"

Evelyn turns the photo over. Two words, WE KNOW, printed in the same red ink as Silvey's name on the envelope.

"What the…" Silvey steps back. "Mom, leave it. Let's go inside."

Evelyn hesitates.

"Mom!" Silvey says.

"Fine," Evelyn says, following Silvey inside.

Silvey locks the front door and dials Baxton's number. It rings four times before it goes to voicemail. "Shit!"

"What's going on?" Evelyn asks.

"Baxton isn't answering. I'm calling his cousin's wife Rozanne." Silvey paces the entryway as the call connects and starts to ring, but it goes to voicemail too. "No, no, no!" She dials Andrea.

"Silvey," Andrea says, answering before it rings.

"Baxton and Rozanne aren't answering," Silvey says, breathless. "Do you have Gage's number?"

"What's wrong?" Andrea asks.

Silvey explains the delivery and the contents.

"Oh, that's not good," Andrea says. "Scott, get in here!"

Silvey listens to Andrea convey their conversation to Scott and her phone dings.

"Scott just texted you Gage's number," Andrea says. "Call me back."

Silvey taps her new message and dials the number. It rings once before going straight to voicemail. "No!"

Evelyn waves her hand drawing Silvey's attention.

Silvey holds up her phone. "Voicemails! All three went to voicemail."

"Do you know where they live?" Evelyn asks, holding her phone up to her ear.

"Who are you calling?" Silvey asks.

"The cops," Evelyn says.

"Wait," Silvey says.

Evelyn shakes her head and points to the front door. "That's a threat, and they are unaccounted for. We shouldn't wait."

"Mom," Silvey says.

"Their last name was Auburn, right?" Evelyn asks, walking towards the kitchen.

Silvey nods and leans against the front door. She slides to the floor and calls Andrea.

"Hey," Andrea says.

"Mom's calling the cops," Silvey says. "Gage's phone went straight to voicemail. Do you know where they live?"

"A few miles past Wabash," Andrea says. "From Rozanne's description, it's tucked back away from the road."

"A perfect place to ambush without witnesses," Silvey says.

"What?" Andrea asks. "You don't think…"

"The picture was taken outside. He was staring at the lens."

"Silvey!" Evelyn yells.

Silvey scrambles to her feet and runs towards the kitchen, crashing into Evelyn.

"The police were called to the Auburn house thirty minutes ago," Evelyn whispers, covering the receiver on her phone.

"Why?" Silvey asks.

"Yes," Evelyn says, holding up a finger. "I'm still here." She holds a hand over her heart. "Yes. I understand. Thank you." She ends the call with a shaky finger.

"Mom, what did they say?" Silvey asks, placing her phone on speaker and taking her mom's trembling hand.

"They received a call from Rozanne's number," Evelyn says.

"What are you not saying?" Silvey asks, looking her pale face over.

"There were shouts in the background telling the caller to get down on the ground or we'll…"

"We'll what?" Andrea asks.

Evelyn glances down at Silvey's phone. "Shoot."

"Oh God," Andrea and Silvey say in unison.

"An officer is coming here to pick up the photo and envelope," Evelyn says. "We need to get you somewhere safe. They obviously know you are here."

Silvey shakes her head.

"We can't just hide out while Bax and his family could be in trouble," Silvey says.

"Evelyn's right," Andrea says, switching the call to video mode. "Silvey look at me!"

"No," Silvey says, looking down at the phone. "You can't be serious."

"Go to Scott's godmother's house," Andrea says. "Do you remember how to get there?"

"Yes, but," Silvey says.

"No buts." Andrea points at Silvey. "You can't hide out here in town. They'll track you down. Leave your phone. There is a landline at the house. Only call if you absolutely need something. I'll call you every hour with updates."

"Is it safe?" Evelyn asks.

"It's the only place close but not linked to any of us on paper," Andrea says. "Plus, there are multiple ways out of the house if it comes to that."

Silvey nods. "She's right." She points towards the front door. "Mom, after the police pick up the photo, go to your friend Pam's house. It's not safe here."

Evelyn stomps her foot. "You are not going alone!"

"Evelyn," Andrea says, waving at the camera.

Silvey turns the phone towards her mom.

"Scott's godmother is a former city cop and she's armed to the teeth."

Scott comes into view. He waves. "She's a great shot. I promise Silvey will be very safe."

Evelyn pinches her lips together. "I'm telling Buzz. He needs to know what's going on."

Silvey grins. "That's great mom. I'll go pack and I guess take your car?"

"No," Andrea and Scott say in unison.

Silvey holds up the phone. "Then how?"

"Don't hate me," Andrea says. "Justin is on his way over."

"Oh, hell no!" Silvey says.

"Silvey," Andrea pleads. "He knows the road out there and he's in a dealership car this week."

"And would rather see me six feet under than safely tucked away," Silvey says.

Evelyn swats Silvey's arm. "He loves you."

"And cheated on me a billion times or have you forgotten."

Evelyn flares her nostrils. "No, I can't forgive and forget the bastard, but Silvey you two were oil and water from the beginning. Like Buzz and I."

"Mom," Silvey says.

Evelyn waves her hand. "Buzz would never physically hurt me, and Justin knows Buzz would obliterate him if anything ever happened to you."

Silvey rolls her eyes. "I hate all three of you right now."

"Silve…" Andrea says.

Silvey ends the call and hands her mom the phone. "I'm going to pack a few things."

"Silvey," Evelyn says.

"I can't believe this is happening," Silvey says, stomping out of the kitchen. "When you talk to dad, tell him this was not my idea."

Evelyn starts towards Silvey, but there is a knock on the front door. "Coming." She swings open the front door. An officer is holding the photo and envelope. "We didn't touch it with our hands." She holds up her black-gloved hands.

He nods. "I'll need a description of the vehicle you saw."

"Sure, a blacked-out SUV," Evelyn says, taking off the gloves.

"Ford, Chevy?"

"Tahoe, I think," Evelyn says.

"Headed in which direction?" the officer asks.

She points to the right. "Towards town."

"Approximately what time was this?" the officer asks.

"Twenty-five minutes ago, or so," Evelyn says.

"And your relationship to the man in the photo?" the officer asks.

"My daughter Silvey worked with him out at the old nike base."

The officer's jaw falls open. "She was the one abducted from the hospital?"

Evelyn nods. "Unfortunately."

"Does she know anything about Captain Wilson?" the officer asks, stepping up on the threshold to the house.

"No sir," Evelyn says. "Please let us know if you have any more questions or leads to this delivery." She closes the front door and locks it before the officer could ask another question.

"Is he gone?" Silvey whispers from upstairs.

"Not yet," Evelyn says, pulling back the curtain a hair. "He's calling someone."

"Tell Andrea I'll meet Justin at the back gate," Silvey says, sneaking past the front door. "I've got three days of clothes." She pats the backpack. "I'll do laundry there. The second you hear anything about the Auburn's whereabouts call Andrea."

Evelyn pulls her into a hug. "Be safe."

8

"Scott," Andrea says, pointing to yellow crime tape draped across a driveway. "Can you pull over?"

Scott signals and pulls off onto the side of the road. "You think this is their place?"

"Rozanne said they lived two miles past Wabash." She points at the mailbox. "Auburn." She releases her seat belt.

"Where are you going?" Scott asks.

"I need to know how much shit Silvey is in," Andrea says, opening the passenger door. "Coming?"

Scott sighs. "Sure, why not." He checks for traffic and hesitantly swings open his door.

Andrea and Scott jog across the county road and duck under the crime tape. They cautiously walk to the accompaniment of their feet crunching on the gravel.

"Do you think they've cleared the scene?" Andrea whispers.

Scott frowns. "We don't know enough to assume there was a scene to clear."

"True, but you heard what the dispatcher told Evelyn."

They pause when the narrow-wooded drive opens to the plot of land surrounding the home with a picturesque wrap-around porch.

"It's stunning," Andrea says.

Scott nods. "It's very nice."

"Understatement," Andrea says, walking towards the front door. "That's Rozanne's car and Gage's truck. Maybe they're home."

A crash of brush to the left makes Andrea jump.

Scott whirls and searches the line of trees. "Who's there?"

"Are you alone?" a woman calls.

"Rozanne?" Andrea asks, searching the trees. "Are you hiding up in a tree?"

"Are you alone?" Rozanne calls again.

"It's just Scott and I," Andrea says, pointing to Scott.

"Were you followed?"

"No," Scott says.

"Are you okay?" Andrea asks.

"No," Rozanne says. "But physically fine."

"Where are you?" Andrea asks, searching the trees again.

"Up here," Rozanne says, pulling back a few willow branches. She waves down at them.

"Why are you in the tree?" Andrea asks. "And why is there crime tape draped over the driveway?"

"Gage made me run when they came up the hill," Rozanne says.

"They?" Andrea turns and looks around.

"I'm coming down," Rozanne says.

Andrea and Scott jog over to the tree.

"Is it just me or is that tree winking at me?" Scott asks.

Rozanne climbs down the back of the tree. "My Great Grandma's idea of a prank that's held up for nearly a century."

Scott chuckles and examines the structure overhead. "A treehouse?"

46

"Yep, courtesy of a drifter a few years back." Rozanne hops off the last rung and wipes her hands on her jeans.

Andrea looks her over. "How long were you up there?"

"Two hours or so," Rozanne says, shaking her head. "I need something strong to drink." She turns and marches towards the house.

"What happened?" Andrea and Scott ask in unison, following Rozanne.

"They took Gage and Bax," Rozanne says.

"Who are 'they'?" Scott asks.

"I wish I knew," Rozanne says. "Bax caught a drone hovering over the pond this afternoon. Gage shot it down and when they went to fish it out, several men came up the hill beyond the pond with guns pointed at Bax and Gage."

"What the hell!" Andrea mutters.

"I called for help but dropped my phone as I sprinted for the trees," Rozanne says. "And by the time the cops came they were gone, and I stayed hidden because…"

"You don't know who you can trust?" Andrea asks.

Rozanne nods and holds open the front door. "Come in, please."

"That's awful," Scott says. "How can we help?"

"I am happy you're here," Rozanne says, closing and locking the front door. "But not sure how you knew something was wrong." She gestures for them to follow her.

Andrea pulls out a chair from the small table. "I'll get it. Have a seat."

Rozanne sits.

"I'll serve," Scott says, pointing to the other chair. "You explain."

Andrea grins.

Scott bows a little and winks. "Tea or coffee?"

"Irish coffee," Rozanne says.

"Same, please," Andrea says, sitting across from Rozanne. "Silvey received a photo of Bax with the words 'WE KNOW' written on the back. It was delivered to her front door."

"We know?" Rozanne whispers, furrowing her brow.

Scott takes down three mugs and places the filter in the basket. "The photo was likely taken by the drone. Silvey mentioned it was a closeup of him." He scoops the coffee into the filter and fills the pot.

"Is Silvey ok?" Rozanne asks.

Andrea nods. "Yes, for now. Silvey's mom, Evelyn, called to report the photo and the dispatcher told her they had just received your call for help."

"I saw the cops' bag my phone," Rozanne says.

Andrea nods. "When we couldn't reach anyone, we chose action. We couldn't just sit at home and wait for answers."

Rozanne frowns. "I don't know who to call for help at this point."

Scott switches the coffeemaker on. "Based on the drone, the photo, and the abduction it sounds like the agents are still on the hunt."

Rozanne stands. "Bax kept the card for Agent Carlton. Give me a second." She walks out of the kitchen.

Scott pushes off the counter and crosses the kitchen to Andrea. "Do you believe the agents are responsible?"

Andrea nods. "They were aggressive enough to corner Bax in the hospital lobby and to bribe security to take Silvey. I believe they are more than responsible, and the only direction we should look."

"Got it," Rozanne says, running back into the kitchen. "Can I borrow your phone?"

"I don't think they can be trusted," Andrea says. "We should call the agents that showed up at the hospital after Silvey was abducted. Scott, you took his card. What was his name?"

"Arnold," Scott says, patting his back pocket. He pulls out his wallet and retrieves the card. He taps it against his chin. "I still don't like this. The shift of the military taking over the base plus the tail we experienced this morning…I don't know where we should turn."

Rozanne's eyes well over and tears fall down her cheeks.

"We have to choose," Andrea says, standing and hugging Rozanne. "We'll get them back."

"What about the reporter?" Scott asks.

Andrea leans away from Rozanne. "Heather did help put heat on the local officials and we got a swift response from the hospital."

Rozanne wipes her face. "We can try, right?"

"I don't think there is a right answer in all of this," Andrea says, nodding to Scott. "Call her."

Scott nods and pulls out his phone. "She'll want an exclusive with Silvey."

Andrea sighs. "I'll talk Silvey into it…if we get Gage and Baxton back."

Scott nods once and taps his phone.

Andrea pulls Rozanne a few feet away from Scott. "Did Bax tell you about twisting hercules?"

Rozanne nods. "Yes. He told us what Silvey found after they left the base."

"Did they search the house?" Andrea asks, looking around the living room and down the hallway. All the furniture and pictures look neat and tidy.

"Not the ones that took Bax and Gage," Rozanne says. "But the local deputy walked in as if he owned the place." She chuckles. "I could see him and his bald spot from the tree. It was the same deputy who came out when we saw a missing girl out near the pond."

"And you don't think you can trust him?" Andrea asks, watching Scott pace between the counter and the kitchen table.

"I wasn't about to find out," Rozanne says, nodding towards the full coffee pot. "Looks like it's finally done brewing." She walks past Scott and swings open the fridge. She pulls out a dark glass bottle and shakes it on the way to the counter. She pours the coffee into the three awaiting mugs and tops each one with a splash from the glass bottle. She hands a mug to Scott and Andrea before taking a long sip.

Scott taps his phone and hands it to Rozanne. "I've put her on mute. But she has a few questions for you. Are you ok to answer?"

"Liquid courage," Rozanne says, raising her mug and tapping the phone.

Scott and Andrea step into the living room. He takes a sip of the coffee and looks around. "It appears they didn't trash the place."

"Only the deputy came in and looked around," Andrea says, nodding towards Rozanne. "Is Heather going to help?"

Scott grins. "She was in the middle of roasting the hospital staff that tried to block us from finding Silvey." He laughs. "I'm pretty sure they were hoping for some redemption."

"They can go straight to hell," Andrea says.

"Pretty much," Scott says, "but Heather was very interested in helping." He points to the clock above the fireplace. "She's got a slot on the next news broadcast. She was going to run the hospital piece, but if we could give her something fact checked, she would run the abduction story instead. Her assistant was already calling the local police and sheriff to get the 911 call made by Rozanne and their statement."

"Nice," Andrea says, taking another sip. "Bax told them about twisting hercules."

Scott lifts an eyebrow. "Let's hope Gage and Bax can keep that information to themselves."

"You think they are going to be interrogated?" Rozanne asks, handing the phone back to Scott.

Scott frowns. "Sorry, but why else would they trespass and take two grown men?"

Rozanne glances out the back door. "I don't know…"

"I'm pretty sure one reason is to find Captain Wilson," Andrea says.

"True," Scott says. "What did Heather say?"

"She's going to send you a text if they can validate everything before she goes live," Rozanne says. "Why didn't Silvey come with you?"

"We didn't know if she was in danger," Andrea says. "I made her go somewhere close to home but unrelated to any of us. Just in case."

Rozanne nods. "Smart." She looks down at her mug. "I don't want to think of what they will do to Gage and Baxton. But I feel relieved that they can't use Silvey as bait for them."

9

"Say another word and I will jump out of this moving car," Silvey says, pointing at Justin's face.

"Seriously?" Justin asks, slowing the car to a stop.

"What are you doing?" Silvey asks.

"Trying to apologize," Justin says, throwing his hands in the air.

"Drive," Silvey says, pointing to the gravel road ahead. "You are just a means to a destination, Justin Birchwood Grayson."

"Whoa," Justin says, punching the gas. "Noted Silvey Lynn Rhoades. Silence it is." His phone lights up and starts to vibrate in the cupholder. He glances down. "It's Dre."

Silvey taps the phone to answer. "Hey."

"Are you at the house?" Andrea asks.

"Not quite," Silvey says, glaring at Justin. "He took the long way so we could—talk."

"Oh, good God," Andrea says. "Is he still breathing?"

"For now," Silvey says. "What's the latest?"

"We are at Rozanne's house," Andrea says. "Gage and Bax were abducted a few hours ago."

"What? By whom? Why?"

"An armed team surprised them out by their pond. The guys were fishing out a drone Gage shot down."

"The agents?" Silvey pounds her fist against the center console.

"Maybe, but thankfully, Rozanne was able to hide in the woods."

"This can't be happening!"

"I know," Andrea says.

"Can we trust anyone to ask for help?" Silvey asks, aggressively rubbing her hand in circles around her knee.

"Rozanne stayed hidden when the local deputy came by," Andrea says.

"She thinks they are in on it?" Silvey asks.

"Not necessarily, but she didn't want to take any chances."

"That's probably a good idea," Silvey says. "Mom had to shut and lock the door in the local cop's face when he found out the connection between me and the Captain." She fidgets with the button for the window. "Now what?"

"We've contacted the news anchor that helped with your abduction," Andrea says. "They are going to fact check a few things, then hopefully share their abduction this evening."

Silvey sighs and bites her quivering lower lip.

"It should help," Andrea says.

"Or stir the pot even more," Silvey says, wiping away a falling tear.

"If anyone saw something," Andrea says, "this could get the ball rolling."

Justin turns down a narrow, tree-lined driveway on the left.

"We are pulling up to the house," Silvey says, reaching in the back and grabbing her bag. She whacks Justin on the side of the head.

"Dude," Justin mumbles, brushing her bag away from him.

Silvey rolls her eyes. "What channel should I watch?"

"Five at five," Andrea says. "Tell Myra hello."

52

"I will," Silvey says. "Keep me in the loop."

"Will do," Andrea says.

Justin brakes and starts to shift the car to park.

Silvey hops out of the car before it is fully stopped and tosses the phone on the passenger seat. "Thanks!" She turns her back on him and the car. She walks to the front porch of the red brick two-story cottage.

Myra steps out on the porch and nods to Justin.

He frowns and turns the car around.

"Any trouble finding the place?" Myra asks.

"No, the jerk," Silvey says, pointing her middle finger at the retreating car. "He thought it was a great time to take the long way so he could," she holds up her fingers in air quotes, "talk to me."

Myra grins. "Did you two date in high school?"

"Yes, unfortunately."

"First loves never quite burn out," Myra says, ushering Silvey inside.

"Resentment, hostility, and rage are the only emotions I will ever associate with that piece of walking flesh."

"Noted," Myra says, pointing up the stairs. "I've made up the guest room, first door on the right. Make yourself at home, and if you're hungry, I've made homemade macaroni and cheese."

Silvey sniffs. "It smells like a dream come true. Thanks. I'll be right back down." She takes the steps two at a time and opens the first door on the right. A queen size sleigh bed is flanked with two antique side tables placed under large windows overlooking the distant hills and fields beside the house. "Not another house in sight. Perfect." She hangs her bag on the hook on the back of the door and turns to survey the room again. "Hey Myra?"

"Yea?"

"Have I slept in this room before?"

"Yes," Myra says. "It had two twin beds before, and the paint color was…"

"Mustard yellow!" Silvey says, laughing and descending the steps. "I remember now."

Myra laughs. "You can thank the original owners for that choice. I never had a reason to change it until recently."

"What changed?" Silvey asks, following Myra to the kitchen.

"My godson promised me a weekend visit once a year," Myra says.

"And has Scott actually fulfilled said promise?" Silvey asks, watching Myra uncork a bottle of wine.

"Two years in a row," Myra says, pulling out two glasses. "Wine?"

"Yes, please." Silvey looks around the kitchen. "You've changed the color down here, too?"

Myra nods and pours the wine.

"I really like the olive cabinets. It fits the space so well."

"Thanks," Myra says, handing her a glass of wine. "It was a choice I wasn't sure about for weeks. I would love it one day and hate it the next."

"Was it all white before?" Silvey asks.

"It was white on white on white with the exception of the mustard yellow bedroom upstairs."

Silvey grins. "Cheers to new colors." She raises her glass to Myra's.

Myra clinks her glass. "Cheers to keeping you safe."

"Thank you," Silvey says, taking a sip. "I really hope it won't be long."

"You can stay for as long as you need," Myra says. "The plates are there." She points to the cabinet above a foil covered casserole dish. "Help yourself. And the silverware is here." She pulls out a drawer near the stove.

Silvey nods and swallows a sip of wine. "Perfect."

"You know it's ironic that you're here with all this news about Captain Wilson and your association with him," Myra says.

Silvey lifts an eyebrow. "Why?"

"His family owned the land a few fields over," Myra says, nodding towards the front door.

"Um," Silvey says, "but wait, how do you know that?"

"My neighbor Sue," Myra says. "The captain was interviewed last week on TV. Sue stopped by to drop off eggs and shared the news. Her dad was a local historian and was obsessed with the history surrounding their land and the founding of Elmira."

"Ok," Silvey says.

Myra pulls out her phone and taps it a few times. She turns the screen towards Silvey. "He framed all the land deeds he could find for their parcels."

Silvey leans closer and squints at the black-and-white image. "Robert Wilson." She shakes her head. "That's a pretty common name."

"That's what I told Sue," Myra says, swiping the screen. "But she's a lot like her father and she pulled up the census." She turns the phone back towards Silvey. "She circled the line for Robert and Caroline Wilson with a son, Darryl, living here in this county. And the dates match the deed."

"Shit," Silvey mutters.

"Are you ok?" Myra asks. "You just lost all your color."

"They'll come looking," Silvey says, pointing to the front door. "If a local found this out—the feds will too. He's still out there and could make his way back to something familiar."

"He, as in the captain?"

Silvey nods.

"I see," Myra says. "Do you think the captain is dangerous?"

"No," Silvey says. "He's just as innocent as we are."

Myra raises her eyebrow. "Innocent?"

"We didn't break any laws," Silvey says. "Wrong place, wrong time situation with the damn tornado."

"Scott mentioned some overbearing reporters," Myra says, shaking her head. "But the feds as in the FBI are after you?"

"They are very aggressive," Silvey says, nodding and swirling the remaining red wine. "Two FBI agents cornered Baxton while I was laid up in the hospital, and then they paid hospital security to abduct me from the ICU. Plus, Baxton and his cousin Gage were taken from their house by an armed group of people a few hours ago."

"What did you guys find to stir up a black ops team?" Myra asks.

"They are looking for information on Captain Wilson that we simply don't have."

"Have you met him?" Myra asks.

"Yes, but it's complicated."

"At the nike base, right?" Myra asks.

"Yes," Silvey says.

"And you were there for work?"

"Yes. It was purchased by Greening Up to convert into a vertical farm."

"Did the new owners have any idea what kind of property they bought?" Myra asks.

Silvey shrugs. "From our initial conversation, no. They saw an old silo that could be converted into a vertical farm less than an hour from a major city."

Myra nods. "But later?"

"They found a few things that weren't on the original deed, but it was connected to the property."

"So, it's true?" Myra asks.

"What is true?"

"They unlocked a worm hole or time machine?"

Silvey snorts and then laughs. "Is that the latest gossip flying around town?"

Myra laughs. "Among other extraterrestrial theories."

Silvey snorts again and sets down her glass. "Oh man, small towns."

"I've been here for fifteen years," Myra says, "and I live in a bubble. I never really know or follow the local gossip unless it comes to my front door with eggs."

"My mom's a hairstylist," Silvey says, pulling out a bowl. "It's a daily conversation that starts with: 'Did you know…' or 'I heard today…' and if you think that is bad, try being a part of any local construction crew."

Myra chuckles. "Not to change the subject, but I have a heavy hand with pepper and paprika."

Silvey smiles and peels back the foil. "Fine by me. I like anything spicey and it looks amazing." She opens the cabinet and grabs a second bowl. "I am not eating alone." She hands Myra a bowl.

"Yes, ma'am."

Thirty minutes later, Silvey pushes back from the table. "Do you have channel five?"

"All the local channels are on the set down here. Why?"

"Sweet," Silvey says, taking Myra's bowl. "Andrea mentioned they may roll a segment about the abduction of Gage and Baxton."

"The press knows?" Myra asks.

"We aren't sure whom we can trust," Silvey says, washing the bowls and forks. "And this reporter helped when I was taken from the hospital."

"I've got a few contacts with some higher ups…"

Silvey holds up one of the forks. "I've dragged enough people into this mess. Thank you for the offer and the hospitality, but I don't want to add anyone else to it yet. If we don't get any leads on Baxton or Gage by tomorrow, I may change that tune a bit."

Myra nods. "I usually do my evening walk of the property about this time. Do you want to join me?"

Silvey glances over at the clock. "Tomorrow yes, this evening I want to stay close to the phone and watch the news."

Myra takes out a hand towel. "The remote is on the coffee table. I'll dry and go on my walk."

"Thanks," Silvey says, rinsing the last bowl.

10

The door flies open to Agent Vickers assigned room. She throws her towel at Agent Carlton's face.

He dodges the towel.

She flings her still damp hair in his direction. "Neil! Knock first!"

Neil raps two knuckles on the door. "No time. I snuck out." He closes the door and steps closer to her.

"Why?" she asks, stepping away from him.

"What did you tell them?" he whispers.

"Nothing. You?"

"Same, but I've heard of Project Q."

Agent Vickers folds her arms across her chest. "And?"

"I had our newest consultant—" He covers his mouth and whispers, "You know the hacker."

Agent Vickers rolls her eyes.

"They ran a search on the dark web for anything related to Captain Wilson and the Nike Air Base. And there were several hits, mostly conspiracy theories, but two threads that used the keywords Project Q."

"Get to the point."

"I didn't get time to dig any further."

Agent Vickers sighs. "Wow, and you barged in here for that important tidbit of news?"

"At least it's something," Neil says, folding his arms over his chest.

"It means nothing," Agent Vickers says, sliding on a pair of shoes. "We are their puppets, and we must dance at their command."

"That's it?" Neil asks. "You've given in?"

"Our backs are nailed to the wall, Neil! Not pinned. Nailed. Get it through your thick eyebrows and head. We've hit beyond rock bottom and our careers are now what they dictate. Unless you want to start your midlife off in a new career with nothing to show for the last decade."

Agent Carlton opens his mouth but snaps it shut as the door to her room swings open.

"Does anyone here have any manners?" Agent Vickers asks, glaring at the man shadowing her threshold.

"Follow me," the man says.

"Sir, yes, sir," Agent Vickers says, pushing Neil out of her room ahead of her.

Neil grunts but he follows the man down the hallway and up a flight of stairs.

Agent Vickers flicks Neil's arm. He glances over his shoulder, and she glances up to the corner of the stairwell.

Neil follows her line of sight spotting a camera and returns his focus forward.

The man stops outside of a glass-walled conference room. "Have a seat in here."

"And then?" Agent Vickers asks before the man shuts the door.

"The Director will be in."

The door clicks shut.

"You think they have eyes and ears everywhere?" Neil asks.

"Duh," Agent Vickers says, waving her hands around. "Of course. Look around, stone slab and steel accented walls. Even the shiny hardware on the glass door. It's all top of the line and screams private funding. Plus, the location is off grid."

"What makes you think that?" Neil asks.

"I took the shower vent apart to get a look outside," Agent Vickers whispers, holding a hand over her mouth. "I could see an array of solar panels, rainwater storage tanks and none of the armed guys carry phones or radios."

"Interesting observation," Neil says, pulling out a chair.

"Better than your conspiracy theories," Agent Vickers says, pulling out a chair next to him. "Please keep those to yourself."

"Oh, the irony."

"How so?" Agent Vickers asks, leaning away from him.

"You've always been the hot-headed crazy one in this partnership."

"Wow," Agent Vickers says. "You are unbelievable."

"Heads up," Neil says, lifting his chin.

Director Gia pushes open the glass door. "Agents."

They nod.

"We've received some new information regarding Captain Wilson," Director Gia says. "Did you know his parents had land in Ray County?"

"Yes," Agent Vickers says, leaning forward. "But they died before he joined the service. How is this relevant now?"

"A man matching his description was spotted near said land," Director Gia says, looking down at her watch. "Less than ten minutes ago."

Agent Vickers leans back. "Great, then our services are no longer needed."

"Not so easy," Director Gia says. "You need to establish what Baxton Auburn saw, heard, or knows about the site."

"I'll take the first stab at him," Neil says, holding up a finger. "I made first contact with him at the house."

"And the other one?" Agent Vickers asks.

"We've got no reason to question him," Director Gia says. "His test came back clean."

"What test?" Agent Vickers asks.

Director Gia smirks. "That's, um, what you would say…classified."

"Seriously?" Neil scoffs.

"The less you know going into this interview the better," Director Gia says. "Just get the basics. No leading questions. Got it?"

Agent Vickers nods and pushes back from the table.

"One more thing," Director Gia says. "General Hall will be monitoring your interviews. Tread carefully."

"Is that a threat?" Agent Vickers asks.

"Let's call this an audition to keep your role," Director Gia says, standing and opening the door.

A man, wearing a black fitted long sleeve shirt and tactical pants, steps inside the room.

"Oscar will escort you while you are on property."

Oscar nods to the agents.

"He didn't skip a leg day," Agent Vickers mutters.

"What was that?" Director Gia asks, glaring at Agent Vickers.

Neil laughs. "My partner was admiring Oscar's fit bod."

Agent Vickers elbows Neil in the ribs.

"Hey!" Neil says, rubbing his ribs.

"I see professional behavior is not a trait I should expect from either of you at this point."

Agent Vickers shakes her head and stands. "Says the woman giving orders while wearing a neon yellow hoodie."

Director Gia tugs on the string hanging from her hoodie. "My casual appearance offends you?"

"Nah," Agent Vickers says, leaning forward and placing both hands on the table. She narrows her eyes. "What's offensive is being drugged and manipulated to do your bidding."

"Here," Director Gia says, pointing to the table. "You do as you're told, when you're told." She levels her eyes to meet Agent Vickers. "Not because of arrogance, but because humanity may depend on that action."

Agent Vickers laughs. "Right and…"

Neil leans close to her. "I don't believe she's joking."

Agent Vickers rolls her shoulders back and tugs her shirt down. "Regardless, blind or not, we'll get the job done."

"Follow me," Oscar says, turning and walking out the door and down the hall.

Agent Vickers walks by Director Gia without a glance.

Neil nods to the director and follows them closely until he is in step with Agent Vickers. "You should probably cool off a bit."

"You mean just stand in the corner while you start with the kid?" Agent Vickers asks, stopping beside Oscar outside of a tinted glass door.

"Precisely," Neil says, pushing ahead of her through the door. He glances around the room. It's smaller than the conference room, but just as nice.

"Rude," Agent Vickers mutters.

Baxton pushes his hair behind his ears and locks eyes with Neil.

"Mr. Auburn," Neil says, holding up both hands. "I come in peace. No needles or weapons, just a few questions and you'll be free to go with your cousin."

"Where's Gage?" Baxton's eyes dart between the two agents.

"In a room nearby," Neil says.

"And her?" Baxton asks, pointing at Agent Vickers.

"Harmless," Neil says, pulling out the chair across from Baxton.

"You've got some nerve," Baxton says. "Attempted kidnapping was one thing, but the danger you put Silvey in is far beyond."

"Yes, yes," Neil says, interrupting him. "We're terrible humans. But we were just doing our jobs."

Agent Vickers leans against the wall behind Neil and clears her throat.

Neil ignores her and continues. "We have a few basic questions and this whole drama can come to a quick end."

Baxton shakes his head. "Nah. I'm not speaking to either of you." He nods to the camera in the corner. "If you want information. Get these two out of the room."

"So, you do have information," Agent Vickers says, pushing off the wall and circling the table.

Baxton stands and steps away from the table. "Don't step behind me." His tall frame towers over her. "My information is about you bribing the hospital security to kidnap a civilian from the ICU." He points to her. "Plus, your aggressive harassment of Silvey's family and friends."

"Silvey, must be something special?" Agent Vickers asks, nodding to Baxton. "Do you know where she is?"

"That is none of your business," Baxton says, stepping further away from her and the table. "I'm done talking."

"And if we have Silvey?" Agent Vickers asks, widening her stance and placing her fists on her hips.

Baxton tilts his chin up and rocks back on his heels. "You wish." He shakes his auburn curls away from his face.

"Clearly we've started off this interview on the wrong foot," Neil says. "Please have a seat."

Baxton shakes his head. "More like interrogation."

Agent Vickers backtracks to the far side of the table and sits next to Neil. She leans back in the chair and folds her arms across her chest. "Just answer three questions."

Baxton raises an eyebrow.

"Are you feeling, ok?" Agent Carlton asks, looking Baxton over from head to toe.

"Annoyed." Baxton glances at Agent Carlton. "That's one."

"Why did you return to the base?" Neil asks.

"To look for my car." Baxton rocks up on his toes and back down on his heels. "That's two."

"What did you discover?" Neil asks.

"The tornado took my car elsewhere," Baxton says, snapping the hairband around his wrist. "That's three. We're done." He pulls his hair up into a messy bun.

"Mr. Auburn," Neil says.

Baxton narrows his eyes at the camera in the corner. "D-O-N-E."

The door opens. And Oscar fills the threshold.

"Agents," Oscar says. "A moment."

Agent Vickers rolls her eyes and stands. "If you were smart, you would cooperate."

"If?" Baxton smirks.

"Agent Vickers," Oscar says. "Now."

"Come on," Neil says. "Let's give him a moment to cool off."

Agent Vickers points at Baxton. "Big mistake."

Baxton smiles. "We'll see."

11

Silvey changes the channel to five and watches the end of the weather broadcast. She presses down on her bouncing knee. *Get a grip! It's only the news.*

"Tonight, we have an exclusive story," the reporter says as the camera pans to a dark-haired woman wearing a black blazer and purple top. "Two local men were taken by a group of armed men from a home in Clay County this afternoon. The men were retrieving a downed drone from their pond that was hovering outside of their private home."

The screen splits keeping the reporter in frame and showing a picture of Gage and Baxton side by side.

Silvey turns up the volume.

"Tonight, we need your help to locate Gage and Baxton Auburn. The local police confirmed that they received a call from Gage's wife, Rozanne, at the time of the incident." A picture of Gage and

Rozanne appears on the screen. "You may recognize Baxton Auburn's name in relation to our calls for help to locate and recover Silvey Rhoades who was taken from the hospital ICU yesterday morning." The camera flips back to the reporter showing her name, Heather, on the left and a picture of Silvey on the right. "We believe the people that conspired to take Silvey and those that took Gage and Baxton are related. The local FBI office declined to comment at this time."

"Of course they did," Silvey says.

"If you have any information to the whereabouts of Gage or Baxton Auburn, please contact our help line." A number comes up on the screen. "Local authorities have stated they are setting up a search team to comb the area for any evidence and will follow any credible leads."

"It's going to be a circus," Silvey says, turning the volume back down. She reaches for the cordless phone, but the back door swings open.

"Hey Silvey," Myra says. "Can you come outside a moment?"

"Sure," Silvey says, leaving the phone on the coffee table. She walks through the kitchen to the back door and spots a second person backlit by the sun.

"You have company?" Silvey hesitantly steps out onto the deck.

"I ran across this man," Myra says, positioning herself between Silvey and the man. "He claims to be a friend of yours."

The man steps up and the light catches his familiar face. "Hi Silvey, sorry to barge in on you here."

"Captain Wilson, how did you? Why are you…"

"I was dropped off about a mile down the road," Captain Wilson says, pointing his thumb over his shoulder. "And your friend Myra spotted me."

"Well, that's kind, but not true," Myra says, patting her hip holster. "I held him at gunpoint until he revealed who he was and how he found you."

Silvey's mouth falls open, and her eyes widen. "What?"

"He was technically trespassing," Myra says.

"How did you find me?" Silvey asks, stepping beside Myra.

"I wasn't actually looking for you," Captain Wilson says. "I was looking for an old cave near a mine shaft. I played in it as a kid."

Myra nods. "The intel about your family owning land around here was accurate?"

"Intel," Captain Wilson asks, backing up a step. "Who do you work for?"

"Retired cop," Myra says. "My neighbor Sue owns the land that your parents had."

"And you had no idea I was here?" Silvey asks.

He holds up both hands. "Honestly, I didn't."

THUMP THUMP THUMP

"That's a chopper," Myra says, pointing up. "It's flying way too low. You two inside! And stay away from the windows!"

Silvey and Captain Wilson stop just inside the kitchen. They duck below the countertops, and slump to the floor.

"This is all my fault," Captain Wilson says, shaking his head.

"What happened after we left the base?" Silvey asks, scooting around to face him.

"Just after your friends left," Captain Wilson says. "Charlotte and Eli locked the chamber, and we split up. I saw them get captured."

"How did you get away?" Silvey asks.

"I hid under an old tractor bucket in the tall grass until it was dark, but they moved in big field lights and set up a perimeter around the base. I had to move low and slow through the field until I got to a tree line. I walked until I found a gravel drive."

Myra steps inside and closes the door. "The chopper is coming back. Who dropped you off?"

"Jean Bowing," Captain Wilson says.

"Was her son in the car?" Myra asks.

"Yes."

"We need to go now," Myra says, zipping up her jacket and nodding to Silvey. "Get your bag."

"Why?" Silvey asks, getting to her feet.

"Her son is training to be a first responder, and he would have messaged any number of local authorities."

"Oh Silvey," Captain Wilson says, shaking his head. "I'm so sorry."

"You couldn't have known," Silvey says, taking the steps two at a time.

"She came here to get away from the people that took her friends," Myra says, pointing a finger in his face. "You are compromising her safety, and now mine."

"Her friends?" Captain Wilson asks.

"Gage and Baxton."

"No!" He buries his face in his hands. "I don't know where to go, who to trust, and frankly I'm so exhausted."

The buzz of the chopper rattles the back door.

Silvey ducks down on the steps. "Are they trying to take off the roof?"

"Let's go!" Myra says, glaring at him.

Silvey rushes over staying low and helps Captain Wilson to his feet.

Myra opens a floor-to-ceiling cabinet with a hiss. Damp air wafts in the kitchen. It reveals a narrow entry to a set of rough, uneven stone steps descending into darkness.

"Whoa," Silvey whispers, covering her nose. "Is that vinegar?"

"Ah, yes, I dropped a jar of pickles last week."

"Where does it go?" Silvey asks, stepping closer and looking down.

"It goes to the root cellar and there's a path down to a cave," Myra says, taking a camp lantern from a hook anchored to the wall. She turns it on and hands it to Silvey. "I'll follow you in a few once I have diverted them via the four-wheeler."

Silvey shakes her head. "We should stay together."

"No," Myra says. "Silvey, trust me."

Silvey nods and holds up the light. "Be careful, please."

"I will," Myra says. "And kill the light once you get to the cave entrance."

Silvey takes the first step down and looks back at Captain Wilson. "Stay close and watch your head."

Captain Wilson shuffles in behind her. "Got it."

Myra closes the cabinet door, muffling the sound of the incoming roar of the chopper.

Silvey makes it to the bottom and reaches back for Captain Wilson. "You good?"

"Am I?" He shuffles beside her. "I don't know if I can ever answer that question honestly again."

Silvey lifts the lantern to his face. She leans closer to inspect his red-rimmed eyes. "Have you slept since I saw you at the base?"

He adverts his eyes away from the light. "No. I've been on the move ever since your friends left."

"My friends," Silvey whispers, moving the light away from his face and holds it up, illuminating the mason jars stocking the shelves.

"Silvey, I'm sorry," Captain Wilson says. "I had no idea they would be taken."

"I know," Silvey says, panning the light methodically from left to right. She pauses and raises the lantern highlighting an old wooden door frame. "This way."

The worn dirt path leads them into a narrow shaft between two giant stalagmites. Silvey walks through straight ahead her petite frame unimpeded, but Captain Wilson must turn his broad shoulders and walk in sideways. He sucks in his belly just squeezing through before the path makes a sharp right.

Silvey glances back. "It widens out up ahead."

"That's good, because I don't think I can get any smaller." He taps the top of his head and waist.

"Tall people problems," Silvey snickers. "Something I've never had."

He chuckles.

She turns back towards the path. "I don't think it's too far."

"You've been to the cave before?"

"A few times," Silvey says. "but not via the root cellar. You've met my friend Andrea. Her husband's godmother is Myra. We spent a few weekends camping out here after high school. And you?"

"I recalled a cave near my father's work at the mine," Captain Wilson says. "My father only took me by it once, so I thought…"

"You thought it would be safe?" Silvey asks, running her hand along the rough stone.

"Yes."

"You weren't wrong," Silvey says. "It's a pretty perfect place to hide out, but your mistake was trusting a local. I believe a local cop who came by the house to pick up evidence would have charged in the front door to get any information about your whereabouts. Thankfully, my mother is a force to be reckoned with."

"Why do they care about an old G.I.?"

Silvey stops and turns.

He takes a step back.

"You said they found the chamber that fixed me." Silvey waves a hand over her body.

He nods.

"And they know you were locked inside of it for sixty years," Silvey says, holding up one finger and then holds up a second. "Two, you haven't aged." She waves a hand over him. "You don't think they are interested in poking and prodding you with every device to reverse engineer the chamber?"

He sighs. "They've known about the tech for sixty years. Hell, for seventy-five years. Why didn't they utilize it?"

"The program was buried under Kennedy's administration," Silvey says.

He shakes his head. "I want to live my life in peace and visit with my wife with what little time she has left."

Silvey reaches up and squeezes his shoulder. "If anyone can help you lie low, it's Myra."

12

Baxton paces the interview room in three long strides. "Release me!" He points to the door. "Now!"

The door opens.

Baxton barges out into the hall.

"Bax!" Gage shouts, running in a full sprint.

Baxton turns and jumps out of Gage's path. "Dude!"

"Run!" Gage shouts.

"Why?" Baxton asks, falling in step beside Gage.

"I may have broken out and tripped a few alarms," Gage says, rounding the corner without looking. He skids down the first few steps before regaining his footing and flying down to the landing. "Hurry!"

"Right behind you," Baxton says, skipping the last two steps.

They rapidly descend four additional floors before halting at dull steel doors.

"Ready?" Gage asks, heaving in a breath.

"For?" Baxton asks, leaning down and bracing his weight on his knees.

"I'm not exactly sure what's on the other side of this door."

Baxton straightens. "Anything is better than being drugged or locked inside another room."

Gage holds up a dark ring to a black sensor to the right of the door. The door silently opens outward.

Baxton ducks his head to shield his eyes. "We're out!"

The sun is dead ahead on the rocky horizon.

"And it's going to be dark soon," Gage says, squinting. "Let's try to find some cover there." He points towards the foothills ahead of them.

Baxton looks left at the long cement building ending at a fence line topped with razor sharp barbed wire. He looks right taking in the scattered concrete buildings. He shrugs. "We can try."

Gage takes off.

The steel door closes with a loud thud.

Gage risks a look back.

Baxton catches up with him. "Where did you find that fancy ring?"

"On the counter next to the bathroom sink."

"Hmm," Baxton says, shortening his stride to stay in line with Gage. "And you just casually used it to walk out?"

Gage nods and glances back. "I saw the guy use it to unlock the door to the room I was being held in." He takes a breath and picks up his pace. "When he was called away, I took a chance."

Baxton leaps over a large rock and looks back. "Did you encounter the agents from the hospital?"

"No!" Gage slows and folds his arms over his head. "They're here?"

"Yes," Baxton says, slowing to a jog. "Come on. I'll explain when we are out of sight." He points back to the complex and up at the dusky pink sky.

"Got it," Gage says, catching up to Baxton.

They reach the rocky foothills as a low, long siren moans out from the complex.

72

"They know we've flown the coop," Baxton says, panting.

Gage squints back at the complex. "I see a few men heading in our direction."

"Let's keep low and try to find somewhere to hunker down." Baxton crouches low and tries to run, but stumbles over a rock. He narrowly misses a face plant into pink flowers surrounded by the long needles of a cactus.

"Whoa," Gage whispers. "Be careful dude. That thing looks lethal." He gives the cactus tree a wide berth.

They hurry over a slight rise leading to a sea of odd rock formations jetting out of the desert.

"Is it just me," Baxton whispers, running towards the rocks, "or do the rocks look like giant mushrooms?"

Gage tugs Baxton behind the first wide rock with a large, shadowed crevice.

"I've seen these before."

"Where?" Baxton asks, peeking around the rock.

Two men pop up over the rise, holding large flashlights.

Baxton slinks back and holds up two fingers. He covers his pursed lips with one finger.

Gage nods and silently moves into the crevice slightly concealed behind a bushy cactus tree. He scoots back until his back is flesh against the rock.

Baxton ducks his head and steps inside. He sandwiches himself between Gage and the rock.

A bulky man sweeps the ground with his light. He slows just beyond the concealing cactus tree and kneels to the ground.

Baxton shrinks back even further.

"I've got something," the man shouts.

"Dead end over here," the second man says. His light bounces up and down, briefly illuminating the crevice.

Baxton meets Gage's wide eyes.

The second man sidles up to the bulky man. "What is it?"

"A set of footprints," the bulky man says, standing. He points his light down on the outline of the prints in the sandy dirt. "Let's go. The chances of them making it past the next perimeter is basically zero."

"We've got them heading west towards the valley," the man says, tapping his earpiece. "Yes, ma'am."

The two men jog away and continue sweeping the ground ahead.

Baxton counts to sixty before he risks a look out and extends his neck until he can see between the cactus branches. "I can't see them." He inches out of the crevice.

"Good," Gage says, twisting his neck from left to right. "That was close. Too close."

"Do you know where we are?" Baxton asks, shifting his weight from side to side.

"It looks like the valley of…" Gage says, waving a finger around. "Nightmares or dreams. Ugh, something like that."

"Not ringing any bells," Baxton says.

"Roz started a road trip wish list last year," Gage says, pointing up and down. "There's a picture of mushroom rock formations like these in a book on our coffee table at home. Roz tagged it as a pit stop on the way to the Grand Canyon." He taps his finger on his nose. "I believe it was near Albuquerque."

"As in New Mexico?" Baxton asks, surveying the dark landscape. "It could be."

Gage turns in a slow circle. "According to the men looking for us. East is out, west sounds like a trap. South or north?"

"North?" Baxton suggests.

"North it is," Gage says.

They carefully walk between the rock formations.

"We should occasionally walk in circles," Baxton says, "to muddy our tracks."

Gage nods and walks around the next stacked rock formation. "These look fake like a prop from a science fiction movie." He pats the rock.

"Where is area fifty-one?" Baxton asks.

"Oh dude," Gage whispers. "You don't think…"

Baxton shrugs. "I don't know what to think."

"Why did they let them walk out of here?" Agent Carlton asks, throwing his hands up.

Agent Vickers looks up at the camera in the corner. "How did they manage to get out?"

"Well," Director Gia says, standing in the open doorway. "We didn't exactly stop them."

They turn and face Director Gia.

"Why?" the agents ask in unison.

"We have cameras with sound covering the area," Director Gia says. "I hope they share something useful."

"And how long are you going to keep them out there?" Agent Carlton asks.

"They're headed north," Director Gia says, turning on the TV in the corner. "They'll hit a steep drop off in three miles. We have a team in place to ensure they don't go over in the dark."

The screen displays the night vision camera feed. It paints the men's silhouettes and the surroundings in eerie hues of green. They watch them navigate a labyrinth of colossal mushroom-shaped rocks, rising like ancient sentinels from the arid earth.

"What are those things?" Agent Vickers asks, stepping closer to the screen.

"Rocks," Director Gia says.

Agent Vickers rolls her eyes. "Seriously, where are we?"

"New Mexico," Director Gia says, turning up the volume. "Now, if you will please sit and watch."

"Gage," Baxton says, stopping. "Did you see Silvey here or hear them mention her?"

"No," Gage says, facing him. "You think they took her too?"

"They agents dangled that tidbit out there," Baxton says, releasing his man bun. He shakes his head and lets his curls fall over his face.

"Dude," Gage says. "Sorry, they never mentioned her, and the only person I saw after we arrived and were separated was the guy I took the ring from."

Baxton pulls his hair back up and looks around. "Do you feel like the landscape has changed?"

"Not really," Gage says, kicking the sandy dirt. "Although the sand is another layer thicker here than back there." He points over his shoulder.

"At least we have some moonlight," Baxton says, trudging forward. "And we aren't being chased."

"But we are being watched," Gage says, pointing up at a camera fixed to the side of a rock.

"Seriously," Baxton says, glaring up at the camera lens. He flips it off. "We were never free."

"Now what?" Gage asks, looking around. "They obviously know we are here."

"Let's make them come to us," Baxton says, sitting on a large, smooth rock.

13

"Rozanne," Andrea says, waving her over to the couch. "I believe your rug may be thread bare after another minute of pacing."

Rozanne looks up from Andrea's phone and stops moving. "I've been through this before."

"What do you mean?" Andrea asks.

Rozanne shakes her head and hands Andrea the phone. "A few years ago." She gestures towards the kitchen. "I stepped out the back door and was thrown in a trunk."

Andrea nods and holds up the phone. "I remember the media blast that came from that incident."

"It was a giant mess," Rozanne says, coming over to the couch. "I never thought it could happen again—especially to Gage or Baxton."

Andrea wraps a supportive hand around Rozanne's trembling hand. "We will find them." She nods towards the television in the corner. "The broadcast will be uploaded and shared across all social media channels. Somebody saw something. We'll have a lead soon."

"Thank you." Rozanne nods. "I need to call my boss and let them know."

"Call us?" Monroe asks, standing at the open front door.

Mary charges around Monroe. "Rozanne, what's happening?"

Rozanne's bottom lip quivers. "Hi." Her eyes well over and tears stream down her cheeks. "I should have called before now, but they took my phone."

Mary waves her hand and pulls Rozanne into a tight hug.

"Hi Monroe," Andrea says, standing. "We met last week at the hospital."

"Andrea?" Monroe asks, pointing at her.

"Yes," Andrea says.

"We met a man in the driveway," Monroe says.

Andrea raises her hand. "My husband, Scott. He left to pick up an order from Wabash. Can I get you two something?"

"No," Mary says, releasing Rozanne. "We brought over a casserole."

"Oh," Andrea says.

Monroe nods. "We keep a few in the freezer."

"You never know," Mary says. "They come in handy a few times a week at our age." She winks at Monroe.

"She calls them 'death' casseroles," Monroe whispers. "Speaking of which, I'll fetch it from the truck."

Mary heads for the kitchen. "I'll put on a fresh pot of coffee and pre-heat the oven."

Rozanne wipes her cheeks. "Thanks Mary."

Andrea nods. "They're amazing."

"Yes," Rozanne says. "They really are."

Andrea's phone lights up with an incoming call. "It's Scott. I'll step out on the porch." She scoots past Monroe and swipes to answer the call. "Hey. What's up?"

"I met a truck on the way out," Scott says.

"Mary and Monroe," Andrea says. "Rozanne's boss and wife."

"Good," Scott says. "I also got a cryptic text from Myra."

"What do you mean?" Andrea asks, walking away from the open front door.

"Word for word," Scott says. "He's here. Chopper tracking me now."

"What?" Andrea exclaims. "Where's Silvey?"

"I don't know," Scott says. "I called her land line, and it goes to her answering machine. Her cell phone goes straight to voicemail."

"But the message said he not she?" Andrea asks, leaning against the porch railing.

"He," Scott says. "I don't know if it's a typo, but a chopper. Seriously, how much worse could this be?"

"Shit."

"I know," Scott says. "I just pulled up. I'll call you back after I pick up the order."

"Ok." Andrea mumbles.

Rozanne steps out onto the porch. "Coffee with—whoa Andrea. What's happened?"

Andrea pushes off the railing and shakes her head. "Scott." She pockets her phone. "Myra texted, and we can't make heads or tails of what it means."

"Run it by me," Rozanne says.

"He's here. Chopper tracking me now."

Rozanne lifts an eyebrow. "He not she?"

"Right?" Andrea shakes her head. "And she's not picking up."

"Dang," Rozanne says. "This is all too much."

"Chopper can only mean helicopter," Andrea says, pulling out her phone and scrolling through her contacts.

"I believe so," Rozanne says.

Andrea types out a message, and hits send. "I have a friend who lives on the other side of Elmira. I'll check to see if they've heard anything." Her phone dings. She swipes to open the message. "Shit." She turns the phone towards Rozanne.

"Two helicopters circled over Elmira about twenty minutes ago," Rozanne reads aloud. "One nearly buzzed the roof off my barn."

A second message dings. *"How did you know they were in town?"*

Andrea quickly types out a response and calls Scott.

"Hey," Scott says, "thanks. Hey Dre, sorry I was paying."

"Confirmed, two helicopters spotted in Elmira about twenty minutes ago."

"Not good," Scott says. "I'm on my way back. Sit tight."

Andrea ends the call.

"I'm so sorry," Rozanne says. "I don't know what to do."

"Come in," Mary says, standing in the foyer. "Eat and drink something."

They walk inside and Mary hands them each a mug of warm, fresh coffee.

"Thanks," Andrea says, sipping the coffee. "Scott is on his way back."

"How does he like his coffee?" Mary asks, taking out a fifth mug.

"Blonde," Andrea says, sniffing a waft of something familiar beyond the coffee and cream.

Mary laughs. "Cream with a splash of coffee."

"Is it just me," Andrea asks, "or do you smell bacon?"

Monroe grins. "Oh yes. My Mary makes comfort food casseroles."

Mary rolls her eyes. "It's just a cheddar, bacon, mushroom, and hamburger casserole."

"Gage's favorite," Rozanne whispers.

"Yes, love," Mary says, wrapping her arm around Rozanne. "The smell of this will bring him home."

Rozanne frowns. "I wish it was that simple."

HONK HONK

Andrea rushes to the door. "It's Scott."

Scott speeds up the driveway stopping next to Monroe's truck.

Andrea steps out onto the porch.

Scott hangs his head out the window. "We've got to go now."

"But," Andrea says, looking back at Rozanne.

"I've got Mary and Monroe," Rozanne says. "Go get Silvey."

80

Scott holds a white styrofoam container out the car window.

Andrea jogs to the car and retrieves the food. She returns it to Rozanne as Mary comes out on the porch. "Save my number."

Mary hands Andrea a pen.

Andrea writes her phone number on the styrofoam. "Call me from their phone." She hands the pen back to Mary. "I'll save the number. We'll call if we get any tips that could lead to Gage or Baxton."

"Thanks," Rozanne says, lifting the box a bit. "Keep us posted."

Andrea gives Rozanne a quick hug and hops off the porch.

Scott holds his head out the window. "We'll find them."

Rozanne forces a smile and nods.

Andrea waves from the passenger seat as Scott puts the car in reverse. "What's happening?"

"Myra called," Scott says. "She found Captain Wilson near her property."

"What? How?"

Scott speeds down the driveway. "His parents owned land near hers."

Andrea shakes her head. "What are the chances?"

"Small world."

"Wait! But his parents died when he was in his teens."

"He was heading towards one of the caves to hide out," Scott says, turning out onto the main road. "But he hitchhiked to Elmira with a local who alerted the authorities."

"Geez," Andrea whispers. "Where's Silvey now?"

"Hiding with the captain," Scott says. "Myra took the helicopters on a little wild goose chase via her four-wheeler. She stopped at her neighbor's house to call me."

"Did she lose her phone?" Andrea asks.

"No," Scott says, taking a corner a little fast.

"Whoa," Andrea says, grabbing the handle overhead.

Scott corrects the wheel. "Sorry, I'll slow down." He reaches over and takes her hand. "Myra called me from the neighbor's line just in case they were tracing hers."

"Smart," Andrea says, squeezing his hand, "but highly unlikely."

"She still thinks like a cop," Scott says.

"Are we meeting her at the neighbors?"

"We're not," Scott says.

Andrea throws up her hands. "Where are we going?"

"By the crooked river fork just west of her place," Scott says, accelerating onto a two-lane highway. "The bank is covered by trees to the highway."

"It will definitely be dark."

Scott's stomach growls. "Can you toss a few fried mushrooms in my mouth?"

Andrea reaches into the bag at her feet. She opens the first container and fingers a piece of meat. "Brisket?"

"Sure," Scott says, opening his mouth.

Andrea eats the piece and grins at Scott's glare. "Hmm, so good."

Scott's stomach audibly growls louder. "See, you've made even my stomach jealous."

Andrea rolls up a strip of the brisket and holds it out for Scott. "I wasn't hungry until I smelled it."

Scott snatches the meat and stuffs the whole piece in his mouth. "Thanks."

Andrea pops open the small box of fried mushrooms and sits it on the console between them. "Any ranch?"

"Should be in the bag," Scott says, grabbing a few fried mushrooms.

Andrea rummages in the bag and finds the clear container. She sits up and holds a hand in front of her eyes to block a sudden glare. She twists to look back. "Are we being followed?"

"I don't know," Scott says. "The headlights are round, possibly a jeep. They've been behind us since we started down three-mile lane."

"It could be a local."

"Let's hope," Scott says, slowing at the stop sign. He signals left before turning. "There are only a few back roads to turn on from here to Elmira. And most of them are dead ends."

Andrea eyes the driver's side of the jeep slowing to a stop. The flashing light doesn't give much away, but she makes out the familiar lift and paint job on the jeep. "Dang it."

"What is it?" Scott asks, watching the jeep turn left and speed up to them.

"The local busybody," Andrea says, "it's Troy."

Troy Larkin was always in everyone's business since second grade. He announced his father's affair with a teacher at a school assembly. He could never keep a secret and would blab to anyone that would listen.

"Dude," Scott says. "Does he live out this way?"

"I don't think so, but his friend Seth has a small house near the cemetery." Andrea checks her mirror. "Let's make a loop around Elmira before you stop, just in case."

Scott nods and eases up on the accelerator. "Maybe I can get him to pass us?"'

They watch the jeep's headlights roll closer, but he doesn't signal to pass, he just slows to their pace.

"I don't think he's going to take the bait," Scott says, speeding back up.

Ding

"Can you check that?" Scott asks, handing her his phone.

Andrea swipes open the message and gasps.

"What is it?"

"We have a lead!"

Scott glances at his phone.

"The farm near Rozanne's place had trail cameras and caught the men taking Gage and Baxton." Andrea presses play on the first video. Three black SUVs roll into frame and several men in tactical gear hop out and surround a small case. The next clips show them fanning out and leaving one man behind with a controller.

"That must be the drone operator," Scott says. "Who sent me the footage?"

"Heather, the reporter," Andrea says. "The footage came in via the tip line."

"Tell me they got a plate number or something," Scott says, slowing even further as the road turns to gravel. He checks the rearview mirror and watches Troy make a left at the top of the hill. "Looks like Troy is headed to Seth's house."

"That's good," Andrea says, scrolling through the message. "Heather forwarded this information to the local police and county deputies."

"Progress," Scott says, pulling their car into a narrow driveway. He backs up and heads towards the river.

"I'll forward these to Mary's phone," Andrea says.

"Let's hope it's not a dead end," Scott says, pulling off the highway at the bottom of the hill. He pops the trunk. "Grab the flashlight from the trunk."

Andrea hits send, but the message failed notification pops up. "There's no signal down here."

"We won't be here long," Scott says, checking his mirror before opening his door. "Dang it."

"What is it?" Andrea looks back at the approaching headlights. "Oh, it's Troy."

"Yep," Scott says, "and he's stopping."

Andrea hops out of the car.

"Hey, you guys lost?" Troy asks, rolling to a stop next to their car.

"No," Andrea says, closing the trunk. "Just checking the trunk." She holds up the flashlight. "This was rolling around making all kinds of weird noises."

"Are you Silvey's friend Amanda?" Troy asks.

Andrea flips on the flashlight and points it directly at Troy's face. "It's Andrea. Take a hike Troy."

"Whoa," Troy says, holding up his hand to block the light. "Just trying to do a good deed."

"Sure, thanks for checking," Andrea says, pulling open the passenger door and clicking off the light. "Have a good night, Troy." She slides into the car and shuts the door.

"Smart," Scott says, watching the jeep take off.

"Not him," Andrea says, shaking her head. "I've literally known him since preschool, and he can't remember my name."

"Ever think he gets it wrong just to get under your skin?" Scott asks, cautiously opening his door.

Andrea scoffs and gets out of the car. "Let's get Silvey and get out of here."

14

"Silvey?" Myra calls.

"Hey," Silvey says, clicking on her light. "We're over here."

"The helicopter is gone," Myra says, maneuvering up the rocky path to the cave. "I've called Scott. They were at the Auburn's place and are headed this way."

"Have they found them?" Silvey asks.

"No," Myra says.

"How did you lose the helicopter?" Captain Wilson asks, stepping into Silvey's light.

"I led them to the opening of an old mine shaft two miles up the road," Myra says. "I left the four-wheeler at the entrance and hiked up to a neighbor's farm to make the call to Scott."

"Do you still have your phone?" Silvey asks.

"Only the sim card," Myra says, patting her pocket. "They are probably pulling my background and phone records, and I didn't want to risk it. They only know about the Captain, not that you are here too."

"True," Silvey says, shaking her head. "They could have spotted me on the back porch, though."

"Well, either way, my place is blown," Myra says. "We're going to walk down by the river to the fork. Scott and Andrea will pick you up."

"And go where?" Captain Wilson asks.

"A house over near Watkins Mill," Myra says. "My old boss has a brilliant nephew that restores old farmhouses and has a few up for sale. The properties deeds are under a trust and will be hard to trace back to me or either of you."

"Wow," Silvey says. "And they are ok with us squatting?"

"I made the arrangement with him months ago," Myra says. "I help victims in abusive situations that need a safe place. He sends a coded message once a week with the coordinates of a property that we can use. It's temporary, but the fridge is stocked with the basics and there are two furnished bedrooms."

"You're amazing," Silvey says, pulling Myra in for a hug.

"Captain Wilson," Myra says, releasing Silvey. "I'm putting my trust in you to protect her at all costs."

"Call me Darryl," he says, "you have my word."

"Great," Myra says. "Let's get moving."

They follow Myra down a steep path to the river's edge, carefully walking over fallen logs and large rocks in the dark until they hear an engine idling and voices up ahead. Myra kills their light. They duck back behind a few trees and wait until the rumble of the engine moves on.

"I'm telling you," a woman says. "He's the worst."

"I think that's Andrea," Silvey whispers, tapping Myra's shoulder.

"Wait for the signal that it is clear," Myra says.

"Hand me the flashlight," Scott says, taking Andrea's free hand and helping her down the loose gravel to the riverbed. He clicks the flashlight on and off three times.

Myra whistles once. "It's clear. Let's go." She clicks back on the lantern.

"Silvey!" Andrea says, running ahead of Scott.

"Hey Dre," Silvey says, jogging to meet her in the middle. "Any news?"

"Yes," Andrea says, giving her a quick hug, "but we can talk about that in the car." She makes eye contact with Captain Wilson. "Captain."

"Please, call me Darryl."

"Well," Scott says, catching up with Andrea, "Darryl, we need to get you two up to the car and to a safe place."

"I've got that arranged," Myra says, pulling out a white index card from her pocket. "Put these coordinates in your GPS. The lock box code is on the card. If you feel like you're being followed don't stop until you get to a well-lit public parking lot with people around."

Scott takes the card and gives Myra a hug. "Sorry for the drama filled evening. And thanks for this." He holds up the card. "I'll call you tomorrow."

Silvey turns towards Myra. "Thanks again. I owe you big time."

"Come back for a visit anytime," Myra says. "Darryl a word?" He nods and steps closer to her. "You know how to assemble and shoot a firearm?"

"Of course," Darryl says. "In the blue bedroom, there is a safe in the closet with a pistol. The code for the safe is hidden in the nightstand next to the bed."

"Understood," Darryl says. "I'll keep them safe."

"We should get moving," Andrea says. "Nosey Troy spotted us on the side of the road."

"Ugh, he's the worst," Silvey says.

"See," Andrea says, pointing at Scott.

Scott rolls his eyes. "Let me climb up first and make sure the coast is clear." He scrambles up the short embankment and investigates the darkness towards town and the lights of a house on the hill. "Alright. Come on up." He extends his hand towards Silvey. She ignores him and ambles up the rocks to the pavement.

Andrea takes Scott's hand and slides a few times before she rights herself on the surface. Darryl follows without assistance. The four of them pile into the car and Scott starts the engine.

"Spill it," Silvey says, sniffing. "What's the latest with Bax and Gage? And do I smell barbeque?"

Andrea laughs and hands Silvey the white box. "Help yourself."

"I'm full," Silvey says, handing Darryl the box.

"Thanks," Darryl says, carefully opening the box.

Silvey nods and pats her abdomen. "I had a big bowl of Myra's homemade mac'n cheese."

"Jealous." Scott types in the coordinates as a car slows but drives by. "Dang it." He hands the card and phone to Andrea. "Talk and type. I can't sit here." He puts the car into drive and punches it onto the highway.

Andrea finishes inputting the coordinates. "Head towards Watkins Mill." She turns towards the back seat. "About Bax, we received a lead just before we got here. Speaking of which, I need to try to send that message again."

"What message?" Silvey asks, watching Andrea fumble with Scott's phone.

"Trail cam footage caught the men that took Gage and Baxton."

"That's great!" Silvey exclaims. "Do we know who took them? FBI, Military, or CIA?"

"Not yet," Andrea says, tapping her phone. "Finally, it sent." She looks up from her phone and narrows her eyes. "Darryl, how and why did you crash the safe house we arranged for Silvey?"

"I was headed to a cave near a mine shaft. It was the only place I could think of that could still be standing."

"Dre, he hasn't slept for a few days," Silvey says, resting her hand on his. She feels his slight tremor. "I'm safe. And thanks to Myra we've got a place for tonight."

"How did she manage that?" Andrea asks.

"She's an advocate for abuse victims," Scott says. "She has access to a few safe houses in the northland. We discussed this as an alternative for Silvey."

Andrea raises an eyebrow. "Is she still a cop?"

"No, it's a non-profit."

"That's very cool," Andrea says, checking her side mirror. "We've got an approaching vehicle. It's coming up fast. You two," she points to Silvey and Darryl, "duck down."

Silvey and Darryl scrunch down below the windows as the headlights illuminate the interior.

"Damn," Silvey says, sinking further behind Dre. "Are they running with their high beams on?"

Scott adjusts his mirror and speeds up.

Andrea's phone lights up. "Rozanne's calling." She swipes to answer. "Hey Rozanne. You've got your phone back?" She tugs on Scott's arm. "They've tracked the vehicles to a small airport in Mosby. Hang on let me put you on speaker."

"Hey Rozanne," Silvey says.

"Was that Silvey?" Rozanne whispers.

"Yes," Andrea says. "We're being tailed at the moment."

"By whom?" Rozanne asks.

"No idea," Andrea says, checking the side mirror. "We are about to turn onto three mile lane and head towards Lawson."

"There's a deputy here now," Rozanne says. "Do you want help?"

"Wait," Scott says, slowing and turning at the flashing light. "Dre, can you try to get a vehicle description?"

Andrea turns around in her seat, straining to see through the foggy rear window.

A diesel engine roars and tires squeal as the vehicle punches it around the corner.

"Ford F250 or 350, silver with mud caked on the passenger side."

"Got it," Rozanne says. "Hey deputy, we may have a lead on a silver Ford F250 or 350 truck heading towards Lawson. Can you help?"

A muffled man responds.

"Thanks," Rozanne says, "he's calling it into the local police."

"We'll do a lap around town square," Scott says, slowing as they reach city limits. "If it follows, it will lead the truck directly to the police station."

"And the captain?" Rozanne whispers.

"Safe," Andrea whispers. "Tell me about your lead."

"Two black SUVs with matching plates from the trail cam footage were abandoned near a hangar at the Mosby airfield. A small jet departed about four hours ago and they are working on getting the flight plan."

"Wow," Andrea says, looking back at Silvey's pale face and wide eyes. She mouths, *"You okay?"*

Silvey gulps and shakes her head. She glances at Darryl's frown. He squeezes her hand.

"Keep us posted," Andrea says, checking the mirror as Scott turns off the highway. "We'll call you after we get these two sorted. The truck took the bait. We are leading them towards the police station."

"Be safe," Rozanne says.

Scott slows through the center of town. All the shops and businesses are dark and closed for the evening, minus the one light on inside the Post Office. There are only three cars parked down the street near the tavern, but he spots a police cruiser idling outside the station on the far side of the park. He makes a right-hand turn just past the old bank.

The truck rides up inches from their bumper.

The police cruiser speeds across the parking lot of the city square. It flips on their swirling red lights and the siren whoops twice.

Scott brakes hard just past the entrance to the parking lot. He braces for impact as the truck barrels within a hair of their car.

"Silvey stay down," Andrea says.

Scott makes eye contact with the officer.

The officer nods and signals Scott to keep going.

"Go!" Andrea says. "If the driver suspects that we have Silvey or the captain, that cop will waste no time calling it in."

Scott checks the rearview mirror as the truck attempts to go around the police cruiser now blocking his path.

"Go, go, go," Andrea says.

Scott turns right at the next street and speeds towards the highway. He takes a left.

"Take a left past the gas station," Andrea says.

"Why?" Scott asks, checking his mirror again.

"Lose the highway," Andrea says, "just in case we're blown."

"Silvey," Scott says, turning left. "How well do you know O'Neal?"

Silvey groans. "Too well. He was the cop?"

"Yep," Scott says. "Are you two on friendly terms?"

"Oh, you mean since I was the electrician that called out his brother's dodgy work and got him canned from a job two years ago. I doubt it."

Andrea laughs. "Silvey, you are a magnet for this kind of drama."

"What can I say?" Silvey asks, cautiously sitting up. "My charming personality is like oil and the electrician industry is water."

Darryl softly chuckles, righting himself in the back seat. "You are charming."

Andrea snorts. "Oh dear. You've got the wool pulled firmly over his eyes."

"Hey," Silvey says, nudging Andrea's shoulder. "I thought you were always on my side."

Andrea turns and winks at Darryl. "Always."

Scott turns right just past the golf course. "Can you check the directions?" He glances at the rear-view mirror. "I think we can cross over the highway and take the long way through the county gravel roads."

Andrea taps his phone and checks the route. "I believe we go straight past the entrance to Watkins Mill and turn right about a mile after.

Scott nods. "Ten minutes?" He slows at the stop sign. He waits for a car to pass before he crosses the highway.

"Seven," Andrea says, checking her own phone. "No new news."

Silvey's knee bounces rapidly. "How was Rozanne holding up?" She presses her hand on her knee.

"Scared," Andrea says. "Her boss Monroe and his wife Mary came over right before we left. So, she's not alone."

"That's comforting," Silvey says, nodding. "But what is absolutely terrifying—why did they take them to an airport?"

"Hey Darryl," Scott says. "Did you manage to pick up any chatter about who was in charge before you retreated from the base?"

"Only that there was a flood of new arrivals descending on the land," Darryl says. "Eli and Charlotte were escorted away into a white van."

"There goes any chance of your job," Scott says, looking back at Silvey in the mirror.

Silvey shrugs. "I'm pretty sure the owners can't be at fault for what the government abandoned and buried on their property."

Darryl shakes his head. "They didn't really try to get away. They distracted them long enough so I could hide."

"My only priority at the moment is finding Bax," Silvey says, letting her knee bounce. "And Gage."

"Turn here," Andrea says, pointing to a narrow gravel driveway. "I believe that's the house."

Scott rolls the car to a stop beside a two-story white house. "The place looks brand new, but old at the same time." He double checks the coordinates on the index card from Myra with his phone. "This is it. Stay put while I do a sweep of the house."

"While we do a sweep of the house," Andrea says, getting out of the car. "Is there a lock box on the front door?"

"Not sure," Scott says, jogging around the car. He surveys the dark tree line around the property. "It's isolated. I can't see a neighbor from here." He climbs up the front porch and flicks on the flashlight app. "Here." He points to a blue and black box with rotating metal numbers.

Andrea kneels. "What's the code?"

Scott holds up the card. "1-9-8-7." He holds his light over the lock.

Andrea adjusts the metal dials, and the lock box clicks open. She pulls out the keys and closes the box. She scrambles the numbers and stands. Scott holds open the screen door as she unlocks the front door.

The smell of fresh paint and cleaning solution hits them in the face. Andrea flips on the light switch and walks around the vaulted foyer. She touches the freshly polished dark wood banister; her eyes follow it up to the large stained-glass window on the landing.

"This place is nice, very nice."

"Considering our house is wrecked by a tornado," Scott says, bumping her shoulder. He frowns at her glittery wide eyes. "Oh no, I know that look. We are not moving."

Andrea laughs. "I can admire a place without picturing our lives here."

"Sure," Scott says, "and I can admire a taco without eating it."

Andrea laughs again. "Come on." She walks through the dining room and flips the light on.

Scott groans. "Is that the same table and chairs we have?"

"It is," Andrea says, smiling. "Let's check out the kitchen."

Scott mumbles under his breath.

"What was that?" Andrea asks, looking back at Scott and entering the kitchen. She flips on the light and gasps.

"Nothing important," Scott says.

Andrea nods and fixates on the sparkling new appliances, including a six-burner gas range and ornate hood, white oak cabinets that extend to the ceiling and a large butcher block island.

Scott reaches up and places a finger under Andrea's chin. "Here," he nudges her chin up, "let me close this gaping hole."

She swats his hand away. "It's so…"

"Expensive," Scott says. "Heading to the second floor."

"I'll be sure to, um, check out the rest of the first floor."

Scott heads upstairs as Andrea wanders around the first floor. They meet back in the foyer a few minutes later.

"All clear?" Andrea asks.

"Yes," Scott says, opening the front door.

Silvey and Darryl are already on the front porch.

"Sorry," Silvey says. "I couldn't wait any longer. I need the bathroom." She gawks at the expansive foyer.

"There's one here," Andrea says, motioning to the right of the steps, "under the stairs. And another near the kitchen."

"Stairs," Silvey calls and rushes towards the small door.

Darryl rocks back on his heels. "Which way is the kitchen?"

Andrea points. "Through the dining room."

Darryl nods. "Thanks again for getting us here safely."

"Let's hope it stays that way," Andrea says.

Darryl nods again and turns towards the dining room.

"How many bedrooms?" Andrea asks.

"You are not allowed upstairs," Scott says.

"Why?" Andrea asks.

"Yeah, why Scott?" Silvey asks.

"Because your best friend is about to blow through all of our savings on this place," Scott says.

"Ha," Silvey says. "Is he wrong?"

Andrea looks around. "I mean…"

"Yeah," Silvey says, "sorry buddy. You're screwed." She pats Scott on the shoulder. "Let's go, Dre." She hops up on the first step. "Show me your new master suite."

Andrea laughs and follows Silvey upstairs.

"Not funny," Scott says, throwing up his hands.

"Trouble?" Darryl asks, leaning against the entry to the living room.

"Probably for my bank account," Scott says. "My wife is enamored with the house."

"It's pretty nice," Darryl says, tapping the wood floor. "And the wood."

"No, man, not you too."

Darryl fights a yawn. "Sorry. Are the bedrooms upstairs?"

"Yes," Scott says. "I'll bring you a few changes of clothes in the morning."

"Thanks," Darryl says, looking down at his stained khakis. "I believe that may be necessary."

"Dre," Scott calls. "We should let them get some rest."

"Coming," Andrea says, laughing. "Silvey thinks that we could bump out the closet into the next room to create a walk-in closet with built-in cabinets." She saunters down the steps with Silvey grinning ear to ear.

"Come on," Scott says, shaking his head. "You two are the worst."

"Scott, it's got great potential," Silvey says, holding up her fingers in air quotes, "to be your forever home."

"Ha," Scott says, handing the keys to Darryl. "Good night, folks. I'll be in the car."

Andrea hugs Silvey and nods to Darryl. "See you in the morning."

15

"Baxton!" Gage whispers.

Baxton lifts his head and blinks a few times. "Did I fall asleep?"

"Yes," Gage says. "We've been sitting ducks for an hour and it's getting colder. I can't sit here any longer."

Baxton unfolds his long legs and stands. He stretches from side to side. "Where too?"

Gage stands and gestures back to the compound. "It's not great, but if we go back…"

"No," Baxton says. "We can't trust them."

Gage points up at the camera. "What if it's not them watching? They would have come by now."

"Then who?" Baxton asks.

"Park rangers?"

"What?" Baxton asks, shaking his head.

"It was a national park book," Gage says, pointing up to the rocks. "Maybe we are on the outskirts of the park."

"Ok," Baxton says. "Let's keep moving." He looks past the rock formation. "At least it's a clear night with a bright moon."

"Good and bad," Gage says, falling in step with Baxton. "We are clearly visible."

"I gave them the option to come and find us," Baxton says. "Now, if they want us, we can give them a run for their money."

"Woo buddy, let's go!" Gage says, bumping his elbow into Baxton's side.

"Easy," Baxton says, rubbing his ribs.

"My bad," Gage says, jogging next to Baxton. "Pretty sure Rozanne is going out of her mind at the moment."

Baxton smirks and nods. "Your wife is turning over every stone and then some."

"And if Silvey knows she is doing the same for you."

Heat fills Baxton's cheeks. "Dude, you think?"

"For sure," Gage says, glancing at Baxton. "Are you blushing?"

"Nah," Baxton says, dipping his head. His curls fall hiding his face. "Are we still heading north?"

"I think so," Gage says. "We can pick up the pace a bit."

"Ma'am, they are heading straight towards us," a man says. His voice comes from the speaker in the middle of the ceiling of the conference room. "Engage?"

Director Gia taps her ring. "No, follow at a distance."

"Why are you stalling?" Agent Vickers asks, pointing at the screen. "They've shared nothing useful over the last two hours."

Director Gia smiles. "According to your initial reports from the hospital records, Baxton had injuries from the tornado and had to have abdominal surgery plus a few broken ribs."

Agent Carlton nods. "And a gash repair on one of his arms."

Director Gia taps the table. "It will be a week tomorrow since the tornado touched down."

"And?" Agent Vickers asks.

"Do you think you could run with broken ribs?"

"No," Agent Carlton says.

"Did you notice a bandage or stitches on either of his arms?" Director Gia asks, directing her attention at Agent Vickers.

Agent Vickers shakes her head. "What are you implying? He can heal fast, so what."

Director Gia rolls her eyes. "Plus, we've received intel from our crew in Missouri. Silvey Rhoades was spotted walking and talking in the local diner. Her list of injuries was quite extensive. Correct?"

"Yes," Agent Carlton says. "We had a medical team ready for her when we received orders to take her from the hospital."

"So how are they walking, talking?" Director Gia asks, gesturing to the screen feed showing Baxton and Gage jogging around the rock formations. "And running?"

"They used the chamber," Agent Carlton whispers.

"Finally," Director Gia says, waving her hands. "All the pieces are coming together."

Agent Vickers pushes back from the table. "The chamber with the white particles in the second room."

Director Gia nods.

"You think the chamber's ancient tech is what healed him?" Agent Vickers asks.

"That's classified."

"Has Project Q's team taken over the base?" Agent Carlton asks.

"Yes," Gia says.

"What do you think they know?" Agent Carlton asks. "Why take them?"

"We need to know what they experienced or if they took anything from the base," Director Gia says.

"We've run out of mushroom rocks," Gage says, slowing to a walk.

Baxton jogs in a circle. "Just thicker sand between here and what?"

"Man, no idea." Gage scuffs his shoes in the sand.

Baxton sighs. "Any idea if we are still heading north?"

Gage looks up and points. "I believe that is the north star."

"Alright," Baxton says. "My tank is about empty. I never did get a chance to eat today."

"Oh," Gage says. "That's right, you were warming up food when we caught sight of the drone."

"And then all of it went to hell," Baxton says, walking beside Gage. "It's probably after midnight at home."

"Is it just me," Gage says, "or did the air just shift?" He moves further ahead and halts. "Dude."

Baxton rushes to his side.

Gage throws out an arm blocking Baxton. "Careful! I can't see the bottom."

"We are beyond in over our heads," Baxton says, looking down at the sheer cliff. "Do you think there is a bridge or a path down?"

"Maybe," Gage says, looking left and then right. "But I can't see the other side. It's either a big valley below or we are…"

"At a dead end," Baxton whispers.

"Ma'am they've reached the cliff," the man says over the speaker.

"Approach," Director Gia says, tapping her ring. "Bring them both back to base with the promise of a warm meal and showers. And no more questions till morning, if they come willingly."

"Is this how you keep people away from here?" Agent Carlton asks.

"It's not an inconvenience to have natural barriers," Director Gia says, watching the two men pace the edge.

"We've only wasted time," Agent Vickers says. "This little adventure was less than helpful. I hope General Hall takes notice that your incompetence is evident."

"I don't agree," General Hall says from the open door.

Agent Vickers whips her head around and her mouth falls open.

"Project Q will no longer need your assistance," General Hall says. "Please bear in mind the contract you signed on your flight home."

"Wait," Agent Vickers says. "Please, let me explain."

"I've heard enough," General Hall says. "Oscar will escort you to the tarmac."

Oscar fills the doorway. "Ma'am."

Agent Vickers pushes back from the table and glares at Director Gia. "Unbelievable."

"Agent Carlton," General Hall says. "Do you wish to remain here, or would you like to leave with Ms. Vickers?"

"I'll stay," Agent Carlton says. He avoids Agent Vickers' menacing stare and looks down at the table.

"Safe travels," Director Gia says.

"Oh, go screw yourself," Agent Vickers mumbles, following Oscar out of the conference room.

"She's normally not like this," Agent Carlton says after the door closes. "I'm not sure what's come over her."

"I understand," General Hall says. He nods towards the screen. "I believe the team have reached the men."

"Hi guys," a man says.

Gage turns around. "Who's there?"

Four men emerge from the darkness.

"We are here to help you," the man says.

100

Gage glances over at Baxton. "Dude."

"We're screwed," Baxton whispers.

"Who are you?" Gage asks. "And how did you find us?"

The shortest of the four men steps forward. "We've been instructed to bring you back to base with the promise of a warm meal, showers, and no questions until morning."

"You work for them?" Gage asks, stepping in front of Baxton.

The man nods. "Do you wish to comply?"

"What choice do we have?" Gage asks.

"Um," the man says. "We would advise this to be the safest option. A mile west, it drops into another deep ravine, south only goes further into the edges of a national park about twenty miles away from civilization and well you've seen where north leads."

"That may be the first honest thing we've heard," Baxton says. "Who do you work for?"

"The US Government."

"What branch?" Gage asks.

"That's classified," the man says.

"Ha," Gage says. "So much for honesty."

"Sir," the man says. "I've got orders. Do you comply?"

Gage looks over his shoulder. "Dude."

Baxton sighs. "I want to return home. Is that an option?"

"Tomorrow," the man says. "The Director will make that call."

"Director of what?" Baxton asks.

"Our department," the man says.

"What department?" Gage asks.

"That's also classified," the man says.

"Bax," Gage says. "I really want to slug this man."

"I get it," Baxton says, patting him on the shoulder. "Let's just follow them back. I can't think straight without food."

"Food," Gage whispers. "That's what is on your mind."

"My tank is beyond empty," Baxton says.

"Lead on," Gage says.

The men assemble, with two in front and the other two following Gage and Baxton.

16

Silvey throws back the covers and sits up. *Why can't I sleep?* She walks to the window and pulls back the curtains.

The moonlight gives the yard an eerie brightness ending with the dark tree line.

"Bax, where are you? What have they done to you?"

Silvey pulls her long blonde ponytail down and massages her scalp. She closes her eyes and takes in a deep breath. *One sheep, two sheep, thwee.*

Silvey chuckles and opens her eyes. Distant thunder rolls and lightning streaks across the cloudless night sky. She cranes her head to look towards the west and watches a cluster of clouds light up.

"Just what this town needs," Silvey mutters. She walks towards the bedroom door but pauses with her hand on the knob. Footsteps thump away from her door.

"Darryl?" Silvey whispers loudly.

"Guilty," Darryl says.

Silvey swings open the door. "What are you doing?"

"I heard someone talking," Darryl says. "I was concerned that we had unwanted company."

"I was just restless and talking to myself," Silvey says, looking at his dark-circled eyes, stooped posture, and rumpled shirt. "You need to sleep. I'm wired. I'll stay up and keep watch if it means you can rest."

Darryl shakes his head. "To be honest, the idea of sleep scares me awake."

"What do you mean?" Silvey asks.

"I might wake up back inside the base," Darryl says.

"Dang," Silvey says. "That would be a mind f…"

"Yea, it's messed up."

"I hear you," Silvey says. "But we are safe here and I don't see any worm holes around."

Thunder rattles the house.

Darryl cowers and covers his head.

Silvey points up. "There's a storm rolling in."

Darryl straightens and shakes out his arms. "Right. Sleep. I'll try."

"Good," Silvey says, patting him on the arm. "I'll be here and wake you if I see anything fishy. I promise."

Darryl nods and walks towards the room down the hall. "Good night."

Silvey watches him until he closes the door behind him and jumps when thunder rattles the house again. "Dang that's close." She pulls her hair back up into a messy bun as she walks downstairs.

She wanders through the dining room to the kitchen. She opens and closes every cabinet. "Soft close cabinets. Fancy." She pulls open the door in the corner and the light overhead clicks on. "Motion lighted pantry. Bravo." She backs out of the pantry as lightning strikes and lights up the window over the sink. "That was close." She wanders to the back door and watches the rainfall. A few trees bend and sway. "It's ramping up." She rubs the chills rippling over her arms. "I hope we are safe." She opens the door across from the back door; steps descend into darkness. "Oh, good a basement."

Silvey flips on the light. "And a finished basement. If Andrea saw this, she would be at home packing." She descends and lets out a low whistle. She runs her hand over the shiny polished bar with an epoxy in lay to the pool table and admires three big flat screen TVs. "This gives new meaning to a man cave." She plops down on the sectional sofa and stares up at the smooth white ceilings with recessed lighting. Her gaze falls on a tiny red blinking light. "Oh shit, that's a camera." She quickly stands, grabs a barstool, and climbs up. She pops off the white ring around the light and pulls out a tiny sensor attached to a tiny camera. "Who's watching a vacant house?" She pops out a black wire and the red light stops blinking.

Silvey surveys each light in the basement for any additional cameras. She works her way back upstairs, carefully inspecting every fixture and switch. She moves through the living room and an office. *No cameras.* But curses when she finds one over the foyer. She quickly moves back through the dining room to the kitchen. *If you were a step ladder, where would you be?*

The thrum of the rain drowns her pounding heart.

Silvey opens every door and cabinet until she decides on a chair from the dining room. She centers the chair under the hanging light fixture and climbs up. She stands on her tippy toes and reaches but falls short. *Damn it!* She gives the camera a middle finger and hops down. She carries the chair back to the dining room and lets it thud on the wood floor. She grimaces and listens for Darryl. But the rain is beating against the windows, muffling her own footsteps. She inspects the light fixtures upstairs and checks every room, but the one Darryl is sleeping in. *Just the foyer and the basement.* She slumps on the bed she started in.

"Let's hope these are just for the security of the home and not linked to anything online," Silvey mutters. "I didn't find a modem in my search for cameras. It should be fine. Don't be dramatic Silvey."

17

Gage swallows the last bite of his burger and leans back. "I'll give them some credit. That burger was amazing."

"I'm not sure I tasted a single bite," Baxton says, patting his waist.

"That's what happens when you inhale food." Gage stretches his arms overhead. "Ready to hit the hay?"

"I believe I could sleep in this chair," Baxton says.

Gage laughs. "Rock, chair, floor—you could always crash anywhere and everywhere since we were kids."

"I'm resourceful," Baxton says. "You're lucky I didn't crash in the shower."

"Lucky," Gage says, shaking his head. "If we're lucky, we'll get to leave this place in the morning." He stands and walks to the bunk bed in the corner. "I'm calling dibs on the bottom."

"Have you ever taken the top?" Baxton asks, pushing back from the table.

"I'm consistent," Gage says, crashing down on the single bed.

Baxton walks over and climbs onto the top bunk. "Let's just hope this was all a bad dream and we'll wake up at home."

Gage yawns. "That's a lot of wishful thinking."

Baxton closes his eyes and sighs. "I know, dude."

"Agent Carlton," Director Gia says, clicking off the TV. "Oscar will take you back to your assigned room."

"Can I ask one question?" Agent Carlton asks, pushing back from the conference table.

"Sure," Director Gia says, looking over at General Hall.

He nods.

Agent Carlton straightens his back and lifts his chin. "When will I be read into Project Q?"

"We've discussed what is relevant to share at this stage," General Hall says. "Our goal is to study and understand the items found at the base."

Agent Carlton leans forward. "The Auburn men's role in this is?"

"If they know and share what the chamber is," Director Gia says. "Can you imagine the pandemonium?"

"Depends on what the chamber can actually do."

"Imagine a world where disease and injuries were instantly healed," Director Gia says.

Agent Carlton's jaw falls ajar.

"Now, when I add in the factor that the white particles recovered from the chamber are made from a raw material that dried up in the eighties."

"It's one of a kind," Agent Carlton whispers.

106

"Precisely," Director Gia says. "A tech with vast healing power, but only one for eight billion plus people."

"Oh hell," Agent Carlton mumbles. "And nothing else can replicate it?"

"We don't know yet," Director Gia says. "But if this leaks before we have the answer…"

"We're screwed," Agent Carlton says.

General Hall leans forward. "Do you understand the urgency required?"

"Yes sir," Agent Carlton says with a quick nod. "Thank you for sharing." He stands and follows Oscar from the conference room.

Director Gia holds up her crossed fingers. "Let's hope that wasn't a mistake."

"We'll see how it pans out by morning," General Hall says. "Gia, do you know what Agent Vickers shared with Oscar on her way to the tarmac?"

"No," Director Gia says, raising an eyebrow. "Do tell."

"If they only knew, they let go of the non-conspiracy agent," General Hall says.

"Oh dear," Gia says. "Why did you let me share any details with him?"

"If he knows of any online chatter or theories," General Hall says, "it could lead us to the outlet that leaked the page from the original documents related to the chamber."

"Interesting," Director Gia says, nodding. "Would you like to tackle that questioning personally?"

"In the morning," General Hall says. "I have our team on standby if either of the Auburn men should need anything. We should hit the racks until zero six hundred."

"Yes sir," Director Gia says, pushing back from the table. She stands but hesitates by the chair. "Have you received a new report from the lab?"

"No, I've sent everyone there to bed," General Hall says. "I don't want weary eyes to miss something important. They are to start again in the morning."

Director Gia nods. "Good night, sir." She pulls up her hoodie and leaves the conference room.

"Sir," Oscar says, stepping inside the conference room.

General Hall stands and nods. "Oscar."

"Agent Carlton was silent," Oscar says. "But the pilot radioed the tower. Agent Vickers has been demanding that they turn the jet around."

"Did she say why?" General Hall asks.

"She says she kept something out of the initial report because it was too absurd."

"About?"

"Something Captain Wilson found after the tornado, but it's now clear he was telling the truth."

General Hall chuckles. "When we find Captain Wilson, we'll be sure to ask. Do not turn the jet around."

Oscar nods. "I'll let the tower know."

"Thanks," General Hall says. "After that, hit the rack. We'll start again at zero six hundred."

"Yes, sir," Oscar says, standing aside for General Hall to exit the conference room.

18

Silvey rolls off the bed and walks to the window. The sunlight streaks through the tree line and glimmers on the wet grass.

"We survived," Silvey whispers.

She turns away from the window and assesses the bed. The covers are twisted in a knot in the middle. *Apparently, I didn't sleep so peacefully. Let's hope Darryl had better luck.*

"Silvey?"

Silvey swings open the bedroom door and walks to the banister.

Darryl waves from the bottom step. "Good morning. How did you sleep?"

"Ok, you?" Silvey asks, descending the steps.

"I woke up in this century," Darryl says, nodding. "I call that a win."

"How long have you been up?" Silvey asks.

"About an hour."

Silvey stops on the last step and points up. "I found two cameras in the house last night. One here and one in the basement."

Darryl stares up at the light fixture. "I don't see anything."

"Grab a chair from the dining room," Silvey says.

Darryl sets the chair under the fixture.

"I was too short to disable it," Silvey says, "but you should be able to reach it." She points to the small red blinking light.

Darryl climbs up and grasps the small black device. "What do I do?"

"Pull the black wire out from the back," Silvey says.

He pulls it out and leaves it dangling by the red wire. "Do you think someone was watching?"

"Hope not," Silvey says, shrugging. "My best guess is the owner had them installed to monitor realtor traffic through the home."

The rumble of a car has Darryl off the chair and scrambling away from the windows in a flash.

Silvey ducks down beside him and peeks out the dining-room window. "It's Andrea."

Darryl sighs holding a hand over his chest. "My goodness. I believe my heart stopped for a few seconds."

"She is pretty heart stopping," Silvey says, winking at Darryl and rushing to the front door. "Good morning, Dre."

"You're both up?" Andrea asks, walking in with a white box of donuts, a full cardboard drink carrier and a plastic bag of clothing.

Darryl takes the drinks from her and walks ahead of her to the kitchen.

"I've only been up about twenty minutes," Silvey says, trailing behind Andrea. "Darryl got up an hour ago. I smell coffee."

"I brought you coffee and donuts," Andrea says. "Scott will be by later with some groceries and toiletries. But I did bring a few changes of clothes for Darryl and your bag from the car." She turns and slides the backpack off her shoulder. She opens the white box and turns it towards Darryl. "You get first dibs."

Darryl grins. "Well, hmm, I think I'll take this one." He picks up a cinnamon roll and takes a napkin from the drink carrier.

"Sweetener and cream should be there too," Andrea says, taking a cup and handing it to Silvey. "Your dad called this morning on his way to his appointment."

"Is that what woke you up?" Silvey asks, picking out a chocolate glazed long john.

"No," Andrea says. "We had a bit of a leak with the rain last night. I was up dumping the water bucket."

"Oh no," Silvey muffles over a full mouth.

"It's bound to happen until we can get the kitchen fixed and a new roof put on."

"That sucks, so sorry, Dre," Silvey says. She pops the lid and pours in a creamer. "What did my dad want?"

"Buzz was checking on you and he mentioned his buddy, Tom, lives out past the base. There has been non-stop military traffic there since they told everyone to stay away."

"No surprise there," Darryl says.

"I did a bit of snooping around here after you left," Silvey says. "The basement is beautiful and finished."

Andrea smiles. "Do tell."

"But I did find a camera, well actually two. One in the basement and one in the foyer."

"No way," Andrea says, pulling out her phone. She frowns. "There is barely any signal here and no Wi-Fi in range."

"That's great news," Silvey says, sipping the coffee.

"Is Wi-Fi the internet thing?" Darryl asks.

Silvey grins. "Yes. How weird is our technology?"

He chuckles. "From the guy that managed to time travel. Odd."

Andrea laughs.

Silvey chokes and coughs on her sip of coffee.

"Easy there tiger," Andrea says, patting Silvey on the back.

"I'm good," Silvey says, raising her hand. "Have you heard from Rozanne?"

"They've tracked down the air controller for Mosby Airfield. He wasn't able to give the authorities the flight destination, but he did confirm two men were handled quite forcefully onto the small jet. And one matching Baxton's height and hair."

"Damn it!" Silvey says. "How's Rozanne holding up?"

"She was somber last night," Andrea says. "The local sheriff searched the area and found a cut chain near the gate they used to enter the field beyond their property."

"Are the feds answering?" Silvey asks.

"Dodging involvement—for now."

"Ugh!" Silvey walks to the back door and swings it open. She steps out onto the back porch.

"AHHHHHHHHHHHH!"

Darryl jumps and spills a little coffee. "Is she ok?"

"She will be," Andrea says. "Coping mechanism of being the only child of a nasty divorce. Keep the peace and scream once it peaks."

Silvey returns to the kitchen and chugs her coffee. "Alright. Any other news?"

Andrea nods. "Myra got a knock on her door from the Military Police."

"No," Darryl says, fumbling to sit down his coffee without spilling more.

"Unfortunately," Andrea says. "But she's a pro. She told them to take a hike and if they trespass on her property without a warrant, she'll consider them a hostile intruder."

"Go Myra!" Silvey says, raising her empty cup.

"We need to be extra careful," Andrea says.

"Is there still a car watching your house?" Silvey asks.

"I noticed one reporter van at the dead end and one black car near the house, but the driver was dead asleep when I rolled past him."

Silvey nods. "Can you ask Myra if we should worry about the cameras?"

"Absolutely," Andrea says.

"Great," Silvey says, taking her bag. "I'm going to run up and change. And tell Scott to go hard on the sweet and salty snack game."

Andrea laughs and looks at Darryl. "Any requests?"

He runs a hand over his scruffy face. "Razor and shaving cream. Plus, a toothbrush and paste."

"No food requests?" Andrea asks.

"I, um, can't think of anything."

Andrea nods. "What did you crave for dinner when you had a long day at work?"

"My Millie's chicken pot pie," Darryl says without hesitation.

"We can make a chicken pot pie for dinner," Andrea says.

Darryl smiles and nods adverting his watery eyes. "That would be lovely. Thank you."

"No problem," Andrea says, dialing Scott. She steps out onto the back porch.

"Hey," Scott says. "Just pulled up to Price Chopper."

"Great, Silvey has a request for sweet and salty snacks to add to the list. And Darryl made a request for a razor and shaving cream."

"Got it," Scott says.

"And I am sending ingredients for a chicken pot pie."

"Let me guess that was Darryl?"

"Definitely not junk food Silvey."

"Hey, I resent that," Silvey says, from the doorway.

Andrea turns and winks. "Am I wrong?"

"I can eat veggies and fruits," Silvey says.

"Sure," Scott says, "smothered or dipped in something."

"I heard that!" Silvey says, flipping up her middle finger and steps back inside.

"She just flipped you off," Andrea says, laughing.

"Shocker," Scott says. "Anything for you?"

"Just stick to the list I made, and you should be fine. But text before heading to check out."

"Got it," Scott says. "Love you."

"Love you too." Andrea hangs up and walks back inside to an empty kitchen. "Silvey?"

"Downstairs!" Silvey yells.

Andrea descends and freezes on the last step. "If Scott sees this, we are moving tomorrow."

19

"Bax," Gage whispers.

"Gage," Baxton says, leaning his head over the bunk.

"Oh, good you're up."

"How does Roz sleep in the same room with you?"

"What do you mean?"

"You snore and grunt in your sleep."

"Grunt," Gage says, laughing. "That's a new one. Roz hasn't added that to my list."

"You've got a list?" Baxton asks, jumping down from the top bunk.

"Of course," Gage says, sitting up and pushing back the cover. "Just wait. I'm sure Silvey will have one for you soon."

Baxton grins. He pulls his hair back and ties it up. "If we ever make it out of here."

Gage nods and digs in his pocket. He holds up the black ring. "They haven't taken this yet."

"Shh," Baxton says, looking around at the dull grey walls meeting the white vaulted ceilings. "They could be watching."

Gage shakes his head. "They found us in the middle of nowhere. I'm pretty sure they have been watching us the whole time."

Baxton sighs. "What can we say that will get us out of here?"

"Nothing about the thing," Gage says, tapping Baxton's abdomen.

Baxton nods. "Duh. And we can't let them split us up."

"Deal," Gage says. "But we know they know we were at the base. Thoughts?"

Baxton snaps. "I told them I went to the base hoping to find my car or a piece of the car post tornado. And we ran because we were running late to Micah's funeral."

"Cool, cool, but why did we go through a field?" Gage asks, tying his shoe.

"We, um, heard the road was blocked by debris from the tornado."

"And Silvey," Gage says, straightening. "Do we know where she is?"

"No," Baxton says. "But they wouldn't dare take her again with all the media exposure from the hospital abduction."

"Hopefully," Gage says, nodding to the door. "Pretty sure we've got company." He points to the shadow in the gap under the door.

Bax swings the door open, and a man with his fist raised steps back.

"They're ready for you," the man says.

"Who are you?" Bax asks, folding his arms across his chest. "And who are they?"

"I'm Oscar and they are General Hall and Director Gia."

"A general?" Bax asks.

"I would give you his first name if I knew it," Oscar says.

"Hold up," Gage says. "You don't know who you work for?"

"General Hall is above my paygrade," Oscar says. "But he did mention, I could share that Agent Vickers has been dismissed."

"Great news," Gage says. "One down, but one still super sketchy agent to go."

Oscar nods. "If you will follow me." He gestures down the hall without losing eye contact with Baxton.

Gage pats Baxton on the shoulder. "Let's go see what they want. I need to get home to Roz."

Bax tilts his chin up. "Lead on."

They follow Oscar up a flight of stairs and into a glass walled conference room with two strangers sitting at a table. A bald middle-aged man, dressed in a black t-shirt and jeans, and a young woman with dark hair, dressed in a neon orange hoodie and jeans. They stand as Gage and Baxton enter.

Oscar remains at the threshold of the room.

Gage cuts Bax a look with an eyebrow raised.

Bax shrugs.

The tall bald man nods to Oscar and he steps away.

"I'm sorry," the woman says, sticking out her hand. "We've not been properly introduced. I'm Director Gia and this is General Hall." She nods to her right.

"Proper?" Gage asks, opening and closing a fist. "You think snatching and drugging two people from private property, and then flying them to New Mexico is polite?"

Director Gia tilts her head to the side. "Why do you think you're in New Mexico?"

"Why are we here?" Baxton asks. "And no games. Ask us what you think we know."

"I like him," General Hall says. "Have a seat. I will not waste any more of your time."

Gage and Baxton pull out the chairs across from them and sit.

"We have a witness that spotted the two of you sprinting away from the base two days ago," General Hall says. "Why were you there?"

Baxton leans forward. "My car was outside the silo when the tornado hit. I was hoping to salvage what I could. But we didn't find any scrap of the car."

"Then why run and come via the field?" Director Gia asks.

"We were told the roads near the base were blocked with debris," Gage says. "And we were running because we lost track of time. We had a funeral to attend."

116

Director Gia nods. "Your boss, Micah?"

Baxton nods. "And friend."

"I am sorry for your loss," Director Gia says, "but according to Agent Carlton, you were hospitalized after the tornado."

"That is none of your business or his," Baxton says.

"You don't want us to play games," General Hall says. "Tell us why you were really at the base."

"We did," Gage says.

"You'll be interested to know that the owners of Greening Up confessed to their involvement of Ms. Rhoades abduction from the hospital," General Hall says.

Gage leans forward. "And your involvement with our abduction?"

"Guilty," General Hall says. "It was my team that took you two."

"And drugging us?" Baxton asks.

"Standard protocol," Director Gia says. "Did you enter the base after the tornado?"

"No," Baxton and Gage say in unison.

General Hall taps the table. "All cards on the table. We ran a test on both of you during the transport to this facility."

"You did what?" Gage asks.

"What kind of test?" Baxton asks.

"A tiny blood sample," Director Gia says.

"Seriously?" Gage asks, examining his arms. "When we were unconscious?"

"It was necessary," Director Gia says. "Baxton yours came back positive for a substance that has only ever been linked to tiny white particles. Like the ones you saw at the base."

"Ha!" Baxton shouts. "I was hit with all sorts of flying particles during the big ass tornado. That test proves nothing!"

"And your healed injuries," Director Gia says. "A miracle?"

"Again, my health is none of your business!"

General Hall shakes his head. "I hear your frustration, but there is this." He taps his ring. The screen at the end of the table turns on and a grainy black-and-white image of a document appears blurry and then clears. Project Rainbow is written in bold across the center of the page beneath the seal of the eagle holding arrows and an olive branch.

Baxton squints at the screen and bites the inside of his cheek.

"Your name, along with Ms. Rhoades, appear on a list of participants." General Hall taps his ring flipping the page of the document and it pauses. He magnifies a list of names. "This document was sealed for sixty years until Captain Wilson was found after the tornado."

"I'm pretty sure there are other people out there with my name," Baxton says. "Same for Silvey."

"A coincidence," General Hall says, folding his hands together. "Mr. Auburn."

"You believe that my cousin," Gage says, throwing his hands up, "who's clearly not a day older than twenty-five is part of a government thing from sixty years ago. I'm pretty sure you two are one screw loose from the looney bin."

Director Gia smirks. "Do you remember doing a background check for the Navy?"

Baxton sits back and sighs. "I was seventeen and didn't enlist."

"It's still in the database," Director Gia says.

"And?" Baxton twirls a finger.

"We have your fingerprints on file and have a set matching yours inside the base."

"I worked there," Baxton says. He taps his forehead. "Remember?"

"In the silo," Director Gia says.

Baxton nods. "Yes."

"But not inside the suspension chamber," Director Gia says. "Along with a long blonde hair and we are betting it matches Silvey Rhoades."

Director Gia taps her ring. The screen darkens to an image of Silvey sitting in the back seat of a car with her hand in front of her face. "This was taken yesterday just before noon."

Baxton audibly swallows. "Did you take her?"

Director Gia shakes her head. "But between her and Captain Wilson we'll need to have a conversation about what you and

118

your cousin found at the base and are refusing to share with the room."

"One," Gage says, holding up a finger. "You've never told us who you work for or why us? Two, the hostility in which we were taken is beyond any trust building rapport. And three, we didn't find his damn car!" He pushes away from the table and stands. "Let us go. Now!"

"Mr. Auburn," General Hall says. "I am happy to release you. If you sign a non-disclosure agreement about your visit to our facility."

Baxton laughs. "Pardon me."

"You're serious?" Gage asks.

General Hall nods. "We are preparing the jet now."

"I'm not signing shit," Gage says. "Let's go Bax."

Baxton stands and turns for the door.

Oscar steps inside the doorway.

Baxton looks him up and down. "Move or be moved. Your choice."

Oscar shakes his head. "Sir."

Baxton towers over Oscar. "Now."

"Mr. Auburn," Director Gia says. "You've not been dismissed."

Baxton whirls and points a finger at Gia. "I am not yours to dismiss!"

Director Gia smirks. "You forfeited that right when you stepped inside the suspension chamber."

Baxton reels back. "You are insane."

"But I'm right," Director Gia says. "Admit that you were there inside the base and used the chamber. And we'll tell you who we are and why you were taken."

Baxton shakes his head. "You can't hold us here forever."

Agent Carlton walks up behind Oscar.

Gage spots the loitering agent and points. "This is your fault!"

Agent Carlton holds up both hands. "I'm sure it's a big misunderstanding."

"Agent Carlton, please," General Hall says, standing and gesturing towards the table.

Oscar briefly steps aside to allow Agent Carlton enough room to pass within an inch of Baxton.

Baxton glares down at them.

Oscar immediately takes his place back at the door.

"Please, have a seat," General Hall says, looking directly at Baxton and Gage.

"Not a chance," Gage says.

"Agent Carlton, can you please tell them who you work for?" General Hall asks.

Agent Carlton hesitates before sitting down. "Sir?"

"Go ahead," General Hall says.

"I work for the State Department," Agent Carlton says, taking a seat.

"Great," Baxton says, "more lies. You showed me your FBI badge when we first met. So, which is it?"

"I was reassigned to the state department as of yesterday," Agent Carlton says.

"What state department?" Gage asks.

"Science and technology," Director Gia says.

"A state department has the right to kidnap civilians?" Baxton asks, shaking his head.

"We have the right to protect technology that could be weaponized," General Hall says.

Gage laughs and points to Baxton. "We, Baxton and I, are accused of harboring tech?"

"Search us," Baxton says, turning out his pockets. "We've got nothing."

"We searched you upon capture," General Hall says. "We know you were inside the base on Saturday. And what you did, saw and/or used while inside."

"Tall grass, a few pieces of debris like vinyl siding, roof shingles, and an old tractor," Gage says. He snaps. "And a shed with an ambulance."

Agent Carlton leans forward. "They have recovered the footage from a camera inside the base. Just tell them what you saw and did."

Baxton flattens his lips in a firm thin line. "No."

"Who are you protecting?" Director Gia asks.

"No one," Gage says.

"We know you were inside," General Hall says, gesturing to Agent Carlton. "We gave you ample opportunity to share the truth, but you've chosen to lie, over and over." He taps his ring and the image of Baxton, Gage, Andrea, and Scott appear on the screen. "Why?"

"Trust," Baxton says, pointing to Agent Carlton.

"Baxton," Director Gia says. "I know that you used the suspension chamber while you were inside. And we know that you've traveled to 1961."

"Traveled?" Agent Carlton whispers, looking over at Director Gia.

"Later," Director Gia whispers.

"Cool," Gage says. "You know everything, right?" He points to the door with his thumb. "We can go now."

General Hall leans back in his chair. "Oscar, please escort the gentlemen to the tarmac."

Gia shakes her head. "Sir."

"It's my call," General Hall says. "We know and they know. End of story. Right, Mr. Auburn?"

"Sure," Gage says, pushing Baxton towards the door.

Oscar moves out into the hallway.

Baxton and Gage walk out and follow Oscar.

"Gage," Baxton whispers.

"Don't speak until we are in the air," Gage says.

"General," Director Gia says.

General Hall holds up his hand and taps his ring. "The lab has finished their analysis of Baxton's specimen." He nods to the screen. "They've confirmed the nano technology is active in his bloodstream—just like the owners of Greening Up."

"And you just let them walk out of here," Director Gia says, gesturing towards the door.

"Yes," General Hall says, scooting back from the table. "We've got interventions in place."

"What do you mean?" Agent Carlton asks.

"Their devices will be returned to them upon landing, and we've received permission to track their communications for the next ninety days."

"You're going to spy on them," Agent Carlton says, shaking his head. "Why don't you take all their first amendment rights away?"

"You know what is at stake," General Hall says. "Director Gia please fill him in on his role here at Project Q." He leaves the conference room and swings the door closed.

Agent Carlton throws his hands up. "What the hell?"

"General Hall received a call from ground operations at the base this morning," Director Gia says. "Something they said had him on edge this morning and our game plan went out the window when the lab confirmed our fears."

"What are you afraid of?" Agent Carlton asks.

"Once you use the chamber it stays with you and if you were to donate blood," Director Gia says, "the recipient will get more than just blood."

"It can spread?"

Director Gia nods.

"But that's great, right?"

"To be determined," Director Gia says. "It's essentially the fountain of youth for the five of them. They have a shot of out living their generation by over a hundred years. Minus a death blow to the head, they will be immune to any life-threatening diseases. And forget about them aging."

"Whoa," Agent Carlton whispers.

"Until the lab can reproduce the particles, it may make them walking targets if the tech is leaked."

"And that bit about him traveling to the past?" Agent Carlton asks. "What did you mean?"

"You uncovered a link between Silvey, Baxton, and Captain Wilson in the documents from Project Rainbow."

"It was the only common thread between them."

"We found a journal entry by the original author of Project Rainbow. They documented a strange encounter with a possible Soviet spy and the subject disappeared. The person gave the date and time that Captain Wilson would be found and other future events that had global impact."

Agent Carlton frowns.

"The journal entry was dated in 1961."

"It's half time and half healing machine?"

"The suspension chamber was used as a stasis for the subject," Director Gia says. "And a precautionary measure if the leap did not go as planned."

"Like for Captain Wilson?"

"We would love to know how he was abandoned for sixty years, and it is under investigation. But considering most people involved are now six feet under it could run cold before we have answers."

"True," Agent Carlton says, tapping the table. "Have you read anything about the project online?"

"What do you mean?" Director Gia asks. "Project Rainbow was sealed until last week."

"But there were small leaks about the project after President Kennedy's death." Agent Carlton says. "Two mentions in a Kennedy memoir published in the eighties and at least three investigative journal articles about technology buried by American politicians over the last decade."

"And you know this how?" Director Gia asks, raising a single eyebrow.

"We have a consultant who is super talented when it comes to browsing the web and databases behind lock and key."

"You mean a hacker."

20

Oscar hands the pilot a zipped bag. "Please return these to the men upon landing." He turns to Baxton and Gage standing in the aisle of the small jet. "I know it's not my place, but I do sincerely apologize for the experience here."

"Uh, thanks," Baxton says.

"Have a seat and buckle up," Oscar says. "They are set to taxi as soon as I close the door."

Gage nods and takes the nearest window seat.

Oscar departs and swiftly shuts the door.

Baxton paces the aisle.

"Sit down," Gage says.

"I can't," Baxton says. "That was too easy. Something feels off."

"Good morning," the pilot says. "Our flight time today is one hour and fifty minutes. Radar suggests it should be a smooth flight. Take a seat and buckle up."

Baxton sighs and sits beside Gage. "I can't get over the feeling that this is bad dude. Like really really bad."

"Like final destination bad?" Gage whispers, tightening his seat belt.

"I don't know," Baxton says. "I just can't shake it. They let us go way too easily this morning."

"I know they lied about who they work for," Gage says, waving his hand around. "What kind of state department has a luxury jet?"

Baxton clicks his seatbelt and puts his head in his hands. "The only reason we could walk out is if they had somebody else to answer their questions."

Gage straightens. "You think they have Silvey or the captain?"

"If they've already spoken to Charlotte and Eli about their involvement—who else does that leave?"

"Shit," Gage says, raising the window cover. "But she said they didn't take Silvey."

"Yet," Baxton says.

The jet rocks forward and picks up speed.

Baxton grips the armrest until his knuckles go white.

"Take a breath," Gage says, patting Baxton's hand. "We'll be home soon."

"Dre?" Scott calls from the front door.

"Coming!" Andrea says, running up the stairs. She meets Scott in the kitchen. "Hey, any trouble?"

"No," Scott says, looking her over. "What's going on?"

"There's a basement," Andrea says, smiling from ear to ear. "It's really…"

"Stop," Scott says, resting the bags on the island. "I get it. You love the house, but are you going to shovel snow all the way down the gravel drive in the winter or mow this huge lawn while I am out of town for work?"

Andrea frowns. "There's a finished basement with a bar and pool table."

"Silvey Lynn Rhoades!" Scott yells.

"Whoa," Silvey says, marching up the steps. "That's uncalled for. What the hell did I do now?" She enters the kitchen with her fists raised. "Come on, put them up, put them up."

Scott laughs. "I'm not a cowardly lion. We are not moving and this bug of buying a new house is all your fault."

"It's not new," Silvey says, pointing up at the ceiling. "It's a remodel."

"Not helping," Scott says, tossing a bag of chips at her face.

Silvey catches the bag and pops it open. "You're welcome." She stuffs a chip in her mouth and waves as she leaves the kitchen.

Andrea's phone dings three times. "I guess I didn't get any signal down there." She scrolls the messages. "They're back. Silvey get in here."

Silvey runs into the kitchen nearly choking on a mouthful of chips.

Darryl races upstairs. "Everything ok?" He skids to a stop beside Silvey.

"Gage and Baxton are on their way home," Andrea says.

"Seriously?" Silvey asks.

Andrea hands Silvey her phone. "Rozanne just messaged. The guys landed at the small airstrip out by the golf course in Excelsior Springs."

"Landed," Darryl whispers. "They were released in under twenty-four hours."

"That's great news, right?" Scott asks.

"They know where we are," Darryl says, looking out the kitchen window.

"They couldn't," Andrea says, looking over at Scott. "You weren't followed here."

"No," Scott says. "And I took the long way just in case."

126

"But your phones are on," Silvey says.

"Of course," Andrea says.

"If they managed to track down the footage from the base," Silvey says. "You two were with Baxton and Gage, but what are the chances?" She looks at Darryl's pale face.

"Tracking a signal isn't hard," Darryl says, "and likely easier these days with the number of satellites in orbit."

"How do you know about the number of satellites?" Silvey asks.

"Eli and I covered a lot of current events," Darryl says, "including a man named Elon. We should split up. Do you know the area around here?"

"The property likely buts up against the edge of the state park," Scott says. "It has a four-mile loop around a small lake, picnic and camping areas, plus a few buildings from the old mill. But otherwise, just a bunch of farms or homes on large plots like these in all directions."

"State land or private property," Silvey says.

"Um," Scott says. "But are you sure we should move? Maybe we just wait to see what Gage and Baxton have to say."

"They'll be monitoring all telecommunications," Darryl says. "I know I sound absurd."

"No," Silvey says. "I understand. Scott, take Andrea's phone and yours to the campgrounds. Once you're there, turn them off and take your sim card but toss the phones."

Andrea's face goes yellow, then green. "Silvey."

"I know your life, work and schedule revolve around that thing, so maybe instead of tossing it leave it somewhere hidden. But we need to lead them to the park and away from here."

Scott wraps Andrea in a hug. "It will be temporary, and you have it backed up to the cloud."

Andrea sighs and releases him. "Take it."

"We'll prep the food to go," Silvey says.

"Sorry no chicken pot pie tonight," Andrea says.

"Safety first," Darryl says, walking to the sink. He washes his hands and looks over the bags of groceries on the island. "Put me to work. I need to stay busy, or I might bolt."

Scott nods. "I'll be back in a bit."

"Wait," Silvey says. "Take Andrea's car."

"Why?" Andrea asks.

"Gut feeling," Silvey says.

Andrea shrugs and tosses Scott her keys.

Scott catches the keys and jogs out the door.

"Sandwiches," Andrea says, taking bread and condiments out of one bag and sliced deli meat out of another. "Start on these and I will boil the eggs."

They wordlessly assemble the sandwiches, wash and slice some vegetables.

Andrea drains the boiling water and rinses the boiled eggs with cold water. "I really hate peeling eggs."

Silvey laughs. "I've got it."

"Do you like pickles in your tuna salad?" Andrea asks Darryl.

Darryl wrinkles his nose. "Uh, no. Is that normal?"

"In Scott's family, yes, but in ours we are a divided house." She picks up the jar of sweet pickles. "His choice, but never mine."

Darryl smiles. "If I have a vote. I will stick with ham and cheese or spam any day."

Silvey drops an egg, and it bounces off the edge of the sink and hits the floor. "Get down!"

Darryl hits the floor, but Andrea hesitates.

"Dre! Down!"

"What's happening?" Andrea asks, kneeling next to Silvey.

"Two men dressed in all black just came out of the tree line."

"Shit," Andrea whispers. "We should have left our phones at home. I'm so sorry."

"You can apologize after we get out of here," Silvey says. "Where are Scott's keys?"

"On the counter," Andrea says, scooting around the island. She reaches up and pats the counter until her fingers find the edge of the key ring. "Got them."

"Set off the car alarm," Silvey says, "and then you two run for the basement door, hide in the room we found. It will take them a while to figure out the dart board is actually a door."

"We are all going down," Andrea says.

128

Silvey shakes her head. "I have a plan. Please, just trust me."

"Don't make me regret this," Andrea says, pressing the remote to Scott's car. The blaring alarm goes off immediately.

"Go!" Silvey whispers.

Andrea and Darryl make a run for the basement door. Silvey runs to the back door and locks it. She hits the switch next to the door.

Sprinkler heads rise and spray the approaching men.

Silvey laughs and retreats downstairs.

Andrea holds open the hidden door and looks her over. "Why are you grinning?"

"I found the sprinkler switch this morning," Silvey says, scooting into the room. "They may be a tiny bit wet when they break in."

Andrea pulls the door closed until it clicks. "We are lucky we found this game room or library thing, too." She gestures towards the wall of shelves and a table and chairs in the center.

"I'm guessing it's a poker room," Silvey says, pointing to a built-in humidor next to a beer tap. "Cigars and beer."

"Oh man," Andrea says. "It's like they checked every box for Scott's dream man cave basement. And he doesn't even know about this space."

"Shh," Darryl whispers, pointing up. "They're in the house."

Silvey and Andrea step away from the entry.

"I don't hear anything," Andrea whispers.

"I heard footsteps," Darryl whispers.

Silvey paces around the table. "I wish I would have thought to bring a knife or something from the kitchen."

"Myra gave me instructions to a small safe." Darryl whispers, lifting his shirt and exposing the small pistol.

Andrea's jaw falls open. "That was here in the house?"

"The blue bedroom upstairs," Darryl whispers.

"She's always prepared," Andrea whispers.

"Let's hope we don't need it," Darryl says.

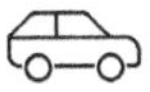

Scott pulls down the driveway and spots the front door wide open. He speeds up and honks the horn. "No, no, no!"

Two men dressed head to toe in black exit the home. One of the men jumps off the porch and sprints towards Scott's car.

Scott banks hard to the left. Gravel and dust kick up in the man's face. He floors the gas and checks the rearview mirror. Two additional men are coming around the side of the house. "Four!" He pounds his hand against the steering wheel and looks forward as a black SUV turns into the driveway. He slams on his brakes and throws the car in reverse.

The man, Scott dusted, waves for him to stop, but he cuts right. The bumper barely misses the man, and he holds the wheel until he is facing the direction of the house. He drops the car in drive, steers through the grass and circles around the back side of the home.

The SUV gives chase.

"Rookies!"

Scott drops the car into all-wheel drive and speeds through the raining sprinklers. The windshield wipers kick in as he rounds the far side of the house and floors it towards the driveway. He makes it back to the driveway and out onto the county road before he takes a chance to look in the rearview mirror. *No SUV.*

"No phone," Scott says. "No access to help. What the fuck!"

"Oh, holy hell!" Andrea says, looking up. "Pretty sure Scott gave them a run for their money."

"Sounds like he circled the house," Silvey says.

"Hopefully he made it back out and can get us help," Darryl says.

130

"Maybe," Andrea says. "But now he doesn't have a phone to call for help. We are on our—"

The muffled sound of men and racing footsteps quiets Andrea immediately.

"I'm guessing he got a way," Silvey whispers.

Darryl motions for them to come to the furthest corner of the room as footsteps race downstairs. They squat down until they are sitting on the floor.

"Clear!" a man shouts.

Silvey covers her mouth to block the snicker of laughter boiling up.

The footsteps ascend, and the basement door is slammed shut. The sound makes Andrea jump.

"Let's hope they give up and leave," Darryl says.

"I still hear a car idling outside," Silvey says.

A loud thud shakes the light fixture above the table.

"I really hope they don't trash the place," Andrea whispers.

"Pretty sure this house will be a hard no for Scott after this event," Silvey says, nudging Andrea.

Andrea frowns.

"We'll fix your house up better than new," Silvey whispers.

Andrea nods. "I'm holding you to the better than new statement."

21

Rozanne runs outside as a dark car drives up to the house. Gage hops out of the car before it slows to park. He sprints and picks up Rozanne. She wraps her arms and legs around him.

Baxton exits and taps the top of the car.

The car immediately turns around and slowly drives away from their house.

"Get up here!"

Gage pushes Rozanne's hair aside and winks at the blonde woman. He carries Rozanne to the porch and sits her down on the top step. "Hey mom."

"Baxton, get in here!" Deanne says, opening her arms for both men.

Gage and Baxton hug Deanne.

Rozanne sniffles and smiles. "Mary and Monroe are on their way back."

"With Bax's mama," Deanne says.

"What?" Baxton asks.

Gage chuckles. "Dude you were injured by a major tornado last week and kidnapped this week. What did you expect?"

Baxton shakes his head. "But how did she get on a plane?"

"Straight determination to get her only son back from the heathens. Anxiety be damned."

"Where exactly did said heathens take you?" Rozanne asks.

"Do you still have that national park book on the coffee table?" Gage asks, darting around his mom.

"I think so," Rozanne says, following him inside. "Why?"

Gage opens the book and turns a few pages.

Baxton comes in and stands behind the couch.

Gage turns the book towards Baxton. "Look familiar?"

"Mushroom-shaped rocks," Baxton says, nodding. "That's definitely similar."

"Babe," Gage says. "Can you google flight times between Albuquerque, New Mexico and Kansas City?"

"Just under two hours," Rozanne says, turning her phone towards Gage.

"We were taken to a base of some sort near this national park," Gage says. "They knocked us out for the flight there and did a blood draw. They know Bax…" He pauses looking over at his mom.

"Know what about Bax?" Deanne asks from the door.

"We went back to the base after the tornado," Baxton says.

"Was it off limits or something?" Deanne asks.

"Not at the time," Gage says.

"They took you with force for trespassing?" Deanne asks.

"They think we saw something we shouldn't have," Gage says.

"Well, did you?" Deanne asks, placing her hands on her hips.

"Mom," Gage says, tapping his ear. He mouths the words. *They can hear everything.* "We are innocent. They had to release us because we didn't do anything wrong."

Deanne looks from Gage to Baxton. "Is that right?"

"Yes, ma'am," Baxton says, turning towards Rozanne. "Have you heard from Silvey?"

"I let Andrea know that you two were headed here," Rozanne says. She thumbs through the message. "It's been read, but she hasn't replied just yet."

Baxton opens his mouth.

Gage raises a finger to his lips and shakes his head.

"We are happy you're home and safe." Rozanne winks at Gage. She walks to the kitchen, grabs a pen and paper from a drawer. She walks back to Gage and hands it to him. "I'll warm up some food. Mary left your favorite casserole here. Baxton go on and get cleaned up before your mom gets here."

"Aye," Baxton says, glancing back at Deanne. "Any chance you brought your shears?"

Deanne laughs. "You're finally going to let me cut your hair?"

"Just need a small trim," Baxton says, holding his thumb and pointer finger less than an inch apart.

"I keep my spare set in my purse," Deanne says, rummaging through her purse. "Go on and get showered. Rozanne, is it okay if we cut his hair on the porch?"

"Trim," Baxton says, walking down the hallway.

Rozanne laughs. "Of course."

"I'll check my car for a cape," Deanne says, walking outside.

Gage sits at the kitchen table and furiously writes.

Rozanne leans over Gage and cups his ear. "No hercules talk in front of anyone."

He nods and turns to give her a kiss. He lingers nose to nose with her. "I missed you."

"I missed you more," Rozanne says. "But we are even."

Gage reels back. "What?"

"The worry, stress, and anxiety you went through when I was taken," Rozanne says. "I get it. I never ever, ever want to go through that again."

Gage stands and takes her face between his hands. His thumb slides over the faint scar on her cheek. "I am thankful for every second I have with you. I won't miss another."

Rozanne's bottom lip quivers. "Mr. Auburn, I believe that is a promise you made on our wedding day."

"And I am so damn sorry I broke that vow," Gage says, wrapping her in a tight hug.

"I forgive you."

The oven dings.

Rozanne leans back and kisses his cheek. "Now finish that." She points to the paper. "I'll get you a drink."

Gage smirks. "Yes, ma'am."

Rozanne takes a few glasses down from the cabinet and fills three out of four with tonic water. She fills the fourth with lemonade. She takes down the gin and adds a shot to the tonic water. She slices a lime and squeezes a slice in each glass.

Deanne comes back in. "I've got a cape."

"Coming," Baxton says, finger combing his wet hair.

Rozanne meets Baxton in the hallway with a drink.

"Thanks," Baxton says, taking the drink. "I'm assuming this is not just water."

Rozanne smiles. "It's twelve o'clock somewhere." She hands the lemonade to Deanne.

"Thanks," Deanne says. "Chop, chop, let's go nephew."

"Just a trim," Baxton says, following Deanne to the porch.

"Sit here," Deanne says, gesturing to the footstool for the glider. "You're too tall to sit in a normal chair."

Baxton pats the top of her poofy blonde hair. He squats low until he's level with the footstool.

Deanne drapes the cape around him and secures it with a snap around this neck. "Rozanne mentioned you fancy a gal from Lawson, Silvey, right?"

"Oh boy," Baxton says. "You may know her mom. She does hair too."

"Oh," Deanne says, pulling out a comb.

"Her last name is Rhoades," Baxton says.

"Evelyn Rhoades?" Deanne asks, combing and parting a section of his hair.

"Yes," Baxton says.

"I've known her and Buzz for twenty years," Deanne says. "Silvey is a lot like her dad, but man she's a stunner."

Baxton smirks. "Understatement."

"Whoa," Deanne says, securing her shears and snipping the first of his ends. "You've got it bad?"

"I know," Baxton says, looking down at the hair fallen onto the cape. "Deanne, how much did you chop off?"

"Just your split ends," Deanne says, taking another snip.

"That looks like two inches or more," Baxton says, picking up a clump of hair. "When it dries, two inches looks more like six inches shorter with my curls."

"Pish posh," Deanne says, snipping a bit more off the back. "I wouldn't do that to your precious curls."

Honk Honk

Baxton turns and spots a car flying up the driveway. "What the—" He stands and hair flies everywhere.

"Who in the devil is that?" Deanne asks, holding up her shears.

Rozanne and Gage come out onto the porch.

"It's Scott," Rozanne says, "and he's alone!"

Baxton rips off the cape and jumps off the porch.

Scott slams on his brakes and gets out immediately. "They found them."

"What do you mean?" Baxton asks, running up to Scott.

"We had them in a safe house," Scott says.

"Had who?" Baxton asks.

"The captain, Silvey and my wife," Scott says. "I went to ditch our phones. But when I got back to the house, they were already inside, and I outran the SUV. I didn't know where else to go, so I drove straight here."

"Who's they?" Gage asks, joining Baxton.

"At least five men, including the driver, dressed in all black."

"Son of a—" Baxton says, "I was right."

"What?" Scott asks.

"I had a gut feeling the only reason we were allowed to walk was because they knew where the captain was or worse, Silvey."

"I'm calling the police," Deanne says.

"No!" Rozanne, Baxton, and Gage yell in unison.

"Sorry, mom," Gage says. "Can you please go inside? I promise." He places a hand to his chest. "I'll explain everything."

"I see," Deanne says. She nods and turns for the front door.

"Sorry," Scott says, watching Deanne retreat. "I didn't mean to add more trouble to your doorstep. I didn't know where to go, but I am happy you two are back and safe."

"Safe is questionable," Baxton says. "We are ninety-nine percent sure we aren't in the clear."

"What do you mean?" Scott asks, looking at Rozanne's pale face and deep frown.

"They handed us our phones upon landing," Gage says. "The pilot gave me a handwritten note suggesting we should toss the phones and get burners. He tapped his ear and winked. We left our phones in the car that brought us home."

"Forget that for a moment," Baxton says. "How can we help?"

Scott sighs. "I don't know what the next smart move is. I just high tailed it here. They could have taken them or—"

"If it is the same guys," Gage says. "We know where they will take them."

"I'll grab a pair of shoes and a shirt," Baxton says. "We'll go to my place and grab a few things from the safe."

"I'm coming with you," Gage says.

"Oh no," Baxton says. "I just got you back to Rozanne and your mom will have a heart attack if you run off and leave. You are staying put. We need boots on the ground here just in case."

"Just in case of what?" Rozanne asks, throwing her hands up.

"We need to be bailed out or something," Baxton says, starting off in a jog to the house.

"This is reckless," Gage says.

"I'm sorry," Scott says. "I shouldn't have come here after everything."

"No," Gage says, shaking his head. "I mean going in without a plan, knowing what you two may have waiting for you."

"Can you describe the men?" Rozanne asks.

"The two that came out of the house were white. Dark brown or black hair, average height, dressed in long sleeve black shirts, pants and boots. The driver looked darker, or maybe that was the window tint. And the other two I saw when I was driving. I can't pinpoint anything other than they were all dressed the same."

"No logos?" Rozanne asks, tapping her phone. She turns or phone towards Scott. "This is the footage of the guys that took them from the trail camera. Do any of them look familiar?"

"I saw this footage while I was driving with Andrea," Scott says, playing the footage. He hits pause and drags it back a few frames. "This is the driver of the SUV." He turns the phone towards Rozanne.

Rozanne taps the screen to grab a screenshot. "Check the others. There are two other videos."

He turns the phone towards him and taps the play icon. He pauses a few seconds later. "This guy too."

Rozanne takes another screenshot.

"Ready?" Baxton asks, jogging towards Scott.

"Identified two of the men," Scott says, watching the footage.

"We can confirm it's the same group," Rozanne says.

"Let's go," Baxton says, rounding the car.

"Where is the safe house?" Gage asks.

"It's out near Watkin's Mill," Scott says, handing Rozanne her phone. "I can't confirm any of the other men, but can you send those two shots to the reporter?"

Rozanne nods. "The press doesn't know that we have the guys back. I owe her an update this afternoon."

Scott nods. "We'll pick up a few burner phones when it is safe." He hops back into the driver's seat. "Are you sure?"

"Absolutely," Baxton says, securing his seatbelt. "Let's go get them back!"

Scott puts the car in reverse and waves to Gage and Rozanne.

138

22

"General," Oscar says.

General Hall looks up from a laptop. "What is it?"

"Our bravo team located a house, but it was empty. One of the civilians, Scott Meyer, drove up to the house while our men were inspecting the home. They let him flee. He was alone in the car."

"Was their evidence that anyone had been inside the home?" General Hall asks, closing the laptop.

"Yes sir," Oscar says. "Two beds showed signs of use, and groceries were left out on the counter. And we found discarded clothes matching Captain Wilson's last sighting."

"Definitely the right house," General Hall says, standing.

"Yes, sir."

"What spooked them?" General Hall asks.

Oscar shakes his head. "Bravo team have expanded their search to the woods surrounding the home and the adjacent state park."

"Does that park have a campground?" General Hall asks.

"Yes, sir," Oscar says. "Three of the six RVs parked overnight have been searched. The other three left before our team arrived. The park ranger gave the team the license plates recorded for all traffic that entered or exited the park for the last twenty-four hours through the main gate, but the footage to the south entrance was blocked by a few overgrown bushes."

General Hall nods. "And Mr. Meyer?"

"His vehicle was tagged as entering the park ten minutes before our men approached the home," Oscar says.

"Who owns the property?" General Hall asks.

"Looks like a trust fund," Oscar says. "But it was recently put on the market, and we've contacted the listing agent, a Ms. Dani Yoakum, to squeeze her for more information."

"And do we know the whereabouts for Mr. Meyer or his wife, Andrea?" General Hall asks.

"Their phones appear to be off," Oscar says. "Last ping was inside the state park around the time Mr. Meyer entered."

Director Gia walks into the room. "Sir, the local reporter just ran a piece that will put the heat on full blast. Two men from the bravo team sighted during the abduction of the Auburn men are now linked to a home invasion near Watkins Mill. A source stated that the US State Department for Science and Technology are suspected in both cases."

"Has there been any action on the Auburn's devices?" General Hall asks.

"A single text to a Rozanne Auburn that they were on their way home," Director Gia says.

"Has our alpha team been able to sync with Mrs. Auburn's phone?" General Hall asks.

"No sir," Director Gia says. "Another woman arrived at the home. We've confirmed she is Gage Auburn's mother."

"It should sync with the men's devices," General Hall says.

"It might have happened if they didn't leave their phones in the car," Director Gia says.

"How long have you known about that?" General Hall asks.

"The driver found them shoved under his seat about ten minutes ago," Director Gia says. "Our contact at NSA is working on a back way to get into Mrs. Auburn's phone as we speak."

"I am regretting this decision," General Hall says. "And I do not say that often. Maybe twice in thirty years."

"There is one glaring omission," Director Gia says. "The one thing the reporter left out of her piece was the men's return."

"That's interesting," General Hall says. "Why are they hiding? Who is watching the house?"

"Alpha Two, sir," Director Gia says.

"Get them on the phone," General Hall says.

"Yes, sir," Director Gia says, tapping her ring. "Connect me with Alpha Two to the general's office."

"Alpha Two, sir," a man says from the ceiling mounted speaker.

"Has there been any traffic to the Auburn residence post the men's arrival?" General Hall asks.

"Yes, sir, a vehicle registered to Scott and Andrea Meyer came in with one male driver, presumed to be Scott Meyer, and left with Baxton Auburn."

"Headed in what direction?" General Hall asks.

"North sir."

"Call command with any additional arrivals."

"Yes, sir."

General Hall circles to the front of his desk. "Pull the two men identified with both cases. I wanted this clean and quiet and it's becoming a circus."

"Yes, sir," Oscar says. He leaves the office.

"The drone footage confirmed Ms. Rhoades and Ms. Meyer on the back porch an hour before our team approached," Director Gia says, pulling up the footage on the large screen mounted adjacent to the general's desk. "A figure nearly the same build as Captain Wilson was spotted." She pauses the frame that has a man at the sink with this head down. "Facial recognition could not confirm."

"Is there anyone at the house now?" General Hall asks.

"One of the men has been posted inside the home," Director Gia says. "If they return, we'll be ready."

"Has the reporter requested a comment from the department?" General Hall asks.

"No," Director Gia says. "But our trace on Agent Vickers phone confirms she may have been contacted by the FBI field office in Kansas City."

"Great," General Hall says. "More interagency politics to balance."

"Also, Agent Carlton has provided the details for the consultant that found the information about Project Rainbow," Director Gia says. "We've made contact and arrangements for travel to our office in San Francisco."

"Good. I just got an update from the federal prosecutor working the case for Charlotte and Eli. They have an attorney, but they are considering the plea deal we discussed before letting them go."

"That's some good news, right?" Director Gia asks.

"I don't know," General Hall says. "They were so forthcoming about their involvement with 'saving' Ms. Rhoades and were proud of their actions. I can see them attempting to plea their case in front of a jury and if Ms. Rhoades testifies on their behalf. It could be a lost cause."

"We'll be sure we get to Ms. Rhoades before they can," Director Gia says.

23

"Are you sure there is still someone upstairs?" Silvey whispers.

Darryl nods. "I am almost certain there is someone pacing the foyer. Listen, about every fifteen seconds you'll hear a creak."

Andrea looks up and holds her breath.

"There," Darryl says, pointing up. "Did you hear it?"

"Barely," Silvey says.

"What are the chances they could hear the door open?" Andrea asks.

"If we can hear a muffled floor creak," Silvey says. "Basically, a hundred percent."

"Ugh," Andrea says, wrapping an arm around her stomach. "The coffee is kicking in."

"Oh dear," Silvey says, looking around the room. "And there is nothing in here. Wait! Do you still have the remote to Scott's car?"

"Yes," Andrea says, digging out the small black remote from her pocket.

"When you absolutely can't hold it any longer," Silvey says. "Press the alarm and on the second blare we'll unlatch the door. On the third run for the bathroom."

"It could work," Darryl says. "But keep the light off and don't flush."

"And if they notice?" Andrea asks. "And come looking?"

"Hide in the tub," Silvey says. "If you can't make it back to the room. Remember, we have Darryl's tiny weapon if we need a distraction."

"Let's hope it doesn't come to that," Andrea says. "Because I can't wait much longer."

Silvey grins.

"What?" Andrea asks.

"It's finally someone else with a poop emergency," Silvey says, bursting into whispered giggles.

"Grow up," Andrea says, wiping away a bead of sweat from her brow. "I nearly got pulled over the last time you had one in my car."

Silvey covers her mouth and muffles her laughter.

Darryl points up. "You're going to give us away."

Silvey tightens her hand across her mouth, her shoulders shake, and tears stream down her cheeks.

"It's going to take her a minute," Andrea says, rolling her eyes. "She has a hard time shutting down a giggle fest."

Silvey releases her hand and blows out a long breath. "I'm good. I'm good."

"Good," Andrea says, crawling towards the door. "Because I'm not." She reaches the door and puts her ear against it. "Here goes nothing." She presses the remote. The blaring alarm starts, and a door slams overhead. It rattles the light fixture over the table. She unlatches the door and peeks out before bolting to the bathroom.

Silvey runs to the door and catches it before it slams shut.

A muffled shout and footfalls pound through the first floor.

Darryl stands. "Get back."

Silvey backs away from the door.

144

"We cleared the house," a man says, opening the basement door. "Yes, I am sweeping it again. The first floor is clear. I am heading to the basement."

"Shit!" Silvey whispers.

Darryl holds a finger over his lips.

The blaring alarm stops and the car engine starts.

"Shit," the man says, "somebody just started the car." He runs back upstairs and through the living room to the front door.

Darryl steps back as the door to their hidden room opens.

"It's just me," Andrea says. "That was too close."

"Do you think he saw anything?" Darryl whispers.

"I don't know. I wasn't going to risk a look just in case.'"

"Feel better?" Silvey asks.

"So much better," Andrea says, "but when we get out of here, do not go in there until I can flush."

"Deal," Silvey says. "But when is when?"

"Scott will come up with something," Andrea says.

"Let's hope it's soon," Silvey says. "We didn't bring any snacks."

Andrea rolls her eyes.

Footsteps overhead lead to the basement door.

"No sir," the man says. "I haven't seen anyone exit or enter the home since I arrived." He runs down the steps. "If you're hiding, come out."

They listen as the man stalks around the basement.

"Oh man," the man says.

The toilet flushes.

"Somebody left an epic deuce down here," the man says. "I don't know if it was here before. I cleared the top floor."

Silvey covers her mouth.

Andrea glares at her.

Silvey drops her hand and mouths the word. *EPIC.*

Andrea drags a finger across her throat.

Silvey covers her mouth with two hands.

Darryl shakes his head.

"I don't know what to tell you," the man says. "No one is here."

The man's footsteps ascend, and a door clicks closed.

Silvey drops her hands.

"Silvey Lynn Rhoades," Andrea whispers, pointing at her. "Don't you dare start."

Silvey runs two fingers over her lips and twists. "Mums the word." She yawns. "Anyone care if I take a quick power nap?"

Darryl shrugs.

"How can you sleep right now?" Andrea whispers.

"When I am stressed, I eat or sleep. Do you see any food?"

"True, but here?"

Silvey shrugs. "Floor, bed, truck, it really doesn't matter." She lays down in the corner furthest from the door. "Wake me up if you come up with a plan that involves an exit or food."

"Unbelievable," Andrea whispers. "Are you sleepy too?"

Darryl shakes his head. "I don't think she slept well last night."

Andrea folds herself onto the floor. "Who do you think he works for?" She points up.

"Project Rainbow was under a new state department for Science and Technology when it was started," Darryl whispers. "According to a conversation with Eli and Charlotte that department has significant funding these days. My guess is that it is still them behind the curtain."

"Hold up," Andrea whispers. "A state department can kidnap people?"

Darryl nods. "A clause written to protect and secure technology that could pose a national threat."

"Wow," Andrea whispers. "The wormhole, yes. I could see that being trouble, but the suspension chamber, no. It's not a threat to heal people."

"It is if it is one of one for the entire world," Darryl whispers.

"But it can be reproduced," Andrea whispers.

"I don't know," Darryl whispers. "My guess is they are worried information about the chamber will leak before they can determine if it can be replicated."

"Making it a target for any foreign government or militia," Andrea whispers. "We are beyond hot water. This is boiling and with no room in the pot."

Darryl smirks. "Pretty much."

The light fixture sways.

"He's coming back," Darryl says, squatting beside Andrea.
Silvey rolls to her side and snores.
Andrea nudges her. "Silvey. We've got company."
"What?" Silvey moans.
"Shh," Andrea whispers.
"Do you hear a car?" Darryl whispers.
Andrea nods. "More than one."
Silvey sits up. "The calvary?"
"Or more trouble." Andrea whispers.

24

A muffled door slams, and then three more.

"That was at least three or more getting out of a car," Andrea whispers.

"Not good news," Silvey says.

"I don't hear anyone inside," Darryl whispers.

"Clay County Sheriff!" a man shouts. "Come out with your hands raised above your head."

"Oh snap," Silvey whispers.

"Oh, to be a fly upstairs right now," Andrea whispers.

The front door opens.

"How can I help you?" a man says.

"Hands above your head!" the deputy shouts.

"Care to tell me what this is all about?" the man asks, raising his hands.

"Turn towards the home," the deputy commands.

The man complies and slowly turns towards the front door. "You're on private property."

"Yes," the deputy says as another deputy pats the man down. "And you're under arrest for breaking and entering said private property."

The man jerks forward. "I live here."

"You do not," a woman says.

The man turns and narrows his eyes at a woman emerging from a truck. "And you are?"

"None of your business," the woman says, nodding to the deputies. "Thanks."

"Check my back pocket," the man says. "You may want to know whom your arresting?"

The woman laughs. "Unless you had a warrant to break in, I believe you still broke the law. Isn't that right, deputy?"

"Yes ma'am," the deputy says, pulling out the man's wallet. "D.O.S.T. Agent Kyle Roberts."

"We'll search the home before we escort you inside," a deputy says. "He's going to county for now. Mr. Roberts, you have the right to remain silent. Anything you say can and will be used against you in a court of law. You have the right to speak to an attorney, and to have an attorney present during any questioning."

Two deputies step inside the home and five minutes later come outside.

"It's clear," the deputy says.

The woman nods. "May I?"

"Yes, but please don't move anything," the deputy says, handing her a pair of latex gloves. "Got it."

"Scott! Andrea!"

"Is that Myra?" Andrea asks.

"Holy shit!" Silvey says, starting for the door.

"Wait!" Andrea says. "The deputies are looking for Darryl. We can't just walk up there."

"I'll stay," Darryl says. "Go. I'll be fine for a bit longer."

"You sure?" Silvey asks.

"Yes," Darryl says.

"We'll be back as soon as possible," Silvey says.

"Let's go," Andrea says, unlatching the door.

Silvey and Andrea close and latch the hidden door before running upstairs.

"Myra!" Andrea shouts as she opens the basement door.

"Oh, thank God!" Myra says, running through the kitchen. "Are you guys, ok?"

"Fine," Silvey says.

"Where's Scott?" Myra asks.

"Not here," Andrea says. "How did you know we were in trouble?"

"When I couldn't reach Scott or you this morning. I called a friend to do a drive by. They reported a few men wearing tactical gear inside a black SUV pulling out of the driveway." She looks over her shoulder. "Is he safe?"

Silvey nods and darts her eyes to the basement door. "Until we give an all clear."

"They'll need a statement," Myra says. "Any idea where Scott is?"

"Probably Rozanne's house," Silvey says. "We had just received word from her. And it was closer than Elmira."

"Can you call her?" Myra asks, walking them to the front porch.

"I don't have her number memorized," Andrea says

Silvey snags a bag of chips from the kitchen island on their way through.

"Ma'am," the deputy says. "Those are evidence."

Silvey frowns. "I'm pretty sure the guy didn't taint the chips. They're not even open." She shakes the bag.

"Silvey," Andrea says. "Give the man the chips."

"Fine," Silvey says, handing over the bag. "You can deal with hangry Silvey."

Andrea snags the bag back from the deputy. "Sorry sir. For your safety and my sanity."

Myra laughs at the slacked jawed deputy. "Deputy Paulson, this is Andrea Meyer and Silvey Rhoades."

Deputy Paulson closes his mouth and focuses on Silvey. "You were abducted from the hospital."

"Yes sir," Silvey says, over a full mouth. "But let's move on. You've caught the bad guys."

"Do you know where Captain Wilson is?" Deputy Paulson asks.

"Now deputy," Myra says. "You are here because of a home invasion. Please respect these kind young ladies and their time. Take their statement."

"Ma'am," Deputy Paulson says.

"Deputy," Myra says, folding her arms across her chest.

"Fine, Ms. Meyer."

"Mrs. Meyer," Andrea says.

Deputy Paulson nods. "Can you follow me?"

"Lead the way," Andrea says, snagging a chip from Silvey and following the deputy to a cruiser.

"Any chance we can distract the men away from the basement?" Silvey asks.

"They'll clear out after your statement," Myra says, nodding towards the house. "And you can confirm there isn't anything missing."

Silvey nods and swallows another mouthful of chips. "I found two cameras."

"Inside?" Myra asks.

"One in the basement and one in the foyer," Silvey says.

"I'll have to ask the owner," Myra says. "It may be a closed loop system for lights in case the realtor failed to turn them off."

"I've heard of that," Silvey says. "Worked on a job out in Lee's Summit a year or so ago. It was a high dollar subdivision. The contractor received an expensive electric bill on the show homes, and he had something similar installed the next day."

"Let's hope that's all it was," Myra says, typing out a message on her phone. She hits send. "I'm sorry this wasn't the haven you two needed."

"We didn't consider that they could track Andrea and Scott's phones until midmorning," Silvey says, wiping the corner of her mouth. "Scott went to dump the phones and that's when the men came out of the woods."

"Silvey," Andrea says, waving her over. "Your turn."

Silvey hands off the bag of chips to Andrea.

"Thanks," Andrea says.

"Deputy Paulson," Silvey says, nodding to the man.

"Ms. Rhoades," Deputy Paulson says, tapping his pen to a notebook. "Walk me through your morning."

"Woke up early," Silvey says.

"Do you know when?" Deputy Paulson asks.

"Before seven or so," Silvey says.

The deputy nods. "Please continue."

"Andrea arrived about twenty minutes later with coffee and donuts. We were hanging out until her husband Scott came by with groceries."

"What time was that?"

"Rough guess, ten or so?"

The deputy nods. "Please continue."

"Scott left to run an errand, and we started to prep some lunch. I was peeling eggs at the sink when two men came out of the woods in the back."

"Can you describe the men?"

"Average height, white, dark hair and wearing all black," Silvey says, looking the deputy over. "One of the men could be your brother."

Deputy Paulson straightens. "I don't have a brother."

"Just saying," Silvey says. "We hid in the basement until you arrived."

"Did they search the basement?"

"Yes, twice."

"Why didn't they find you?"

"I'm the bite size version of an adult," Silvey says. "I can fit in small spaces."

"But Andrea?"

"Is tall, thin and beautiful," Silvey says, smiling.

The deputy frowns. "I mean where did she hide?"

"Oh," Silvey says, shrugging. "I think once in the bathroom and another time under the pool table."

Deputy Paulson flips back through his notes. "Are you sure about that?"

"Not really," Silvey says. "She was hidden before I went downstairs. I gave the men a little shower thanks to the sprinkler switch by the back door."

Deputy Paulson nods. "And you didn't ask where she hid once the coast was clear?"

"No," Silvey says. "Too busy stressing about the food we left sitting out and how long we were going to be stuck down there."

"Hmm," Deputy Paulson says, tapping his pen against the paper. "And it was just you and Andrea alone in the house when it was invaded?"

"Yes, sir," Silvey says. "Although a few minutes after the men entered, we did hear a car and a horn that sounded like Andrea's car that Scott took. We are assuming he caught the men mid action."

"And where is Scott now?" Deputy Paulson asks.

"Pulling up." Silvey waves and immediately notices a second man in the car. "Bax?"

Deputy Paulson turns.

A car slows to a stop behind the cruiser.

A tall man steps out of the passenger seat and Silvey runs into his arms. The man picks her up and she wraps herself around him.

Myra and Andrea jog over to Scott.

"Are you hurt?" Scott asks.

"No," Andrea says, pulling him into a hug. She whispers, "Everyone is fine."

"Ms. Rhoades," Deputy Paulson says. "We still have a few questions."

"Start with Scott," Andrea says. "Those two will need a moment."

"Who is he?" Deputy Paulson asks.

Myra steps into Deputy Paulson's line of sight. "Silvey's man. Obviously."

Andrea and Scott look down and hide their grins.

"Scott Meyer," Myra says. "Deputy Paulson."

"How can I help?" Scott asks.

Deputy Paulson gestures for them to walk closer to the cruiser.

Andrea peeks over at Baxton and Silvey. "Wow."

Myra chuckles. "The chemistry." She winks at Andrea.

"Right," Andrea says, looking at the house. "Think there is a hose hooked up."

Myra laughs.

"What's so funny over there?" Silvey asks.

Andrea smiles and turns to face Baxton and Silvey. "I asked Myra if there was a hose."

Silvey smirks.

Baxton furrows his brow.

Myra laughs harder.

Silvey elbows Baxton in the side. He meets her eyes, and she bounces her eyebrows. His cheeks blush instantly.

"Ms. Rhoades," Deputy Paulson says.

"Coming," Silvey says, pointing to Baxton. "Don't move." She jogs over to Deputy Paulson.

Scott returns to Myra and Andrea. "Myra, this is Baxton Auburn."

Myra sticks out her hand. "Nice to meet you."

"You too," Baxton says, shaking her hand. "Thank you for coming."

"Happy your back," Myra says.

"Thank you," Baxton says.

"Hey Andrea," Silvey says. "We are ready to check the house and see if anything was taken."

Andrea and Silvey follow Deputy Paulson inside.

"What are the chances they put it together?" Scott whispers, leaning close to Myra.

"Depends on the evidence."

"Crap," Scott says. "I bought a men's razor and shaving cream."

"It's yours," Myra says. "You just hadn't taken your stuff out of the bag yet."

Scott nods and bumps Baxton's arm. "That was one hell of a hello."

Baxton shakes his head. "Dude, bro code."

"He's still blushing, Scott," Myra says. "Leave the young man be."

Scott grins from ear to ear. "Hey, can we borrow your phone?"

Myra hands him her phone. "It's a burner."

"Good," Scott says. "What is Rozanne's number?"

"Uh," Baxton says. "Give me the phone."

154

Scott hands him the phone.

"My finger memory is better than my actual memory." He types in the number and hits call. "Hey it's Bax. Yes. No. And yes, they are all good. I'll tell you at home." He listens for another beat. "Sure. I'll see you later." He hands the phone back to Myra.

"Did you just get an earful?" Myra asks, pocketing the phone.

"Yes," Baxton says. "My mother flew in today and I wasn't home when she arrived. She's not happy."

"Ah," Myra says.

Two deputies carry out a few bags marked as evidence.

Andrea and Silvey follow Deputy Paulson back to the cruiser.

"Mr. Meyer," Deputy Paulson says.

"Yes, sir." Scott walks to Andrea's side.

"Does this belong to you?" Deputy Paulson asks, showing a clear bag with a black shirt.

"Yes, sir."

"And these?" Deputy Paulson asks, holding up a bag with stained khaki pants.

"Also mine," Scott says.

"Did you fall or something?" Deputy Paulson asks, examining the pants.

"Sir, my house and neighborhood were directly hit by the tornado," Scott says. "I wore those cleaning up debris around our home. And our washer was sucked out along with our kitchen, so I was hoping we could do a few loads here.'"

"I'm sorry to hear that," Deputy Paulson says, placing the items in the cruiser. "We'll take these items into evidence. They were noted as moved during the invasion."

"No problem," Scott says. "And thanks again for coming so quickly."

"Will you be staying here this evening?" Deputy Paulson asks, looking at Silvey.

"No sir," Silvey says.

Deputy Paulson hands Silvey a card. "If you hear from or see Captain Wilson, please let us know."

Silvey nods and takes the card.

"Myra," Deputy Paulson says. "I need a minute with you."

Myra nods and walks toward the deputy. "Go on inside. See what you can salvage from the groceries."

Andrea and Silvey nod. Scott and Baxton follow the ladies inside. They migrate towards the kitchen.

Silvey grabs a water bottle and a bag of chips. "Be right back, but Dre keep watch."

"Got it," Andrea says, nodding and positioning herself behind the island looking out the dining room window. "Go quietly."

Silvey opens the basement door and closes it quietly. She descends and keeps her footsteps light. She inspects the basement before unlatching the hidden door.

"It's me," Silvey whispers.

"Is it clear?" Darryl asks.

"Not quite," Silvey whispers. "They are still here but outside." She nods towards the stairs. "But if you need the bathroom, go now."

"Thanks," Darryl says, heading to the bathroom.

Silvey sits the water and chips on the table.

Darryl returns and smiles. "Snacks?"

"Always." Silvey smiles. "I'll be back once they are gone."

"Did they have any suspicion of my presence?" Darryl asks.

"Yes, unfortunately."

"Damn it," Darryl whispers.

"Hey Silvey," Andrea says.

"Shoot," Silvey says, backing out of the room and latching the door. She takes the steps two at a time and carefully exits the basement. She peeks around the corner as Deputy Paulson enters the kitchen. "What's up?"

"We've received word from the station," Deputy Paulson says. "The man we apprehended has been cleared of all charges and released."

"What!" Andrea and Silvey shout in unison.

"I know, I know," Deputy Paulson says, holding up his hands. "It is political bullshit, excuse my language, but it appears the higher ups have issued Ms. Rhoades as a person of interest—"

"Hell no," Baxton says, positioning himself between the deputy and Silvey.

Scott slyly passes his car keys to Baxton.

Myra barges in. "Paulson! Are you really going to harass these kids after everything they've been through?"

Deputy Paulson turns to face Myra and Baxton grabs Silvey's hand. They back out of the kitchen and softly run through the living room while Myra is facing off with the deputy. They bolt out the front door and run to Andrea's car.

Two deputies exit their cars and shout. "Wait!"

Silvey and Baxton don't stop until they are inside the car. Baxton starts the car and throws it in reverse turning the wheel hard as the deputies give chase on foot. He shifts the car into drive and punches it, kicking up dirt and gravel.

The deputies hold up their hands to shield their faces.

Silvey looks back as the dust dissipates. Deputy Paulson is running from the house. He is shouting and waving his arms. The two other deputies run for their cruisers.

"What the hell just happened?" Silvey asks.

Baxton glances in her direction. "Twisting Hercules comes with consequences."

Silvey groans. "And we left the captain in the basement."

"Scott and Andrea will take care of him," Baxton says, turning on to the highway. "Is it too soon to meet my mother?"

Silvey laughs. "What?"

"My mom just landed and if—"

"Yes," Silvey says, reaching for his hand.

25

Myra turns to Andrea. "Get the captain, everything of yours and theirs out of here and into the car." She points to Scott. "Start the car and put it in drive. I'm going to block the end of the drive with the truck until you are loaded."

Andrea nods and throws the remaining groceries inside the plastic bags.

"I'll run upstairs," Scott says.

"No," Andrea says. "I want to be ready the second we step outside the door."

The dust from the cruisers still lingers in the air creating a haze around the two remaining cars.

Myra nods to Scott as she turns her truck around and he nods in return. He turns the car and backs up to the house before placing it in drive. He taps the steering wheel and stares at the rearview mirror.

"Come on," Scott mutters.

The front door opens.

Andrea and Darryl sprint to the car. They're barely inside when Scott punches the gas. The car races down the driveway. Scott follows Myra down the county road.

"Can someone please tell me what happened?" Darryl asks, leaning forward.

Andrea turns to Darryl. "The men were agents with the Department of Science and Technology and the man arrested was released. They made Silvey a person of interest whom they need to interview immediately. Myra managed to distract the deputy long enough for Baxton and Silvey to run."

Scott nods. "And at least two of the men at the house today were part of the crew that took Baxton and Gage."

Darryl sits back. "Holy hell."

"Right," Andrea says.

"We have a plan," Scott says. "But we aren't exactly sure where Silvey and Baxton are hiding."

"I'm listening," Darryl says.

"It's actually Myra's plan," Andrea says. "We are going to go public about the department's involvement in Gage and Baxton's abduction and their illegal pursuit of you and Silvey."

"And the tech they are after," Scott says.

"Whoa," Darryl says, holding up his hands. "No, we can't open that up to the public."

"If we don't," Scott says, "this search and harassment will only continue. I don't think we have a choice."

"Did you tell Myra about the suspension chamber?" Darryl asks.

"No," Andrea says. "But she knows something is up after witnessing Silvey's miraculous recovery. She knew how bad she was injured last week."

"If the public knows the US Government stole lifesaving technology and buried it for sixty years," Darryl says. "Our problems would be more than harassment—it would be nuclear."

Myra turns into the gas station and Scott follows.

Myra hops out of the truck.

Andrea rolls down the window.

"I got a call," Myra says, handing Andrea the phone.

Andrea furrows her brow and takes the phone.

"Hello?"

"Rozanne?" Andrea asks.

"Hey, yes, they just pulled up."

Andrea nods and smiles. "They can fill you in on why, but they aren't safe there."

"Do you have a plan?" Rozanne asks.

"A half-baked one," Andrea says, "but we are still not in agreement."

"Do you have a safe place for tonight?" Rozanne asks.

"Hopefully," Andrea says, glancing at Scott's waving hand. "One second."

Scott takes the phone.

"Tell Bax plan C. He'll understand."

"Got it," Rozanne says. "Be safe."

Scott disconnects the call and hands the phone back to Myra.

"You really think they are listening?" Myra asks, taking the phone back.

"We can't take any chances," Scott says. "Head home. I'll call when we are safely tucked away."

"With what phone?" Andrea asks.

"A land line," Scott says.

Andrea raises an eyebrow. "What is plan C?"

"A church camp," Scott says.

Myra laughs. "What?"

"Micah and Baxton finished a project out at a church camp near Polo," Scott says. "He still has the master keys, and it's vacant for another week."

"What happened to pulling back the curtain on the department?" Myra asks.

"To be determined," Andrea says, nodding her head to the back seat. "He's not on board."

"I don't like it," Myra says.

"We have food and water for a few days," Scott says. "And Bax was going to get some supplies from Gage and Rozanne, so we should be fine."

Myra sighs.

"It's going to be rough no matter what we do," Andrea says.

"Please," Myra says. "Just be careful."

26

"General," Director Gia says. "Alpha team has eyes on Silvey Rhoades. Engage?"

"Is she alone?" General Hall asks, closing his laptop.

"No, sir," Director Gia says. "She arrived at the Auburn's residence with Baxton."

"They wasted no time for their reunion," General Hall says. "Have they established a connection to any device inside the home?"

"Yes, sir, but lost the connection after only a few minutes."

General Hall nods. "And did they get anything useful?"

"An outgoing call to a burner phone from Rozanne Auburn."

"And?"

"They believe the recipient was Andrea Meyer," Director Gia says. "They discussed the arrival of Silvey and Baxton, but everything was vague and non-specific."

General Hall pushes back from his desk. "And Captain Wilson?"

"A man matching his description was spotted in a car at a gas station near Lawson. The bravo team are requesting the footage from the station."

"We've been chasing this man instead of being two steps ahead." General Hall stands.

Agent Carlton knocks on the open door. "If I may."

General Hall nods.

"We know Andrea and Scott Meyer have been assisting Ms. Rhoades," Agent Carlton says. "I believe they've been hiding Captain Wilson."

"We've been monitoring them," Director Gia says. "Ms. Rhoades was the only person seen with them since they left the funeral three days ago."

"Any connection to the home in Elmira?" General Hall asks.

"Retired Gladstone Police Captain, Myra Bridger," Agent Carlton says. "Lives alone. No family ties to anyone involved."

Director Gia nods. "But she did threaten our team with deadly force unless they came back with a warrant."

"Agent Roberts," Agent Carlton says. "Described a woman matching Ms. Bridger at the house with the county deputies."

"A possible connection to the Meyers or Ms. Rhoades," General Hall says. "I want her file on my desk and a team assigned to her by dawn."

"Yes, sir," Agent Carlton says, stepping out of the office.

"The bravo team did leave a tracker on the car registered to the Meyers before the deputies arrived at the home," Director Gia says. "The car is heading north of Lawson."

"Sir, ma'am," Oscar says from the open door. "Bravo team confirmed they, the Meyers, are traveling with Captain Wilson."

"Once they've reached their destination," General Hall says. "Apprehend without force. I want them transferred to the base. We are not flying more civilians here."

"The owners of Greening Up, Charlotte and Eli," Oscar says. "Called the number you provided. They have agreed to the deal with one exception."

General Hall nods. "Are they still on the line?"

"Yes, sir," Oscar says, tapping his ring.

"Good evening," General Hall says. "I have Director Gia and myself in the room." He nods to Oscar.

Oscar steps out and closes the door.

"Good evening," Eli says. "Charlotte and I have reviewed the offer, but we can't compromise on one item."

"I'm listening," General Hall says, raising an eyebrow and eyes Director Gia.

Director Gia shrugs.

"We agree to the settlement offer to sign the deed for the Lawson property over to the government," Eli says. "And the subsequent land to replace our loss of business is adequate. But the hush clause about our interactions with Mr. Wilson are where we've come to an impasse."

"Your livelihood depends on your silence," General Hall says. "Captain Wilson does not deserve such sacrifice."

"Sir," Charlotte says. "We've met the man. Have you?"

Director Gia hides her smile with her hood. She glances at General Hall's frown. She taps her ring. "It's on mute. Go on."

"What hold could he possibly have over these people?" General Hall asks.

"An orphan soldier who faithfully served his country," Director Gia says. "Only to be locked away and forgotten for sixty years can swoon even the most cynical person."

"Including you?" General Hall asks.

"Making him a public enemy would not have been my choice," Director Gia says.

"He's a walking time bomb," General Hall says, tapping his ring. "Ma'am, I believe your empathy for Captain Wilson is clouding your big picture judgement of what his very existence may mean to the natural order of our fine country. I will speak plainly. His emergence equals a hailstorm of nuclear proportions to our doorstep. Do you really believe protecting one man is worth sacrificing the safety of millions of Americans?"

"Sir," Eli says. "Captain Wilson is an American and we are not willing to throw him under the hypothetical bus."

"Then we have no deal," General Hall says.

164

"We understand the pressure you're under to hide the truth. And with respect, painting Captain Wilson as anything other than a national hero is a crime. Your actions have consequences. We have submitted a statement to the local and national media. You may speak with our lawyer from this point forward."

The line clicks.

"General," Director Gia says. "I will work on blocking their statement and drafting a response for any leaks."

General Hall moves around his desk. "Before you do that, walk with me."

General Hall and Director Gia walk in silence to the elevator. The door opens and they walk inside. The door promptly closes and the elevator descends to the lowest level.

"Sir," Director Gia says when the doors slide open.

General Hall steps out and scans his ring on the black pad next to the first locked door. The door opens to a sterile white room. Two technicians look up from their stations and nod before resuming their tasks.

General Hall weaves around the work areas covered in test tubes and beakers. He slows and taps on a glass door sealing off a workstation covered in papers and two large monitors.

A young woman turns and gestures for them to enter.

"General," the woman says. "Thanks for coming down."

"Virgil," Director Gia says. "What's the new news?"

"We've discovered an anomaly within the sample from Baxton Auburn that we didn't find within the samples from Eli or Charlotte. And I believe it is the active component we were missing." She taps the space bar on a keyboard and two images appear on the monitors.

"On the left is the sample from Baxton whom we believe used the chamber three days ago." The stains of red blood cells are enlarged with jagged white particles within the nucleus. "On the right, Eli's sample had limited white particles in the nucleus."

"Could this mean the regenerative quantity will dissipate over time?" Director Gia asks.

"I believe a larger sample would be necessary to determine that factor, but it's possible that we are looking at active particles and can observe them in real time."

"This is progress," General Hall says, leaning closer to look at the images. "When you say watching it in real time."

"Oh yes," Virgil says. She taps the keyboard a few times. "We introduced a bacteria strain to the sample from Baxton. Watch."

A recording of the magnified cells appears on the monitor. A blue dyed droplet is administered next to a red cell. The white particle inside the red cells nucleus expands and engulfs the blue droplet.

"Wow," Director Gia says. "It vanishes?"

"Yes," Virgil says, speeding up the footage. "The white particle reduces its size after sixty seconds. We repeated the test three times in a row with the first strain and then tried a second cycle with a viral strain. And a third round with a pancreatic cancer cell. The results were the same."

"In one minute," General Hall says. "It wiped out all three."

"It's a true miracle."

"Thank you, Virgil." General Hall extends his hand towards Virgil.

Virgil firmly shakes his hand.

"Please send the results and your report to our team. I need to inform the President."

"Yes sir," Virgil says.

Director Gia follows General Hall from the lab to the elevator. "Red alert?"

"Yes," General Hall says.

"Oscar has a car waiting," Director Gia says, stepping on the elevator.

"Do you comprehend the gravity of what she just said?" General Hall asks, watching the elevator door close.

"Catastrophic," Director Gia whispers. "Hidden for sixty years—why?"

"Greed."

27

Baxton holds open the passenger car door for Silvey.

Silvey waves to Gage and Rozanne before sliding into the car. Baxton nods to the family as he jogs around the car.

"Be safe," Rozanne says.

"Precious cargo," Baxton says, winking. "Always." He grins and slides into the driver's seat. "Ready?"

Silvey turns to face him. "They're worried. And your mom flew all this way. Are you sure?"

"It's a good plan," Baxton says. "And we have a backup should we even sniff a bit of trouble."

"But your mom," Silvey says.

"She'll be here for a few weeks," Baxton says, resting a hand on hers. "We're more danger to them if we stay."

Silvey sighs. "Alright, I'll trust that you and Scott came up with something solid."

Baxton laughs and turns the car towards the county road. "How do you feel about camp?"

"Like camping?" Silvey asks. "With tents and smores."

"More like summer camp," Baxton says.

"Andrea and I ruled camp one summer," Silvey says. "So much so that we were politely asked not to return the following year."

Baxton raises an eyebrow. "We have about forty minutes. I think I need to hear the epic saga of Silvey and Andrea go to camp."

Silvey laughs. "We dominated the prank war between the dorms. My electrical skills came in quite handy. I managed to disconnect the motion sensor lights around the dormitory during the day. This gave us excellent cover to lay out a plan to cover every door handle with red jelly and shaving gel. And wrap all the sinks and toilets with plastic in the main mess hall."

"Oh man," Baxton says, laughing. "How did they catch you?"

"They didn't and that was the first night," Silvey says, shaking her head. "The second night was a little worse."

Baxton pushes his hair behind his ear and waggles his brows at her. "Are you always trouble?"

"Pleading the fifth," Silvey says, holding up her hand palm out.

"Ha, so what happened on night two?" Baxton asks.

"Whoopee cushions under the mattress for every counselor," Silvey says.

Baxton turns onto a two-lane highway and speeds up. "That doesn't sound too bad."

"Oh," Silvey says, fighting her own laughter. "It is when they were also filled with a smell to raise the dead. Literally smelling salts."

"Whoa," Baxton says, shaking his head. "How did you even manage that?"

"I blew up each cushion," Silvey says. "Dre wore her dad's old gas mask while she inserted the salts." She laughs. "The dorms were evacuated. We had a giant sleep over in the mess hall."

"Did you get caught?"

"Not until the third day," Silvey says. "We had a counselor corner us after they found the gas mask in Andrea's bag. She made up a story about taking the wrong old suitcase from the attic. She claimed she didn't take anything out and threw her stuff in."

"Did they believe her?" Baxton asks.

"Not for one second," Silvey says. "But we covered our tracks well and didn't leave any incriminating evidence."

"Masterminds."

"We got a little cocky on the third day," Silvey says. "We set and hid the alarm clocks for every room one minute apart during shower hour. A few girls started screaming, 'FIRE! FIRE! FIRE!' after the second alarm started. About twenty sopping wet girls ran out of the showers and outside."

"Was this a coed camp?" Baxton asks.

"Yep," Silvey says.

"Oh, that's bad, really bad."

"It was," Silvey says. "And we were caught holding the last alarm clock."

Baxton laughs. "Wow."

"Not our brightest moments of mischief and mayhem." Silvey checks the mirror. "Have you noticed the same car hanging back behind us?"

Baxton checks the rearview mirror. "It pulled out behind us about five minutes ago from a gravel driveway. We'll see if they follow once we turn."

Silvey's knee rapidly bounces.

Baxton lays his hand on the center console. "We'll keep an eye on them. I promise."

Silvey takes his hand. "Thanks. I really just want one day without the adrenaline rush zinging every fiber of my anxiety."

Baxton squeezes her hand. "I won't let them take you."

Silvey looks up at Baxton. "You really mean that."

"I do," Baxton says, locking eyes with hers for a solid second before turning his attention back to the road.

"Do you think we are going to end up as lab rats?" Silvey asks, watching the mirror as Baxton turns right and the dark sedan barely stops before following.

"Crap, they followed."

Baxton speeds up. "Hold on." He double checks for oncoming traffic and cuts the wheel hard to the left. He taps the brake just enough to keep the wheels on the road before punching the gas again.

Silvey turns to look at the car screeching to a hard stop in the middle of the road. "Go!"

Baxton makes the first left off the highway. He kills the headlights and whips the car around onto the shoulder. The overgrown shrubs and a thick holly bush conceal most of the car.

The dark sedan speeds by.

"I can't believe that worked," Silvey says, writing an eight, four, and B with her finger in the dust on the dashboard. "I managed to get a partial plate."

Baxton gently rolls back onto the road and creeps up until he can see the car in the distance. "That's good news. I'm going to wait a few minutes to make sure they don't circle back."

"Smart, but risky."

"I don't want to lead them straight to the camp."

Silvey nods. "I wonder if Dre made it there without a tail."

"Hopefully we can ask them soon," Baxton says, inching further out onto the road. "I think it's clear. I don't see the car anymore."

Silvey leans forward. "No headlights in either direction. Good. Let's try this again."

Baxton turns right and speeds down the two-lane highway until he reaches a gravel road. He turns left and slows. "I'm going to turn back on the headlights. If you notice anyone behind us, let me know."

"Got it," Silvey says, turning to face the rear.

Baxton catches a few strands of her long blonde hair across his face. He inhales and his cheeks flush.

"Sorry my hair has its own life," Silvey says, pulling her hair away from him.

"I get it," Baxton says, pulling on one of his loose ringlets.

Silvey grins and turns her attention back to the rear window. She pats her warm cheek.

170

Baxton speeds over the rolling hills. He slows and turns into a driveway. "No!" He slams on his brakes as the headlights ahead of him pop on.

Silvey whips around. "Oh, no!"

The lights surround Captain Wilson, Andrea and Scott. They are surrounded by five people dressed head to toe in black.

"No, no, no!" Silvey shouts. She turns and spots a pair of headlights nearly on their bumper. "We're blocked in."

Baxton releases the brake and lets the car roll forward. "I'm so sorry."

"It's not your fault," Silvey whispers. "Let's hope they let us walk away, too."

Baxton stops about ten feet away from the group and he puts the car in park. "Get out slowly. I don't see any guns, but I can't guarantee." He turns the car off. "Ready?"

"No," Silvey says, tying up her hair. "Are you?"

"Definitely not." Baxton opens the door. "But here we go."

"Mr. Auburn," a man says. "Step away from the car and come to the front of the vehicle. Ms. Rhoades?"

Silvey opens her door. "Who's asking?"

"Special Agent Ryan Askew."

"Agent in what agency?" Silvey asks.

"Secret Service branch dedicated to the Department of Science and Technology,"

"And you're trespassing on private property, why?" a woman shouts, stepping out of the shadows and cocking a shotgun. She levels the barrel at the men in black.

"Ma'am," Special Agent Askew says, turning to look at the woman. "We are unarmed. Please put down your weapon."

"Do you have a warrant?" the woman asks.

"No, ma'am, but we do have orders to question these men and women."

"Hand them over to the tall young lady," the woman says, nodding her chin towards Andrea.

"The orders aren't written on paper."

The woman releases the safety from the shotgun. "Then you have two minutes to exit this property without my guests. A second less will be considered a hostile intrusion, and I have every right to protect my property as I see fit."

Silvey and Andrea lock eyes.

"Who is she?" Andrea mouths.

Silvey shrugs and shakes her head.

"Ma'am," Special Agent Askew says, holding up his hands. "It is a matter of national security that we detain these individuals for questioning."

"Clocks ticking, mister," the woman says, lowering the barrel level to the man's groin.

"We can't leave without them," Special Agent Askew says.

"I believe you might change your mind," the woman says. Three people emerge from the darkness just behind the convoy of black vehicles. "We have you surrounded."

Silvey makes out two teens, and another woman with weapons pointed at the men in black. "Shit, just got real."

"You heard the lady," Scott says. "Leave or else."

"Thirty seconds," the first woman says.

"File out," Special Agent Askew says.

"Sir," a man says.

"File out!" Special Agent Askew shouts.

The men move back to their vehicles and pile in. They roll out one by one, including the one that pulled in behind Baxton.

Andrea waves away the dust cloud and coughs. "Thank you!"

"Who are you?" the woman asks.

"Andrea Meyer," Andrea says, pointing to Scott. "My husband, Scott, and this is Captain Darryl Wilson." She points towards Baxton. "Baxton Auburn and my best friend Silvey Rhoades."

"We've seen you on the news," a teen says.

"Yes," Andrea says.

Baxton raises his hand. "I worked here two weeks ago installing the new rubber mats inside the kitchen and office areas. My boss Micah was the main contact but Ms. Swafford we've met. Do you remember me?" Baxton walks forward into the beam from the headlights. He opens his hand and jangles the keys.

172

The woman with the shotgun steps closer to the group. She looks Baxton up and down.

"We needed a place unrelated to us to avoid the men we just encountered." Baxton hands her the keys. "We're truly sorry for bringing this mess to your door."

Ms. Swafford takes the keys. "I do recall your tall frame. I'm the first one to admit I am not great with names." She gestures to the three lingering nearby. "My name is Meg Swafford, my sister Lou and her kids Kara and Kevin." They wave. "We are the caretakers and spotted the headlights in the lot." She nods to a small house down the hill. "We came up to investigate just as the men in black rolled up and surrounded them."

"We are super thankful for the assist," Silvey says, joining Baxton. "We'll head out and leave you in peace."

"Nonsense," Meg says. "We've got the perfect place to hide those in need and trust me it's not connected to us or the property here."

"We couldn't impose any further," Andrea says.

"It's not an imposition," Meg says, disarming her shotgun. "And we are here to serve despite my tough guy act."

"Captain?" Silvey asks. "What do you think?"

"I hate to put them in the crosshairs, but we are out of options."

Silvey nods. "Alright, what did you have in mind?"

"An off-grid bunker about two miles from here," Meg says. "It's set up for ten people with running water and electricity thanks to some cleverly disguised solar panels and a well."

"Wow," Andrea says, "sounds like a movie set up."

"Regardless," Silvey says, "we have some supplies and will hopefully only need it a day, or two max."

"Then it's settled," Meg says. "Take what you need from the cars. We'll move them into town. The kids can take you on the side-by-sides to the bunker. There's a radio inside. If you should need help, keep it on channel three. The locals use channels one and two when out here hunting or farming."

"Got it," Silvey says, sticking out her hand. "Thank you. We'll be no trouble from here on out."

Meg shakes Silvey's hand.

Andrea and Scott unload the groceries from the trunk as Kara and Kevin pull up. They help them load the bags under the back seat.

"One last thing," Andrea says. "If they come back. We went to the media and are exposing them and their department for all their harassment."

Meg smirks. "You bet." She takes their car keys. "We'll have a friend keep an eye on the cars in town."

Scott nods. "Seriously, thank you."

Captain Wilson hops in the front next to Kevin. "Nice ride."

Kevin grins. "Are you the real Captain America?"

Scott laughs. "Somebody was bound to make that comparison."

Captain Wilson turns with a raised eyebrow. "Is that a comic book thing?"

"And a movie thing too," Andrea says, sitting next to Scott in the back.

Baxton and Silvey grab the bags from the car and climb into the ride with Kara.

"Hold on," Kara says. "It's a bit hilly up ahead."

Silvey grins. "Bring it on."

"Are you a bit of a thrill seeker?" Baxton asks.

"I'm an electrician," Silvey says. "A little shock is a daily occurrence. As my dad puts it, 'the spice to a dull day.'"

Baxton laughs. "He's an interesting fella."

"You've only met Buzz in the reserved setting of a hospital," Silvey says, bouncing her brows. "His name isn't the only buzz in the room when he walks in."

Baxton smiles. "It's nice you two are close."

"What about your dad?" Silvey asks, swaying into him as they ride over a hill.

"Navy," Baxton says. "He was deployed most of my childhood and my parents divorced when I was eight. He retired last year and got remarried to a woman with two young kids." Baxton shrugs. "We've maintained a friendly semi healthy relationship via text, but I haven't seen him since the summer after high school."

"Seven years?" Silvey asks.

174

"Yes," Baxton says. "His wife wasn't a fan of his previous life and I've kept my distance."

"Dang," Silvey says, "I'm sorry."

"Nah," Baxton says. "It's life and the only one I know."

"Watch your arms," Kara says. "The bush is thick in this part."

"Thanks, Kara," Silvey says, scooting closer to Baxton. He wraps his arms around her.

"Do you know why they built a bunker way out here?" Baxton asks.

Kara looks over her shoulder and smiles. "Where do you think most bunkers are built? Near the highway?"

Silvey laughs. "She's got a point."

Baxton frowns.

Silvey leans up and kisses his cheek. "You'll get them next time."

Baxton laughs and levels his nose to hers. "Ha, ha."

"We're here," Kara says, winking at Silvey.

"Just kiss already," Andrea says, shaking her head.

Silvey raises her middle finger to Andrea. "Mind your business."

"If I did that, I would not be in the middle of the woods right now."

Silvey climbs out of the side-by-side and charges Andrea.

Andrea turns her back and bends. Silvey hops on Andrea's back and raises her fist in the air. "Ah, but we are ride and die for life friends."

Silvey and Andrea laugh and follow Kevin.

Scott fist bumps Baxton. "They are really a two for one deal."

Captain Wilson grins. "It's something."

Baxton nods. "Does it come with an instruction manual?"

Scott pats Baxton on the back. "Oh no, but I should write one."

"What are you two whispering about?" Andrea asks.

"How to survive the twisted sisters," Scott says.

Silvey and Andrea simultaneously turn and glare at the men.

"Oh dear," Captain Wilson says, chuckling. "You two are in deep."

"We are about to be," Silvey says, pointing down at the ladder. "How deep is this thing?"

"Forty feet," Kevin says, turning on a flashlight. "At the bottom of the ladder is a switch. It runs the main power for the bunker, and there are tubes built in to allow in some natural sunlight during the day. It's best to conserve the power for evening and nights."

Kara nods. "We'll come out and check on you in a few days, but you should have everything you need down there." She taps her fist on the door four times, pauses for a beat, and taps again twice. "Only open when you hear that knock."

"Got it," Silvey says, testing her weight on the ladder. "See you soon. And thanks for everything."

Kara and Kevin nod.

"We appreciate the action," Kevin says. "This summer has been rather uneventful."

Silvey grins. "Oh, I wish I could say the same." She starts her descent as the others say thanks and see you soon. She jumps off the last rung and feels the wall. She finds and flips the main switch.

The lights overhead flicker on illuminating the four bunk beds in the corner, a large sectional couch across from the beds, and a small kitchen with an island and table with chairs set up across from a closed off room.

She turns and gasps.

"What is it?" Andrea asks, climbing down.

"It's massive," Silvey says.

Andrea pauses on the last rung. "Geez."

"Beep, beep," Scott says.

Andrea hops down. "Take a look at this."

Scott whistles and hands off the bags to Silvey and Andrea. They take the bags over to the kitchen.

Scott pats Captain Wilson on the shoulder as he hops down. "What do you think?"

"Reminds me of Hawaii," Captain Wilson says, moving away from the ladder to allow room for Baxton. "We had a few bunkers about this size."

"A full circle moment," Scott says.

"True, it was my first duty station." Captain Wilson nods and scratches the scruff on his cheek. "I wonder if they still exist."

176

"The base is still open," Scott says, walking over to the kitchen. "A friend from high school was stationed there for a few years." He pulls out the shaving cream and razor from the bag on the counter. He turns to Captain Wilson and shakes the items. "Do you want dibs on the bathroom?"

"Ladies first," Captain Wilson says.

"No," Silvey says, waving him towards the door. "Help yourself."

Andrea nods. "I'm good. Go!"

Captain Wilson takes the clothes from another bag and grabs the toiletries. "Thanks, five minutes—tops."

Baxton comes to Silvey's side. "What's with the mound of sandwiches?"

"We were interrupted during our prep to leave the house. We didn't know how long it would be until we found another kitchen."

"Oh, dang," Baxton says. "And here I've been blubbering on about Gage and I's trauma."

"Don't minimize the trauma you experienced," Silvey says, nudging Baxton in the side. "The fact we are still standing is a miracle after the last two weeks."

"Amen," Andrea says, opening a cabinet. "I can make the chicken pot pie."

"Double amen," Captain Wilson says, patting his smooth cheek.

28

"General," Special Agent Askew says.

"Tell me you have them," General Hall says.

"Negative, sir. We were held at gunpoint until we left the property."

"They had help?"

"We believe they were the owners of the property. We've tracked their cars to town and have a team scouting the area for their whereabouts."

"I want you to go back to the property and demand answers," General Hall says. "We can't delay this any further."

"Sir," Special Agent Askew says. "The local woman requested a written order to detain the men and women. If we can get something in writing, I believe they will cooperate."

"Done," General Hall says, sending a message to Director Gia. "Check your email in a few minutes."

"Thank you, sir."

"Call me directly," General Hall says, "once you have a lead."

"Yes, sir."

General Hall disconnects the call and slams his fist against the seat. "How far out are we from the base?"

"Thirty minutes, sir," the flight attendant says.

"Thanks," General Hall says, undoing his seatbelt. "I need a few minutes in the back. Please do not disturb me."

"Yes, sir."

General Hall pushes open the door at the end of the aisle and steps through. He secures the door with the latch and walks to the desk. He picks up the red phone and waits.

"General Hall," a woman answers.

"Admiral Tyson," General Hall says. "We've had a delay capturing the assets."

"Define delay."

"The team had them surrounded, but they had assistance from a few locals. And our leads have gone dark."

"Your team couldn't handle locals?"

"The locals were armed," General Hall says. "Our team was instructed to apprehend without force."

"Instructed by whom?"

"My orders," General Hall says. "We need them alive and well."

"For the sample?"

"Yes. Do I have clearance to bring in the crisis team?"

"Is that necessary?" Admiral Tyson asks.

"We have blocked some leaks starting to circulate regarding the technology and the association to Captain Wilson. Director Gia has a team, but they are struggling to keep up with the ongoing threads. We want to control the narrative and need full autonomy to share when we see fit."

Admiral Tyson sighs. "I will approve of the crisis team assisting with the press, but I expect your team to apprehend

Captain Wilson, Ms. Rhoades, and Mr. Auburn by dawn. We need to put a lid on this operation."

"Yes, ma'am. Thank you. I'll notify Director Gia of the approval and have a ready team on standby."

"Dawn, General Hall. Dawn."

"Yes, ma'am." General Hall replaces the red receiver and walks to the door.

A murmur of conversation and fleeing footsteps away from the door have him out and drawing his sidearm. "What's going on?"

The flight attendant looks up from the coffee she is pouring and scrunches her brow. "Sir?" She raises her free hand and slowly puts down the pot of coffee.

"Who was whispering outside the door?" General Hall asks.

"The pilot used the lavatory," the flight attendant says, glancing at her watch. "About five minutes ago. No one else has been near the door this entire flight."

"You're lying." He rushes up the aisle.

She cowers. "I'm not."

He pounds on the cockpit door. "Open up."

"Sir?" the pilot asks over the intercom. "Is everything ok?"

"No! Open up, now."

The light over the door flicks from red to green.

General Hall yanks open the door and raises his sidearm. "Souls on board?"

"Four, sir." The pilot looks beyond the General to the pale-faced flight attendant. "What's happened?"

"Someone was just outside the door," General Hall says.

"Sir, my copilot hit the head about five minutes ago," the pilot says, pointing to the paper logbook.

General Hall checks the time against his watch. "I'm grounding this entire crew upon landing until I can review each of your credentials."

The pilot nods once. "General, we are landing in ten minutes," the pilot says. "You're welcome to search the jet upon arrival, but we are starting our descent. Do you mind taking your seat until we land?"

General Hall looks out the window. "There aren't mountains in Missouri."

"We are landing in Colorado Springs," the pilot says.

"Why the hell are we in Colorado?" General Hall asks.

"We were rerouted due to the storms and lightning strikes in the Kansas City area," the pilot says.

"Why wasn't I informed?" General Hall asks.

"You requested no disruption," the pilot says. "According to the flight attendant."

General Hall turns to the flight attendant. She nods.

"I'm sorry," the flight attendant says. "You did ask me not to disturb you."

"You told me we were only thirty minutes out," General Hall says, pointing a finger at her face. "It would take longer to divert and land in Colorado Springs. Why are you lying to me?"

"I wasn't aware of the cockpit's decision to turn back until now," the flight attendant says.

"Hand me the headset," General Hall says, gesturing to the copilot. "I want to speak to the tower." The copilot hands General Hall the headset and secures it over his ears.

"Kansas City Tower, this is J941US, requesting weather update for approach."

"J941US, Kansas City Tower. Be advised, severe weather conditions in the area. Thunderstorms with heavy rain, wind 270 degrees at 35 knots gusting to 55 knots, visibility 1 mile, overcast at 1,500 feet, temperature 28 degrees Celsius, dew point 19 degrees Celsius, altimeter 29.85. All inbound traffic is currently being diverted. Advise on your alternate airport."

"Copy, Kansas City Tower. We will proceed to our cleared alternate airport, J941US."

General Hall takes off the headset. "Why Colorado Springs?" He hands the headset back to the copilot.

"Kansas airfields are under the same diversion, and we had the fuel to proceed to Colorado."

The copilot secures their headset.

"Permission to begin approach?" the pilot asks, turning his attention to the instruments.

"It would seem I have no choice," General Hall says, leaving the cockpit and heading to the back of the jet. He checks the lavatory and partitioned room for intruders before returning to his seat. "I will find out why you three are snooping around in business you have no clearance for."

The flight attendant nods and busies themselves with securing the galley for landing.

29

"Can you pass the pepper?" Scott asks.

Silvey passes the pepper and looks up. "Does anyone else here dripping water?"

"I thought I heard something too," Baxton says, pushing back from the table. He checks the taps in the bathroom and the kitchen. "I can still hear it." He walks to the ladder and climbs up a few feet. "I think it's raining."

"They said there are sunlight tubes, right?" Andrea asks.

Baxton walks the length of the bunker. He stops in the corner and points up. "Condensation is on the cover. Pretty sure this is the source of the dripping sound."

"Ugh, let's hope the pots and buckets can empty themselves," Andrea says, shaking her head. "The leaking roof is going to give me an ulcer. I can't even call anyone to check on the house."

"Sorry Dre," Silvey says. "We can use the radio to call for help."

"No, it's for emergency purposes only," Andrea says. "Insurance will cover the damages."

"I will start on the dishes," Captain Wilson says.

"No," Andrea says, waving her hand at him.

"I insist," Captain Wilson says. "You cooked; I'll clean. It was tradition at home, and you made a chicken pot pie. My Millie would be jealous of the ready-made pie crust. It was always her least favorite part. Something about the grease and her apron." He smirks. "She never complained to me, but I could always hear her mumbling to herself while scrubbing her apron."

"She sounds amazing," Silvey says.

"Hopefully one day I can introduce you and the others to my Millie." Captain Wilson stands, and Scott helps him clear the dishes from the table.

"I'll dry," Baxton says.

Silvey raises an eyebrow. "Did we just win the lottery?"

Andrea laughs. "Maybe. You did survive a damn tornado."

Silvey points up. "Let's hope that's just rain and not something worse."

Scott nods to the desk with the radio. "There might be a weather radio over there."

Silvey and Andrea walk over to the desk.

Andrea bumps her hip into Silvey's side. "He might be a keeper."

"All mine to keep," Silvey says, winking. She fiddles with the radio and static drowns out the sound of the men doing dishes for five seconds until Silvey finds the volume. "Sorry, hit the wrong switch." She adjusts the dial on the radio and music fills the space. "Is this Bob Marley?"

Andrea nods and sways to the island beat of *Three Little Birds*.

"Better than the weather," Scott says, dancing over to Andrea. He takes Andrea's hand and pulls her close. They sway on beat and smile from ear to ear.

184

Silvey leans against the desk and watches them. She catches Baxton swaying and singing while drying a plate, and her smile matches Andrea's and Scott's.

Baxton looks over his shoulder at Silvey. He blushes instantly but continues singing. "Don't worry about a thing cause every little thing is gonna be alright."

Captain Wilson turns off the water and turns to watch Scott swing Andrea around. He grins and winks at Silvey. "They know how to cut a rug."

"Always the first and last to leave a dance floor," Silvey says, walking around Andrea and Scott towards the kitchen. "It's been like that since we were sixteen."

"I can see why," Captain Wilson says.

Baxton wraps an arm around Silvey's shoulder. "What about you?"

"Do I dance?" Silvey asks.

Baxton nods.

"I've been known to make a crowd part and circle around me," Silvey says.

Andrea laughs. "She's being modest. She could have been a ballerina except you know she stopped growing after sixth grade."

"Hey!" Silvey protests. "Short girls can have tall dreams."

Scott twirls Andrea out from him, and bows. "Dancing is how I wooed my beautiful wife."

Andrea twirls back into his arms and kisses his cheek. "True story."

"Taking notes my friend," Baxton says.

Silvey leans into Baxton. "I saw a deck of cards in the desk. Who's up for a game of rummy?"

"I actually know how to play rummy," Captain Wilson says. "I'm in."

"Fair warning," Scott says. "Andrea and Silvey are super competitive."

Andrea and Silvey shrug.

"Also, a true story," Silvey says.

Baxton shakes his head. "I'll watch the first few rounds. I think I've played before, but I need a refresher."

Silvey skips over to the desk and grabs the deck of cards. "We'll keep score after Baxton joins us."

"I saw paper and pen in the junk drawer in the kitchen," Andrea says, pulling out the end drawer. She rummages through the contents and pulls out a yellow legal pad and a pen. "Let the game begin."

30

General Hall paces the aisle of the jet. He taps his phone to refresh the weather over the Kansas City area. The red warning banner is still at the top of the screen. He dials Director Gia.

"General," Director Gia answers. "We have a leak that I can't plug."

"What's on fire now?" General Hall asks, freezing at the end of the aisle.

"Agent Vickers," Director Gia says. "She went on a national broadcast with the owners of Greening Up, validating their story and agency involvement in the plans to remove Ms. Rhoades from the hospital."

"She wouldn't," General Hall says.

"She did," Director Gia says. "Agent Carlton stated she can be quite vengeful when pushed out."

"Send me the link," General Hall says. "And draft a response of a fired, disgruntled employee."

"Yes, sir," Director Gia says. "I've recorded a statement from Agent Carlton backing our position."

"Good," General Hall says. "I'm grounded until the storm passes over Kansas City. Has the alpha team reported any leads?"

"No, they've interviewed the women involved in the exchange between the team and the subjects. They stated the subjects left after receiving directions to the nearest town. And this checks out—the team located the cars in town."

"They have until dawn," General Hall says, checking his phone and he clicks on the notification. "I just got a new flight plan. Call me the second you have any leads."

"Yes, sir," Director Gia says, ending the call.

General Hall checks the link and waits for the feed to load. "Did they go live for this interview?"

"Sir," the pilot says, "we've been cleared for takeoff."

General Hall pauses the clip and looks up from the phone. "Who are you?"

"Your new pilot, Josh Aniford. My copilot, Christina Oakley, is about to board. She is just finishing the inspection."

"Where are we landing?" General Hall asks.

"A private airstrip in Excelsior Springs," Josh says, checking the log. "We'll be flying without a flight attendant."

"No problem," General Hall says.

Josh nods and closes the jet door after Christina boards. She nods to General Hall before entering the cockpit and Josh follows her inside.

General Hall presses play. The newsfeed starts with a dark-haired woman centered on the screen with a breaking news banner scrolling across the bottom.

"Good day, I am Heather Sanders. We have breaking news in the ongoing investigation into the abduction of two local men and the recent kidnapping of a local woman from a Kansas City hospital. I have former FBI Agent Michelle Vickers here in the studio." The camera angle widens to include Agent Vickers in

a pressed black suit. *"Thanks for joining us here at Channel Five and National Press Live."*

Agent Vickers nods. *"Thanks for having me."*

"Can you share your involvement in the events that lead to the abduction of three local residents?"

"My partner, Agent Carlton and I were assigned to the appearance of Captain Darryl Wilson post the tragic tornado."

"He was found near the old nike base in Lawson, Missouri.

"Yes," Agent Vickers says. *"We first interviewed Captain Wilson in the first aid shelter. He told us he was a soldier working at the base and we thought he was suffering from shock after the traumatic tornado. We sent him to be medically cleared."* Agent Vickers shakes her head. *"We initially didn't believe he was a soldier."*

"What changed?"

"We located his dishonorable discharge papers and found a next of kin, his wife, Millie. It was then—we realized that he had been telling us the truth."

"How does this discovery lead to the abductions?"

"We interviewed everyone working at the nike base, close to where Captain Wilson was first spotted."

"Who is everyone?" Heather asks.

"Ms. Silvey Rhoades and Mr. Baxton Auburn. They were working inside the silo when the tornado hit the base."

"But Ms. Rhoades was severely injured."

Agent Vickers nods. *"She was ejected from the silo and found in a field about a mile from the base. She was life flighted to the trauma center here in Kansas City. I had to wait for her to wake from a medically induced coma before conducting my initial interview. She denied any association with Captain Wilson."*

"And Mr. Auburn?" Heather asks.

"He was also injured during the event but was released from the hospital three days later." Agent Vickers looks directly at the camera. *"He was interviewed at home by Agent Carlton. He claimed to have no knowledge of Captain Wilson or how he ended up at the base."*

"Have you proved that claim to be false?" Heather asks.

"No," Agent Vickers says. *"However, we do believe that Ms. Rhoades and Mr. Auburn met Captain Wilson at the base after the tornado."*

"Do you have any evidence to support this belief?"

"Silvey Rhoades and Baxton Auburn have been recently spotted by multiple witnesses around town—injury free and fully recovered."

"How could that be possible?" Heather asks.

"Because the same technology that sustained and perfectly preserved Captain Wilson's life for the last sixty plus years was used at the base—healing them instantly."

"Let's take a step back," Heather says. *"You are stating a miraculous technology exists and it can heal trauma damage instantly."*

"Not just trauma—disease, cancer, autoimmune conditions, and more," Agent Vickers says. *"The technology was hidden during the Kennedy administration under an operation called Project Rainbow."*

"This sounds more like science fiction than reality," Heather says, raising an eyebrow. *"Why would the government cover up such a miracle?"*

"Money, resources, and power," Agent Vickers says. *"Imagine a disease-free world with a life expectancy of a hundred or two hundred years compared to the meager average age of eighty."*

Heather's mouth falls open, but she recovers quickly. *"That would be amazing, but also unimaginable."*

"And a major industry disrupter," Agent Vickers says. *"Effecting the pharmaceutical, health insurance, for-profit hospitals, nursing homes, social security funding, and medical technology to name a few. Industries built on the backbone of illness and poor health advice distributed over the last sixty years."*

"Shit!" General Hall shouts, pausing the feed.

"Sir," Josh says over the intercom. "We are next in line to take off."

"Finally," General Hall says, pressing play.

190

"Agent Vickers," Heather says. *"That's a pretty heavy statement to consider. Can you inform the viewers how you learned about this massive cover up?"*

"My partner Agent Carlton and I were taken to a secret base in New Mexico after our discovery of the device that held Captain Wilson at the nike base." Agent Vickers shifts in her chair and glares at the camera. *"When we landed, I saw the owners of Greening Up, Charlotte and Eli, being escorted to the jet. I was separated from my partner, then I was drugged by Director Gia of the US State Department of Science and Technology."*

"Drugged?" Heather asks.

"She injected me with a sedative. I woke up in a room with a table and two chairs. There I was told of my reassignment to the US State Department of Science and Technology."

"FBI to the Department of Science and Technology," Heather says, shaking her head. *"Why would a state department need FBI agents?"*

"To serve and protect science and technology that could compromise public safety," Agent Vickers says. *"But we were just pawns."*

"How so?" Heather asks.

"We were there to interview Mr. Baxton Auburn," Agent Vickers says. *"Him and his cousin Gage were taken from their home and brought to the base."*

Heather smiles. *"Gage and his wife, Rozanne, confirmed this statement moments before this interview started."* She nods. An audio recording and transcript begins to roll beside a picture of Gage Auburn.

"My name is Gage Auburn. I was taken by force from my home along with my cousin Baxton Auburn. We were drugged and placed on a jet. When we landed, Baxton and I were separated and transported to a secure base. I was guarded for the first few hours. But I managed to sneak away and find Baxton. He had just been interviewed by Agent Carlton and Agent Vickers. We did attempt to run from the facility but only made it to an edge of a canyon before being escorted back to base. There we were fed and instructed if we answered all questions in the morning, we could promptly return home."

"I'll pause the statement from Gage," Heather says. *"He confirms your presence and involvement. Why would a state department take four people to a secure base?"*

Agent Vickers taps the desk. *"They believe Baxton used the device. They also have witnesses that Baxton and Gage were seen at the base after the tornado."*

"And did they confess?"

"The men confirmed they were at the base to look for Baxton's personal vehicle. It was parked outside the silo when the tornado struck. The two witnesses stated the men were running away from the base. And they said they lost track of time and had to attend a funeral for Micah Hutchins, Baxton's boss, who sadly did not survive the tornado."

"Were you able to confirm their story?"

"The family of Micah Hutchins did confirm their presence at the funeral."

"But you said moments ago you believe that Baxton Auburn used the device to heal him?"

"The area the men were spotted is where our team found the device Captain Wilson described as a suspension chamber."

"Can you describe the chamber?" Heather asks.

"A rectangle shaped glass box filled with tiny white beads set in the middle of a concrete room."

"This sounds like the same device Eli and Charlotte found on the property," Heather says.

Agent Vickers lifts an eyebrow.

"Please welcome to the segment, Eli and Charlotte, owners of Greening Up," Heather says.

The broadcast shifts the feed and splits the screen in three, holding each face in focus.

"Thanks for having us," Charlotte says.

"Can you confirm the suspension chamber found at the base was indeed the same that Captain Wilson used?"

Charlotte and Eli nod.

"Before the tornado struck the base," Eli says, *"my wife and I located a separate set of rooms away from the silo that we had no previous knowledge of and found Captain Wilson inside the suspension chamber."*

192

"You knew he was there?" Agent Vickers asks.

"We did," Charlotte says. *"I screamed for a solid minute. I thought he was dead until we read the note on the lid."*

"That must have been quite startling," Heather says. *"What did the note say?"*

"The project was classified and to trust no one."

Agent Vickers smiles. *"You see, Heather and those watching at home. Whoever decided to abandon Captain Wilson over sixty years ago took that mission to their grave. We have found an original document from Project Rainbow naming participants. Those included Charlotte, Eli, Silvey, Baxton, and Captain Wilson."*

"How could their names be on a list created sixty years ago?" Heather asks.

"They entered the suspension chamber and took it for a test drive," Agent Vickers says.

"We did," Eli says. *"Under the supervision of Captain Wilson and thoughtful consideration—we each decided to give it a shot. Charlotte had a chronic condition that was healed with zero side effects, and I had a bum shoulder for years that was repaired."*

"And you were present when Silvey Rhoades and Baxton Auburn also gave it a shot?" Agent Vickers asks.

Heather holds up her hand. *"Agent Vickers this is my interview. I'll ask the questions."* She pauses. *"Charlotte, how did your names end up on a sixty-year-old list?"*

"According to Captain Wilson the suspension chamber was built to keep trial participants in a state of stasis while time traveling."

"Whoa," Heather whispers. She stills her face and looks directly at the camera. *"We have to take a short break."*

□

General Hall slams his fist against the seat next to him. He dials Director Gia.

"General," Director Gia says.

"This is catastrophic," General Hall says.

"You finished the interview?"

"Yes," General Hall says. "It ended with them going to a short break. Is there more?"

"Not that aired," Director Gia says. "We managed to squash it for now, but the producer said they will air an additional segment this evening."

"What are they requesting?" General Hall asks.

"An exclusive interview with me or you."

"Absolutely not!"

31

Rozanne flips the television off. "Do you think they pulled the rest of the interview?"

"Check your phone," Gage says, nodding. "It's vibrating."

Rozanne shows Gage the incoming call. "It's Heather."

"Hey Heather," Rozanne says, placing the call on speaker mode.

"The producer pulled the rest of the interview," Heather says. "But we have another segment running at nine."

"Did they say why?" Gage asks.

"The producer got a cut it now or else call from the vice president of the network," Heather says. "We are tracking down any possible connection to the Department of Science and Technology. And we have a green light if the department fails to give a statement with proof of no misconduct for their hand in the abduction of you and Baxton."

"Ha," Gage says. "Zero chance they can come up with that."

"Is there any chance my film crew can go live with you at nine?" Heather asks.

"Um," Gage says, looking at Rozanne's frown. "Does it have to be here at home?"

"No," Heather says. "I would ask you to come down to the studio, but with Agent Vickers pacing the hall…"

"Yep, hard pass."

"Tell your crew to meet us at the local hospital," Rozanne says. "Mary sits on the board and has access to the conference room. It's late, so it should be available. I really don't want another reason for anyone else to come on our property."

"Any chance you can have Silvey and Baxton meet them there?" Heather asks.

"No," Gage says, shaking his head. "We are leaving them alone for now."

"But you know where they are?" Heather asks.

"Not exactly," Gage says, lifting an eyebrow. "Are you asking, or is somebody listening to the call?"

"No one, I promise. I had to ask. They are the missing piece for Project Rainbow and the time travel statement made by the owners of Greening Up. Captain Wilson could shed some light on this as well, but I believe he is still underground."

"I see." Gage squeezes Rozanne's knee. "Rozanne will send you the conference room information in a few minutes. Good luck with your producer." He ends the call.

"Do you think she was fishing for their location?" Rozanne asks.

"Highly suspicious." Gage tugs on his collar. "I'm going to go tell my mom and aunt the plan, then change my shirt. Let me know what Mary says."

Rozanne nods and dials Mary. She watches Gage enter the kitchen and go out the back door.

"Rozanne," Mary says, answering the call. "I saw the news."

"Hi Mary. I have a small favor related to the news."

"I'm listening," Mary says.

"They want a camera crew to come and interview Gage and I to follow up on the piece."

"At your house?" Mary asks.

"No, actually, that's the favor. Any chance we can borrow one of the conference rooms at the hospital?"

"I'm sure I can make that happen," Mary says. "Give me a few minutes and I'll call you back."

"Thanks Mary," Rozanne says, smiling.

"Anything for you, darling."

Rozanne ends the call and joins Gage on the back porch. "Mary is going to call me back—she thinks it should be fine."

Gage nods. "They are going back to my mom's house for the evening."

"That's probably the best idea," Rozanne says, looking out at the pond. "I don't want you two here alone, just in case." She wraps her arm around Gage's waist. "We should get changed."

Deanne looks them over. "No word from Bax?"

"Not yet," Gage says.

"Please, be careful."

"We will," Rozanne says, releasing Gage and leaning into Deanne for a hug. "I promise."

"And the second you hear from Baxton we want to know."

"Yes, ma'am," Gage says, hugging his aunt and mom.

Deanne pats his cheek. "Son, shave please."

"Yes, ma'am."

Rozanne laughs and takes Gage's hand. "We'll talk soon." Her phone buzzes and she swipes the screen. "Hey Mary."

"Conference room A is all yours. The key will be at the guest service desk."

"Mary, thank you so much," Rozanne says, heading inside. "We are changing and heading there shortly."

"We'll be watching at home," Mary says. "Please be careful."

"We promise to be extra careful," Rozanne says. "Thanks again."

"All set?" Gage asks.

"Yes," Rozanne says. "I'll text Heather the details."

"I'll get changed," Gage says, patting his cheek. "Or I guess I'll shave first."

"Yes, please."

Thirty minutes later, Gage pulls into the hospital parking lot and spots the news crew van parked a few cars down.

"Are you ready for this?" Rozanne asks, squeezing Gage's thigh.

"No," Gage says. "But I want their feet held to the fire for the stunt they pulled with Bax and I. Plus them crashing the house with Silvey and Captain Wilson."

Rozanne nods. "Let's get this over with."

Gage hops out of the truck. He circles around to Rozanne's side and opens her door. He takes her hand, and they walk towards the news van.

The van's back door slides open, and two people hop out with a few bags, a tripod, and two hardshell cases.

"I'm Liv and this is Zack." She nods towards the man with the tripod. "Are you Gage and Rozanne Auburn?"

"Yes," Gage says. "We have a conference room reserved inside. Do you need any help?"

"We're good," Zack says. "Our field producer is finishing up a call and he will join us shortly." He nods to the passenger sitting in the van.

"We'll be in conference room A," Rozanne says.

"Thanks," Zack says, knocking on the passenger window. "I'll let him know."

"Lead the way," Liv says.

Rozanne and Gage head inside and stop by the guest service desk. The lady in a pink vest stands and hands Rozanne a key.

"Mary called," the woman says, gesturing to a closed door across from the lobby. "Everything should be good to go."

198

"Thanks," Rozanne says. She unlocks the door and turns on the lights. "You can set up anywhere in here. The Wi-Fi is open."

"Great," Liv says. "This won't take long." She assembles her gear and takes a case from Zack. She nods to a man in the open door. "Can you help Zack mic them up?"

"Yes," the producer says, resting his backpack on the table. "I'm Owen." He extends his hand towards Gage. They shake. "We are still on hold, but hopefully we will get the green light soon."

Gage nods. "I understand the gravity of the information we are about to share."

"So, it's true?" Zack asks, handing a mic pack to Owen.

"Depends on what you've heard?" Gage asks, taking the mic pack and clipping it to his jeans.

"Some science fiction miracle cure has been hidden away for the last sixty years," Zack says, clipping a mic to Rozanne's collar.

"Science fiction would imply that it is indeed fiction," Liv says, rolling her eyes. "Sorry, Zack has been going down the dark and bleak internet rabbit hole since this afternoon's broadcast."

"It's ok," Gage says, nodding. "It's more non-fiction."

Zack snaps and points at Liv's slacked jaw. "See, it is true."

Rozanne shakes her head. "Careful dear."

Gage winks at Rozanne. "I believe if we tell the truth, it will only be turned into some major conspiracy theory."

"Honesty is all we ask for," Owen says, swiping the screen of his phone. "We've got a green light in thirty minutes. We'll be live with Heather."

"Great," Gage says, looking up at the clock.

"And it's just you two?" Zack asks, flipping off the overhead lights.

"Yes," Rozanne says.

Liv turns on the lights on the tripods. She holds up a meter and adjusts the lighting aimed at two chairs. "Have a seat."

Rozanne sits down and holds up her hand, shading her face. "Will the lights be this bright?"

"No," Liv says, raising the light. "Making a few more adjustments."

"Thanks," Rozanne says, dropping her hand.

Liv smiles and checks the camera angle. "Have you ever considered being on camera more?"

Gage leans over and kisses Rozanne's reddening cheeks. "Roz has had enough of the spotlight for a lifetime."

"Understatement," Rozanne mutters.

"You were abducted a few years ago," Owen says, checking the notes attached to a clipboard.

"Yes," Rozanne says.

"Heather may bring that up during the introductions."

"Is that necessary?" Gage asks, taking Rozanne's hand.

"It's establishing the trauma response and credibility of Rozanne witnessing the abduction of you and your cousin Baxton," Owen says. "And her name will sound familiar to the viewers. So, either we establish why at the beginning or lose the viewers who will be busy googling her name."

Rozanne shifts in her chair. "It's fine and old news. I just want them to focus on the truth of your abduction."

"And then hopefully Baxton and Silvey can be home without harassment from the media or the government," Gage says.

Owen raises an eyebrow. "You believe that may happen?"

Gage nods. "It's not belief. It's a fact."

"Sorry to interrupt," Liv says. "The camera and lighting are set. Can we do a sound check?"

Owen nods.

Zack puts on headphones. "Rozanne, please just say testing a few times."

"Testing, testing, testing," Rozanne says.

Zack holds up his thumb. "Great. Gage."

"Testing, testing, testing," Gage says.

Zack nods. "All set."

Owen checks his phone. "I'll pull up the live feed on the laptop. Heather will introduce you and then we'll be live. While the camera is connected to the live broadcast, a red light will appear just above the lens." He points to the camera. "And there may be a slight delay in your response time with the live feed. This is normal." He checks his watch. "Do you have any questions?"

"Will Agent Vickers be live with us?" Gage asks.

200

Owen nods.

"Is swearing frowned upon?" Gage asks.

Rozanne elbows Gage in the side.

"Definitely frowned upon," Owen says.

Gage rubs his rib. "I'll try to keep my cool."

"Dre!" Silvey shouts.

Andrea laughs. "What can I say?" She brushes off her shoulders. "I can't lose."

Silvey lays down a hand full of queens and jacks. "I'm sunk."

Scott shakes his head. "I would say she's counting cards, but not sure that would make a difference in rummy."

"Am I still in the game?" Captain Wilson asks, looking at the legal pad.

"Second place," Silvey says, tapping the paper. "Baxton and I are dead last."

"We could come back," Baxton says, nudging Silvey's shoulder.

Silvey smiles and shakes her head. "You're negative sixty at the moment. Andrea is at four hundred and eighty-five."

"Well," Baxton says, shuffling the deck. "Let's hope Gage and Rozanne are having better luck than us."

32

"Good evening, I'm Heather Sanders and I'm coming to you live with a special broadcast update from a segment aired a few hours ago. Our earlier segment was suppressed on orders from our network partner's Vice President. We will no longer be silenced and bring you, the viewers, a first-person account of the abduction of two young men from a home in Clay County." She pauses and taps her ear. "Earlier we heard a recorded statement from Gage Auburn." She pauses. "Please welcome Gage and Rozanne Auburn."

The red light above the camera lens blinks on and Owen points to Gage.

"Hi Heather," Gage says. "Thanks for having us."

"The pleasure is ours," Heather says, placing a hand over her heart. "Can you walk us back through the abduction?"

Gage nods. "My wife, Rozanne, cousin Baxton Auburn, and I were at my home when a drone was flown close to our house."

"Is that a common occurrence?"

"No. We live on a few acres outside of town, so a rogue drone hovering over our property is not common."

"Odd. What happened next?"

"We protected our property and privacy." Gage glances at Rozanne. She nods once. "I shot it down over the pond."

Heather fights a smile. "And after that?"

"Baxton and I went out to the pond to retrieve the drone. As a group of men dressed all in black came up the hill beyond the pond and surrounded us."

"And where were you, Rozanne?"

"I was watching all of this go down from the back porch. Once the first few men crested the hill, I had stepped off the porch. But Gage told me to run, and I did."

"You've had experience with strangers on your property?"

Rozanne nods. "Unfortunately."

"You were abducted from your home."

"Yes, a few years ago. But the people involved are behind bars."

Heather nods. "But the men dressed in black?"

"Definitely professional," Rozanne says. "They took Baxton and Gage with force."

Heather holds up her hand. "What do you mean by force?"

"The men were armed," Rozanne says. "And they tackled them to the ground and zipped tied their hands behind their backs."

Gage holds up his right arm and pulls back his sleeve. "Still missing hair that was rubbed off from the plastic during the confrontation."

Zack zooms in on Gage's wrist.

"Sounds quite scary," Heather says. "Did the men identify themselves or tell you why you were being taken?"

"No," Gage says. "Even though Baxton and I were asking questions. They said nothing."

"So, a group of men fly a drone over your private property, then trespass while armed, and tackle you and Baxton without a word."

"Yes," Gage says. "I was taken down while shouting at Rozanne to run."

"I tried to call for help," Rozanne says. "But dropped my phone while running. When the sheriff responded to the home, Gage and Baxton were long gone."

"And you?" Heather asks.

"I stayed hidden," Rozanne says, looking over at Gage. "I wasn't sure who I could trust."

"You believed the men that abducted your husband and his cousin were working with the police or local government?"

"I wasn't sure at the time," Rozanne says.

"And now?" Heather asks.

"The men were agents with orders from the State Department for Science and Technology," Gage says.

"How did you discover this?" Heather asks.

"Baxton and I met with the heads of the State Department, General Hall and Director Gia. They admitted it was their team that took us."

"And did they explain why you had been taken?" Heather asks.

"They believe we saw and used technology hidden at the base," Gage says.

"Were they concerned you used the suspension chamber that the owners of Greening Up, Charlotte and Eli, found Captain Wilson in at the base?"

Gage nods.

"And did you use the suspension chamber found at the base?" Heather asks.

"I did not."

"Can you confirm that the device exists?" Heather asks.

Gage looks over at Rozanne. She meets his eyes and nods. He looks back at the camera. "Yes, I can."

"Did Baxton use the chamber?" Heather asks.

Gage looks left and then right. "I'm sorry, but Baxton isn't in the room. I don't feel comfortable speaking on his behalf."

Heather nods. "Joining me in the studio is former FBI Agent Michelle Vickers."

The screen splits in three keeping Gage and Rozanne on the left, Heather in the middle and Michelle on the right.

Gage frowns. "She is responsible for Silvey Rhoades abduction! Did she tell you that?"

Michelle glares at the camera. "Mr. Auburn."

"Seriously!" Gage says. "She paid the hospital security staff to abduct Silvey Rhoades from the ICU."

Heather holds up her hand. "Ms. Vickers would you like to comment on your involvement in the abduction of Ms. Rhoades?"

"I was following orders."

"Orders that put the health and safety of Silvey at risk," Rozanne says.

"As I stated earlier," Ms. Vickers says. "We have had several eyewitnesses come forward to say Ms. Rhoades is alive and well."

"That doesn't make it right!" Gage says, pointing at the camera lens. "You also held Baxton up in the hospital lobby. You should be charged and tried for your crimes!"

"Again, I was just doing my job."

"That doesn't mean you get immunity for harassment, assault, and kidnapping," Gage says.

Rozanne places her hand over Gage's closed fist. "We've witnessed the trauma she caused Baxton and Silvey's friends and family."

"I'm sorry," Heather says. "My producer just received a statement from the US State Department of Science and Technology."

The red light blinks off above the camera lens.

Owen turns up the broadcast.

"The US State Department of Science and Technology denies any involvement with the ongoing investigation at the old Nike Air Base in Missouri or any involvement with the abduction of two men. And former FBI Agent Michelle Vickers was fired for gross misconduct. Her statements about our department are false."

Gage shoves his chair back and unclips the microphone. He hands the mic pack to Zack. "This is absolute insanity."

"The segment isn't over," Owen says. "Can you please mic back up?"

"I'm done," Gage says. "They've lied about their involvement and taken no responsibility for their actions."

"The people need to hear your reaction to this statement."

"Give us a minute," Rozanne says. She stands and takes Gage's hand. "Come on." They walk out into the hospital lobby.

"I refuse to give them any more of my time," Gage whispers.

"They," Rozanne says, pointing to the door, "are trying to expose them."

Gage paces away from her. "Roz, they know what they did and won't own up to it. Bax is going to be livid!" He turns towards her. "They basically just called me a liar."

Owen sticks his head out the door. "We have two minutes. Thoughts?"

Gage sighs.

Rozanne holds up a finger. "We need another minute."

Owen nods and closes the door.

"Look, we know the truth." Rozanne taps his chest. "We've got this."

Gage leans his forehead to hers. "I can't promise I'll be on my best behavior."

Rozanne kisses his nose and winks. "Obviously."

Gage laughs. "Alright."

Owen opens the door.

"We're coming," Gage says.

Owen hands Gage the mic pack and clips the microphone to Gage's collar as they walk back to their chairs.

"Fifteen seconds," Liv says. "Ready?"

Gage and Rozanne nod.

"And we're back," Heather says. "Before the commercial break, we heard a statement from the US Department of Science and Technology denying any involvement in their abduction of Gage and Baxton Auburn. Gage, would you like to respond?"

The red light clicks on.

Owen points to Gage.

"I don't appreciate being called a liar and them denying what I know is the truth."

"Was the statement signed?" Rozanne asks.

"It was signed by Agent Neil Carlton."

"Figures," Gage says, shaking his head. "He came into the interview room right before Baxton and I were released."

"And Ms. Vickers," Heather says, "you can confirm that you were with Agent Carlton during the interview with Baxton Auburn."

"I can," Michelle says. "I'm not surprised they are trying to paint me as a disgruntled employee, but I am surprised they are denying all involvement."

"Why is that?" Heather asks.

"They gave the owners of Greening Up a non-disclosure agreement with their seal on the paper."

"Please welcome Eli and Charlotte," Heather says.

The screen shows Eli and Charlotte.

"Hi Heather," Charlotte says. "We do have the non-disclosure here." She holds up a stack of papers. "If we chose to sign, it would have included our silence about the suspension chamber, anything to do with Captain Darryl Wilson, and would forfeit the rights to our silo property in Lawson. They included a deed for a new property in the Kansas City area to replace our business asset."

"They are offering you a new piece of property for your silence?" Heather asks.

"Yes, ma'am," Eli says. "I've asked our lawyer to email your team a copy of the agreement and the US Department of Science and Technology seal is clearly visible in the scanned copy. They are lying about their involvement."

"Why did you refuse to sign the agreement?" Heather asks.

"The main reason was how they've treated Captain Darryl Wilson," Charlotte says. "We've spent time with him, and he has the kindest soul. Considering he must face a new reality—most of the people he knew and loved are long ago deceased. His beautiful wife Millie is almost ninety and in late-stage renal failure. This man has had his entire life ripped from him because he chose to serve his country. They've stated he is a dangerous threat to humanity. It is beyond absurd."

"Empathy," Heather says. "You are putting your faith and possibly your financial future in jeopardy to stand next to a man you've just met."

"Yes," Eli says.

Heather nods. "Tonight, we've heard that the US Department of Science and Technology have a long list of questions to answer for their actions and false statement. I will leave you with this final thought. Why would our government hide a scientific discovery that would have radically changed the health and well-being of every citizen for sixty years and only try to bury their heads in the sand again?"

The red light above the lens flicks off.

"That's a wrap." Owen twirls his finger. "Thank you."

Gage exhales and shakes his head. "Well, that lid has been blown clean off."

Rozanne sighs. "We'll see how they come out swinging soon enough."

Liv nods to Zack. "I know I lost the bet."

"What bet?" Gage asks.

"I thought this was all a big hoax," Liv says, shrugging with her palms up. "I'm a jaded skeptic about anything that has government and possible conspiracy written all over it."

Rozanne laughs. "I don't blame you. It is wild what we've learned over the last week."

Zack smirks. "I do have a few more questions, off the record."

Gage lifts an eyebrow. "I refuse the right not to answer, but shoot go ahead."

"Zack," Owen says.

"It's innocent enough," Zack says. "How many shots did it take to shoot the drone down?"

Rozanne covers her mouth to hide her smile.

Gage holds up a single finger. "One."

Liv laughs. "You are such a strange duck, Zack."

Zack smiles while he disassembles the camera and tripod. "Second question, do you actually believe in time travel?"

"Nope," Gage says, handing back the mic pack and microphone.

Zack nods and takes Rozanne's mic pack. "Cool."

"Is that all?" Gage asks.

"Final question. Do you know if Captain Wilson is safe?"

"I don't," Gage says, frowning. "I wish I knew the answer to that and so much more."

208

33

General Hall releases his seat belt and opens the jet door before the pilots have rolled to a complete stop.

"Sir!" Josh shouts. "We are not parked."

"I've got to go now!" General Hall shouts. He descends the first three steps before he jumps to the tarmac. He glances back at the jet.

Josh is frowning and standing at the open door.

"Stay put and get a crew assembled if you are about to time out."

"Yes, sir," Josh says.

General Hall jogs to an idling black car.

The driver steps out. "General Hall."

General Hall nods. "I'm riding shotgun."

The passenger rolls down the window. "Hop in back. We have company."

"Who the hell do you think you are?" General Hall asks, scowling at the cheeky grin plastered on a shaggy, strawberry blonde-haired young man.

"Trust me man," the guy says, nodding his head towards the back.

"Out!" General Hall shouts.

"Your loss, dude," the guy says, getting out of the car.

"He stays here," General Hall says, sliding into the passenger seat and slamming the door.

The driver hesitates. "Um, he's the hacker."

"What?" General Hall asks. "Why are you with a hacker?"

"He was hired to find the moles leaking information about the technology found at the base." The driver points to the back. "She is the computer tech that figured out how to work the suspension chamber."

General Hall turns in his seat.

"Hi," the young woman says, raising a hand. "I'm Kari Davey." She holds up the laptop. "I have the results from the trial run."

General Hall's eyes widen. "Who gave you permission to start a trial?"

"You did," Kari says, tapping her keyboard. "Our orders were to assess, run, and test the device before we submit a report. I came along to share the report in person."

General Hall gets out of the car. He points at the young man pacing a few feet away. "Get in. But don't speak another word until you learn some proper respect."

The young man nods once.

General Hall gets in the back of the car and slams the door. "Drive."

"Destination?" the driver asks.

"To the Nike Base," General Hall says, pressing the privacy screen toggle on the door. He waits until the screen is up all the way. "Show me."

Kari pulls up a lab panel. "We drew blood from one of our analysts, Patrick. He volunteered to go first. He has type one diabetes and was recently diagnosed with the early stages of

210

kidney failure." She scrolls down and points out the highlighted lines. "These are the abnormal levels before the submerge."

"What do you mean submerge?" General Hall asks, studying the numbers.

"When I activated the device, Patrick sunk into the white particles until he was completely covered." She snickers. "All of his clothing was dissolved."

"Seriously?"

Kari nods. "He was in the chamber for twenty-eight minutes. The device opened automatically, and we pulled him out." She scrolls further down in the document. "Here are the labs after the submersion."

General Hall runs his finger down the list. "These are all with in normal range."

Kari smiles. "It's been two hours, and we've continued to check his glucose levels." She pauses and clicks on the next document. "He hasn't required any insulin and all the scars from years of injections from his pump were healed."

"Is that everything?" General Hall asks.

"No," Kari says. "He has poor eyesight and has worn thick glasses his entire life. He can see perfectly fine without his glasses."

"Did you send this information back to the team for review?"

"Yes, sir." Kari clicks on the response from the lab. "They've reviewed our findings and have requested a few more vials of blood for further analysis."

General Hall scrolls through the documents one more time. "Did the team measure the level of white particles before and after the test?"

"Yes, sir." Kari frowns. "The approximate loss of particles was close to eight percent."

General Hall mutters, "Son of a …"

Kari nods. "The majority of waste was noted from the destruction of Patrick's clothing."

"I need all testing to cease until further notice," General Hall says. "And Patrick will need to be confined to the base for the next seventy-two hours until we transfer him offsite."

"Yes, sir."

"And you," General Hall says, lowering the privacy screen. He taps the young man in the front passenger seat on the shoulder. "What is your name?"

"Jimmy Ladvig."

"What have you found?"

"Your email server was compromised, and any communications sent over the last thirty-six hours were published on the dark web for a hefty price. There were six buyers."

"How in the hell did that happen?"

"Somebody left a back door open," Jimmy says. "It took me less than ten minutes to find and close the door."

"And the six buyers?" General Hall asks.

"Two have covered their tracks well, bouncing their IP addresses all over the world, but the other four will have a knock on their door within the hour."

"A knock from whom?"

"A task force with the FBI and NSA," Jimmy says. "I've been working with the NSA as an independent consultant for the last two years. Our team will be able to track any shared data and trace the original hacker."

"Six people," General Hall whispers. "Was there anything else compromised?"

"Our team found schematics for a nuclear-powered lab from 1958 about forty-eight hours ago. We've been tracking activity for all the users who have looked at or downloaded the schematic from the site. We've burned the site seven times, but a new host creates another within two minutes."

"Is anything contained at the moment?" General Hall asks.

"Not by a long shot, sir."

"We're here," the driver says.

General Hall steps out of the car and scans the white tents, field lights, and command vans dotted around the field. "Chaos."

"General Hall!" a woman shouts.

He scans the darkness until he finds a woman waving a clipboard. He jogs over to her.

"Susan Prew, field supervisor."

General Hall nods. "Ms. Davey gave me her report about the trial. Status update?"

"The nuclear lab's power source appears to have been stripped during the initial decommission. We found the disposal documentation for radioactive waste inside the lab."

"That's good news," General Hall states.

"We would agree but," Susan says.

"But what?"

"The power source was retrofitted to the main power grid connected to the city."

"And no one thought to investigate a surge in power consumption for sixty years?"

Susan shakes her head. "We are still waiting on the records. The electrical grid here has changed providers four times over the last decade alone."

"Is the lab still functionally intact?" General Hall asks.

"So far, but we are still working our way through each console."

General Hall nods. "Any other anomalies that we didn't expect?"

"Only a rogue drone," Susan says. "It has been spotted a few times, mostly at night."

"Nothing is visible from the air." General Hall points to the closest tent.

"No, sir." Susan checks her clipboard. "We have a list of drone pilots in the area. Would you like a team to pay them a visit?"

"No, we need everyone's focus on what's down there." General Hall points to the opening.

"Yes, sir," Susan says. "I'll have an update on the nuclear lab soon."

"Thanks," General Hall says, pulling out his vibrating phone. "Excuse me."

Susan steps away.

General Hall answers a call. "Tell me you have good news and who left a door open to be hacked."

"I wish," Director Gia says.

"What is it?"

"The owners of Greening Up just threw us in the fire."

"How?"

"The NDA had our logo."

"And?"

"They showed it on air after they read our statement during the live broadcast."

General Hall runs a hand over his bald head and down his face. "I thought they pulled the segment!"

"We hoped the statement would have squashed any airtime, but it only made it worse. We are in full damage control and the oval office has called for an explanation."

"What can we explain when we are on fire and sinking at the same time! Who's in charge of the server and how was it breeched?"

"Jerome and Diane," Director Gia says. "They are monitoring the diagnostics on the server now just in case Jimmy's patch doesn't hold."

"Do you suspect a mole on our team?"

"No, sir, but Agent Carlton had a third party looking into Project Rainbow. He disclosed this information after we got the call from the NSA."

"Cut him loose!"

"Are you sure? He could go completely rogue like his old partner."

"If he ends up like her," General Hall says. "We can take them to court or better yet, they can spend a few weeks in no-man's-land for a lesson in integrity."

"Yes, sir. Also, alpha team is tracking a new lead in a town called Polo."

"Is it a solid lead?"

"A kid was overheard bragging to a friend about hiding a few fugitives in a bunker."

"A kid?"

214

"It was a kid matching the description of one spotted at the camp when the locals intervened."

"Credible enough. Send me the alpha contact details and coordinates." He walks back to the car. "Oh, did you see the data from the volunteer?"

"Yes, remarkable."

"Problematic."

"How so?"

"An eight percent waste in the nanoparticles is a lot to lose for a single test."

"But type one diabetes cured in less than thirty minutes," Director Gia says.

"We'll see," General Hall says.

34

"Do you mind if we turn it down?" Andrea asks, yawning and stretching. "I am falling asleep over here."

"It's almost over," Scott says, poking her in the side.

Andrea yelps and leans away from him. "Rude."

"Good, you're awake now," Scott says, pulling her back down to his side.

"I've seen the Goonies a hundred times," Andrea whispers.

"But Darryl hasn't," Scott whispers.

Andrea sighs.

"Hey you guys!"

Darryl laughs.

Silvey smiles. "It is magical to witness a grown man watching this for the first time."

Baxton tightens his arm around her. "It's pretty special."

Silvey snuggles in closer to him and risks a look up.

He smiles and winks.

Her cheeks feel instantly hot. *Busted.*

Twenty minutes later, Darryl stands and throws up his hands. "That was fantastic!"

"One classic film down," Scott says. "Wait until you see a video game for the first time."

Darryl's smile falls. "What's that?"

Baxton slow claps. "Your gaming education will be life changing."

Silvey lifts an eyebrow. "I did not peg you as a gamer."

"I dabble," Baxton says.

"Console?" Scott asks.

"Oh no," Andrea says, climbing over the end of the couch. "This rabbit hole just became a sinkhole. I'm calling dibs on the bathroom."

Silvey laughs. "She's not a gamer, but she provides great snacks."

"That's why I win at cards," Andrea says, tapping her temple. "My brain isn't melted."

"Pish," Silvey says, rolling her eyes. "She's just jealous because she never could beat me at Mario Kart."

"I heard that!" Andrea yells behind the closed door.

Silvey laughs again and stands. She pats Darryl on the shoulder. "We'll go easy on him and start out old school maybe like Pac Man."

CHHH CHHH CHHH

Silvey jumps. "What was that?"

"The radio!" Darryl says.

Scott races over to the desk. "What channel are we supposed to be on?"

"Three," Andrea says, opening the bathroom door.

Silvey and Baxton huddle behind Scott as he adjusts the channel.

"Get out!" a woman whispers.

"Did she say get out?" Andrea asks.

Darryl walks over and takes the microphone. "How many?"

"A dozen," a woman whispers, "maybe more. I'm sorry."

"Let's go," Baxton says, jogging over to the ladder. "I'll go up first."

"Wait," Andrea says. "It's nearly midnight and storming. Can't we just lock the bunker down?"

"Babe," Scott says, grabbing her shoulders. "We would be sitting ducks. I saw some flashlights in the totes by the bunk beds. I'll grab them but go now!"

Silvey looks up at Baxton. "This is going to be a long night."

Baxton looks down. "We'll make it. It was like a ten-minute ride. We've got time to hide."

"Unless they have eyes in the sky," Silvey says, gripping the first rung.

"If that is the case—pray it's still storming," Andrea says, climbing up behind Silvey.

Darryl hesitates on the first few rungs. He looks down at Scott jamming food, water, and flashlights into a backpack. "That's enough. We've got to move as light as possible."

Scott frowns and zips the bag. He jogs over and climbs up quickly matching the others rung for rung until he feels the cool damp air on his face.

"No rain," Silvey whispers. "But they've got wheels." She points towards the worn tracks. An engine revs in the distance. "And they are getting closer."

"That's definitely a dirt bike or two," Baxton says, helping Darryl close the steel hatch.

Scott pulls out a flashlight and hands one to Darryl. "Captain, what do you think?"

"Our tracks will be visible," Darryl says. He lifts his suctioned shoe from the mud. "I'd say ditch this path and take cover in the thicker brush and tree line further down." He turns his light down the hill and walks in a circle to void his tracks.

"Sounds good," Baxton says, taking a flashlight from Scott. "Let's go." He takes Silvey's hand and bounds down the hill.

218

Silvey squeezes his hand. "Hey daddy long legs. Slow down."

Andrea stifles a laugh behind them.

"Sorry," Baxton says, shortening his stride. He looks down at Silvey. "Better?"

Silvey frowns. "I will be once we are hidden again. I don't like being hunted."

"Ditto," Andrea says.

Baxton looks over at Scott and Darryl. They are grinning from ear to ear. "Think of it as an epic game of hide and seek."

Silvey looks over at Andrea. "I was always really good at that."

"That's because you could cram your micro sized body into some ridiculously small spaces," Andrea whispers.

"Small but mighty," Silvey says, puffing out her chest.

They reach the tree line and after about ten paces they are forced to go one by one through thick overgrowth, slowing their progress.

"They are almost upon us," Silvey whispers, pushing through a bush nearly up to her chin.

"They are too close," Darryl says, "we can't risk the light." He clicks off his flashlight.

Scott and Baxton kill their lights.

"Our eyes will adjust," Darryl says.

Thunder rumbles and masks the roar of the approaching engines for a few seconds. They carefully weave around the trees and tread further down the hill.

Baxton tightens his grip around Silvey's hand. "Careful, it's a little damp and slick here."

Despite the warning, Silvey slides down a few feet. "You weren't kidding."

Scott and Andrea struggle to keep upright and slide down the steep slope.

Darryl walks down unphased by the terrain or its condition.

"Are you superhuman or something?" Andrea whispers to Darryl.

Darryl puts a finger over his pursed lips and extends his other arm out to his side. He slowly squats.

The others follow his lead and lower themselves to the ground.

The advancing engines slow to an idle above them.

Darryl turns away from the slope. "We've got about three minutes before they learn that we have abandoned the bunker." He lifts his chin towards the clearing at the bottom of the slope. "Stay under the cover of the trees or risk a sprint across the clearing?"

"Hide!" Andrea whispers.

Darryl looks at Silvey. She nods.

"Ok," Darryl whispers. "Move low and slow to the large cluster of oaks."

They scramble over to the trees and duck behind the trunks just as lights dance through the darkness above.

"Times up," Darryl whispers.

Silvey and Andrea make eye contact.

"You good?" Silvey mouths, watching Andrea try to catch her breath.

Andrea nods.

Scott peeks around the trunk and ducks back quickly. He holds up two fingers.

Baxton stretches his neck to check. He holds up four fingers, shakes his head and then holds up a second hand with two fingers.

"Six?" Silvey whispers.

Baxton nods.

Andrea buries her head in her hands.

Scott wraps his arms around Andrea and pulls her close.

The lights filter through the branches just over their heads.

Baxton ducks down even further and wraps himself around Silvey.

Darryl feels around on the ground. He finds a small but hefty rock, tosses it up, and grins. He gets to his feet and throws the rock towards the clearing.

The rock lands with a thud and the lights swing away from the trees.

Silvey clamps a hand over her mouth and gives Darryl a thumbs up.

Darryl grins and peeks around the trunk. He holds up three fingers, twice, and gestures towards the clearing.

"Now what?" Andrea whispers, cowering as thunder rumbles.

"Move when it thunders again," Darryl whispers. He gets to his feet but stays low.

The four of them ready their position and wait for the next round of thunder.

Lightning streaks across the sky just before the thunder rumbles.

They swiftly move until the sound of thunder subsides.

A branch swings back and nails Baxton in the face just as they stop.

Silvey grabs his chin and gently presses below a scratch. She holds up her finger and thumb about an inch apart. "Tiny scratch."

Baxton frowns. "Blood?"

"A little."

The lightning overhead bursts from cloud to cloud and the thunder intensifies.

They move quietly and quickly between each rumble until they make it to the edge of the tree line.

Rain falls hard and fast.

They huddle together.

"There," Darryl says, pointing across the open field. "I think that's an old pole barn."

Scott looks back. "I don't think we were followed."

The rain picks up.

"Ready?" Darryl asks.

They nod and start their sprint.

Andrea falls hard, but Scott gets her to her feet. Baxton beats Darryl to the barn and lifts the wooden sash from the door. Darryl pushes the door open just wide enough for them to squeeze through.

"I think I fell in a cow patty," Andrea says, frowning and shaking off her muddy, covered shoe.

Silvey twists her blonde ponytail and lets the water drip over Andrea's shoe.

"Going to need a lot more than reclaimed rainwater to save these," Andrea says.

"Sorry, Dre," Silvey says, wringing out her shirt.

"Did anyone else see a light in the distance?" Baxton asks, shaking out his curls.

Scott nods. "It was dim, but I did see it."

Darryl nods. "We stay here until dawn." He covers the flashlight with his wet shirt and clicks it on. He walks the length of the barn. "Just old hay bales." He points the light up. "A few holes need patching, but we should be able to stay dry. If and only if we need to run—we head for that light."

35

General Hall lifts the radio to his lips. "Repeat that?"

"It's clear!" the man says.

General Hall squeezes the radio. "Find them!"

Thunder rumbles and shakes the command van.

"Bring up the map," General Hall says.

The tech sitting at the desk opens the satellite map of the area.

"Where is the team?" General Hall asks.

The tech points to a green dot next to a line of trees and a visibly worn path.

"May I?" General Hall asks, taking the mouse.

"Of course," the tech says, pushing back from the monitor and offering him the chair.

General Hall zooms out. "Five homes with several outbuildings not including the camp. And your team has cleared the camp's buildings?"

"Yes, sir," Special Agent Askew says, standing at the entrance to the van. "We have a man patrolling the camp just in case they double back. And a second team with agents at every intersection surrounding the area."

"I want them to focus on the outbuildings," General Hall says, looking over the map. "It's about to unleash a ton of rain. They'll seek shelter."

"Yes, sir," Special Agent Askew says.

General Hall dials Director Gia.

"Did you get them?" Director Gia asks upon answering.

"No," General Hall says. "What are you doing to navigate the mess from the interviews?"

"We are refusing to comment as we investigate the allegations made against our department," Director Gia says. "And we've received two angry calls from the press secretary."

General Hall sighs. "The press secretary can navigate the response from here on out. I want our team focused on the data breech and securing the site."

"Yes, sir," Director Gia says. "And one other thing."

"Yes?"

"Agent Carlton left a little too quietly," Director Gia says.

"What do you mean?"

"He accepted his dismissal with a simple head nod and did not utter a single word on the way to the airfield. Oscar spoke to the pilots, and they mentioned Agent Carlton remained silent during boarding and fell asleep just after takeoff."

"Silence is good," General Hall says. "Maybe he's learned that speaking out can muddy the waters and create chaos."

"I can't imagine Agent Carlton has ever remained silent longer than two minutes in his entire life."

"Make sure we have eyes on him when he lands," General Hall says.

"We'll have to call in reinforcements from other agencies," Director Gia says. "We are tapped."

"Uh, call in the favor with homeland."

"Are you sure?" Director Gia asks.

224

"It's better than the alternative," General Hall says.

"The FBI is pissed," Director Gia says.

"Keep me posted," General Hall says, disconnecting the call. He turns towards Special Agent Askew. "Status?"

"We've had to recall the thermal drone because of the rain. Our teams are checking the closest barns and sheds now." He nods to the tech. "Pull up the active tracking."

A grid with six moving green dots appears on the screen. The tech overlays the map and adjusts the transparency.

General Hall points to the outbuildings furthest away from the green dots. "Why are they all heading in the same direction?"

"They picked up tracks heading northwest," Special Agent Askew says.

"I need them to split up and cover more area. I want them apprehended before these farmers wake up and realize we are trespassing."

Special Agent Askew nods. "Dodger and Mitchell inspect the buildings to the southeast."

"Roger that," Dodger responds.

Two green dots move to the south.

General Hall zooms in and out of the surrounding area. "Do you have information about the people living in these five homes?"

"Mostly farmers," Special Agent Askew says, pointing to the plots that back up to each other on the northwest corner. "We believe these two are related. This one in the middle was bought under a trust about a year ago. We are still waiting to confirm the owner's name."

"And these?" General Hall asks, pointing to the southwest corner.

"This one is a retired county sheriff," Special Agent Askew says, pointing to the house on the corner.

"You didn't think to lead with that?"

"It's nearly midnight," Special Agent Askew says. "I was hoping we would be long gone before he would be up poking around."

General Hall shakes his head. "What about the last house?"

"Another farmer," Special Agent Askew says.

"If we don't apprehend them in the next hour, I want the team to knock on doors and preempt any trespassing concerns." He points at Askew's chest. "Especially the retired sheriff."

"Yes, sir." Special Agent Askew steps out of the van and slides the door closed.

General Hall continues to track the green dots. "Turn up the radio."

The tech adjusts a dial on a receiver sandwiched between two computers.

"General's given us an hour to apprehend before we start door knocking," Special Agent Askew calls. "Pick up the pace."

General Hall fights a yawn. "Is there coffee?"

"No, sir," the tech says. "But there is a stash of soda and a few energy drinks in a cooler up front."

"We've got movement! Dodger over."

"Resident?" Agent Askew asks, getting back in the van. He shakes the rainwater from his jacket.

"Yes, sir. We triggered motion lights near the outbuildings on the southeast corner."

General Hall takes the microphone. "Were you spotted?"

"No, sir," Dodger responds. "Scratch that. I just spotted a mounted camera."

"Approach the house," General Hall calls. "Keep your hands up with your identification out."

"Darlin, call the neighbors," Obi says, checking the camera feed. "We've got trespassers."

"It's almost midnight," Marge says. "Are you sure it's not just coyotes?"

"Do these two men look like wild animals?" Obi asks, showing her the images on his phone.

"Oh dear," Marge says, reaching for her phone. "I'll start with the Hatfield's and then call Yoakum's."

Obi nods and slides on his pants. "I'm going to go out. Lock the door behind me."

Marge nods and hits call.

Obi makes his way through the dark house to the back door and slides on his boots. He takes the rifle off the hook by the back door and slings it over his shoulder by the strap. He swings the door open and steps out onto the back porch.

"I know you're out there," Obi says, squinting into the darkness. "Come on out."

Two men in full tactical gear emerge from the darkness with their hands raised.

"What the hell are you doing?" Obi asks, shaking his head. "Who are you with?"

"Sir, we are agents for the Department of Science and Technology," Dodger says.

"And the reason to trespass on private property in the middle of the night?"

"We are tracking Captain Darryl Wilson and four citizens that may be in danger."

Obi rocks back on his heels and straightens his posture. "You have sixty seconds to walk to the road and wait for your team. If I catch any men or women walking in the fields without a warrant, I will consider it a threat to my home and personal safety." He pats his rifle.

"Sir," Dodger says. "If we could just clear your barn and outbuildings."

"Forty-nine seconds," Obi says, nodding towards the road. "I suggest you jog. It's about a hundred yards to the road."

Dodger taps Mitchell.

Mitchell nods and they take off at a jog towards the road.

Marge opens the back door. "Reynold checked his property and found tracks of at least two people near the barn."

"It's the same agents that took the two men from Excelsior Springs. I'm calling it in."

"Do you want me to come with you to check the barns?" Marge asks, sliding on her boots.

"No, it's still raining. Call the Yoakum's and make sure they know what's going on."

Marge nods. "Be careful and try not to shoot anyone."

"Ha," Obi scoffs. "Not unless they deserve it."

"Obi," Marge says.

"I'm just kidding." Obi closes the door and walks through the backyard to the first outbuilding. He dials the county sheriff.

"Obi?"

"Hey John," Obi says. "Sorry for the late call, but we've got a problem." A series of motion activated lights illuminate his path and he opens the first shed and looks around the lawnmower and gardening supplies before closing it up.

"Is Marge, ok?"

"Fine, but we had a few trespassers. Agents with DOST looking for Captain Wilson."

"What the hell?" John exclaims. "Give me a few minutes. I'll get the deputies headed over your way while I check out how and why they are in Caldwell County."

Obi clears the feed shed. "Thanks John."

"But just a heads up," John says. "Clay County had a run in with one of their agents earlier today. He was released in less than ten minutes."

"Great," Obi grumbles. "Keep me posted."

"You got it."

Obi flips on the flashlight app and follows the worn path to the old pole barn. He waves his light from side to side as he gets closer. "I'm the owner and I'm armed for my protection. If you are hiding in the barn, please come out. I've told the DOST agents to take a hike off my property. You're safe."

Obi pauses just outside the door. "I'm coming in." He pushes open the door and finds a man standing in front of four people with their arms out and above their heads.

"Sir, I'm Captain Darryl Wilson."

Obi steps closer and shines the light over Darryl's face. "Yes, you are. I'm Obidiah, but you can call me Obi." He turns the light towards the others. "And you are?"

"Scott and Andrea Meyer," Scott says, gesturing to Andrea.

Baxton waves. "Baxton Auburn."

Silvey drops her hands. "Silvey Rhoades."

"I suppose you are soaked through and could use a warmer place than the barn to ride out this storm?"

Andrea sighs. "Yes, please."

"Dre," Silvey whispers.

Andrea shrugs. "Sorry I'm wet, cold, and tired."

"I'll have Marge put on a pot of coffee," Obi says. "Follow me to the house. I have plenty of questions, but if I ask without Marge, I'll have to repeat myself. Trust me when I say I don't have the patience for that tonight."

Scott chuckles. "Wise man."

Andrea pokes Scott in the side.

Baxton reaches for Silvey's hand.

Silvey locks her fingers through his and gives him a gentle squeeze.

Darryl falls in step with Obi.

They trudge through the muddy path to the house and stop at the back porch.

"Marge," Obi calls.

The back door swings open.

"Get inside," Marge says, holding the door open. "You'll catch your death out there in this storm."

Andrea bends to remove her shoes.

"Don't worry about that," Marge says.

"They're pretty bad," Andrea says, scrunching her nose and slipping off her shoes. "I'll just set them out here."

"Alright," Marge says, gesturing to the table. "There are towels and a few shirts. Help yourself. Obi, a word."

Marge and Obi walk to the front of the house.

"I've spoken to the Yoakum's," Marge whispers. "Debbie said their grandson was stopped by agents at the intersection just before their driveway. And the deputy rolled by a few seconds before you returned. Are they a threat?"

"I don't think so," Obi says. "But they've been on the run for a reason."

"And?" Marge whispers.

"I haven't questioned them yet."

"What are you waiting for?" Marge asks.

Obi smiles. "You." He taps her nose. "Let's go."

"Smarty pants," Marge says, swatting his backside as they make their way back to the kitchen.

Darryl steps forward and extends his hand. "We are so sorry for the intrusion and in the middle of the night."

"Pish," Marge says, shaking his hand. "I'm Marge and you?"

"Captain Darryl Wilson," Darryl says, gesturing to Scott. "This is Scott, Andrea, Baxton and Silvey."

"Care to fill us in on what we are now aiding?" Marge asks.

Darryl spends the next thirty minutes going over their safe house invasion, the encounter with Special Agent Askew, his team surrounding them at the camp, and the Swafford's intervention.

Marge nods. "No surprise to hear of Meg and Lou's assistance. They are good eggs."

"We are very thankful for their help," Silvey says. "And the use of the bunker."

Obi nods. "You should have been safe there. I bet Lou's boy was out bragging about it again."

"Obi," Marge says, nudging him in the side. "You don't know how they found them."

"True," Obi says. "You've told us how you ended up on our land and in our neck of the woods, but not the why?"

"Have you seen the news?" Andrea asks.

"We watched the broadcast with Heather and that FBI agent," Obi says. "It was on this evening. We heard about the miracle tech conspiracy and the alleged abductions."

"Not a conspiracy," Darryl says.

"And nothing alleged," Baxton says. "Gage and I were abducted from the house by Special Agent Askew and his men."

"Oh my," Marge says. "I think we are going to need something a little stronger than coffee to unpack all of this."

"Ma'am," Darryl says, placing a hand across his heart. "I don't believe we should put any more burden on you. The more you know could put you and Obi in their crosshairs. And I, for one, don't want to drag any more innocent people into this mess."

Obi's phone rings and startles everyone in the room besides Obi. He looks down at the screen and holds up a finger to his lips. He swipes to answer the call.

"Hey John," Obi says, placing the call on speaker mode.

"Hey," John says. "The deputies just cleared four SUVs blocking the intersections around your land and near Reynold Hatfield. The agents refused to comment on why they were there to begin with and deferred all questions to a General Hall. I've called the number, and it goes straight to a switchboard operator who transferred me to a voicemail."

"Not surprised," Obi says.

"Did you find anyone else on your property?" John asks.

"No," Obi says. "Marge and I are going back to bed."

"My deputies are going to patrol your area until dawn just in case these agents decide to stomp on my soil again without an invitation."

"Thanks, John, we appreciate it."

Obi ends the call and looks Darryl in the eyes. "John is the county sheriff and my replacement when I retired. I've never lied to that man and hope I don't have to again."

Darryl nods. "Understood."

"Do you have a car in the area?" Marge asks.

"Meg and Lou drove them to town," Andrea says. "Do you mind if I borrow your phone to make a call to get us a ride?"

"I've got an idea on a way out of here that won't raise any red flags," Marge says.

Obi lifts an eyebrow. "And what is that, dear?"

"They can take dolly," Marge says.

Obi frowns. "The old RV?"

"Why not?"

"You think an RV rolling out of here in the middle of the night wouldn't be suspicious?"

Marge rolls her eyes. "I didn't mention when they'd be leaving. We've got bunk beds and the sleeper sofa to keep them safe until the dust settles."

"We couldn't impose," Andrea says.

"Nonsense," Marge says. "It's the middle of the night and pouring down rain. I won't take no for an answer."

"Yes, ma'am," Scott says, taking Andrea's hand. "Thank you. We appreciate the hospitality."

"Then it's settled," Marge says. "Obi, pull out the sofa bed and I'll get you sheets and blankets from the hall closet."

Obi salutes and leaves the kitchen ahead of Marge.

Silvey sighs. "I hope this doesn't come back to bite them."

Darryl nods. "I believe it's the only option and we can sleep a few hours."

Andrea fights a yawn. "I could definitely use more than a few."

36

"You were kicked off the property?" General Hall yells in Dodger's face.

Dodger takes a step back. "Sir, he had a gun, and we were trespassing."

"You lost our only credible lead," General Hall says, throwing up his hands.

"We can get a warrant and go in legally," Special Agent Askew says, stepping between Dodger and General Hall.

"Oh, brilliant," General Hall says, "on what grounds?"

Special Agent Askew puffs out his cheeks. "For the owners protection. We've made public claims that Captain Wilson is armed and dangerous."

"You're kidding, right?" General Hall asks. "If they are on that property, it is the retired sheriff. I believe that reasoning would get laughed at by any judge."

"Do I have permission to at least pull the guys back in for the night?" Special Agent Askew asks.

"Yes," General Hall says. "We will start at first light." He steps out of the command van and pulls up his hood.

The rain fall is steady. The puddle beside the van is rapidly filling, and the sky lights up with a few streaks of lightning.

General Hall ducks his head and makes a run for the idling car. He slides in the back. "I need to make a few calls."

The driver nods and pushes the button for the privacy partition.

General Hall pulls out his phone and checks the latest thread of messages from Director Gia. The communications team is actively attempting to squash the rising discourse of mistrust with the DOST, and a few senators are calling for a hearing.

"Admiral is going to lose it," General Hall mutters before hitting dial.

On the second ring, a woman answers. "You're on thin ice Hall!"

"Admiral," General Hall says. "We had them until more civilians interfered with our team."

"Tell me news I don't know!"

"Ma'am?"

"The local sheriff's brother works here at the Pentagon," Admiral Tyson says. "And the other agent has flipped sides."

"What?" General Hall asks, running a hand over his bald head.

"Agent Carlton submitted a formal statement and apology to the Auburn's and Rhode's families for his involvement with your dangerous department and exposing Project Q."

"Submitted it to whom?"

"Every major news outlet."

"And they are running it?" General Hall asks.

"Of course," Admiral Tyson says. "We can't stop this train wreck. I am recalling you and every member of your team with boots on the ground in Missouri."

"Ma'am," General Hall says. "We can't leave the chamber here and the assets are too important to the research to let them run free."

234

"It's time," Admiral Tyson says. "Any delays in your team's departure will be another digit off your funding for the next fiscal year. Is that clear?"

"Yes, ma'am," General Hall says, disconnecting the call. He calls Director Gia next.

"General," Director Gia answers.

"It's over."

"What do you mean?"

"Admiral Tyson is shutting everything down including our team at the base. We are pulling everything we can, but the clock is ticking."

"She can't!" Director Gia shouts.

"She can and did with the threat of reducing our funding," General Hall says.

"And I thought our night couldn't get worse than Agent Carlton's statement," Director Gia says.

"I'll have to circle back with Admiral Tyson—once she's had time to cool off. I want to pursue Vickers and Carlton for their involvement in this going south so quickly."

"We weren't exactly that covert," Director Gia says. "We can own that, right?"

"It was necessary, and we got the samples to prove that!'"

"Without their consent," Director Gia says. "If this ever gets called for review—we are so screwed."

"We had full rights to the technology, and anyone involved with it!"

"I hear ya," Director Gia says, "but the Senators may beg to differ."

"We can handle the lousy politicians," General Hall says.

Director Gia sighs. "I'll get the remaining jets to head your way to pick up what we can safely remove from the site."

"Wheels up in three hours," General Hall says, disconnecting the call. He taps the privacy screen.

The driver rolls the screen down. "Sir."

"We are done here," General Hall says. "Keep the car running. I'll be back in a few minutes."

"Yes, sir."

General Hall steps out of the car and jogs back to the command van's open door. "We're done here. Stand down. Pack it up and head back to the base." He points to Special Agent Askew. "You and your men can assist the field team with packing up."

"Wait, what?" Special Agent Askew asks, stepping out of the van and closing the door. The rain smacks him in the face and soaks his shirt.

"The operation is over. We have been recalled by orders from the admiral."

"Oh shi—" Special Agent Askew pulls out his wet shirt.

General Hall raises an eyebrow.

"I mean, yes, sir."

37

Gage rolls over and reaches for Rozanne. The bed is empty and cool.

"Roz?" Gage calls.

"In the kitchen," Rozanne says.

Gage rolls out of bed and checks the clock over the dresser. "It's early. What's going on?"

"Bax called his mom about an hour ago," Roz says. "Deanne knocked on the door about twenty minutes ago."

Gage jogs down the hall. "Is he okay?"

"Yes," Roz says, handing Gage a mug. "We are meeting Bax and the others in Lawson in about thirty minutes."

"Is it safe?" Gage asks, taking a sip.

"We think so," Roz says. "They were basically hunted last night by the DOST agents."

"What!"

"They're fine and ironically ended up in a barn that belonged to a retired sheriff. The kind man and his wife took them in. The county deputies even got the agents to withdraw from the area."

"That's good news," Gage says.

"And Silvey spoke to her dad," Roz says. "The base was cleared overnight."

Gage lifts an eyebrow. "They abandoned the base?"

"Supposedly," Roz says. "Scott's friend Wayne flew his drone over again. He spotted only one van at the site, and it was leaving the base. All the tents and field lights are gone."

Gage sighs. "That's some relief."

"And then there is this," Roz says, tapping the keyboard to her laptop. She pulls out a chair from the kitchen table. "Have a seat and read this while I change."

Gage hesitantly sits down and places his mug next to the laptop. The bold headline draws his attention immediately.

It's TRUE

I, Neil Carlton, former FBI agent, served the agency for the last seventeen years and was unwillingly transferred to the US State Department of Science and Technology and assigned to Project Q three days ago. I was forced to lie in my statement to the press about Michelle Vickers, the owners of Greening Up and the Auburn's. They threatened my pension and jail time if I shared any information about the Nike Base in Lawson, Missouri and the technology that was hidden inside. Yes, it's true, a chamber I've seen inside the base was used to keep Captain Darryl Wilson in a suspended state for the last sixty years and is still functionally intact. I also want to formally apologize to my partner, Michelle Vickers, for being a coward and not following her out the door when she saw the department for what it was. And I also apologize to the Rhoades and Auburn families for our harassment and involvement

*in the abductions that endangered their lives
and wellbeing. I am aware my actions were
wrong and unjust.*

"Holy crap," Gage says, leaning back away from the laptop.

"Right?" Roz asks, leaning over and softly kissing him. "Go get dressed. We can talk about it on the drive."

Gage lingers with his nose pressed to hers. "Or?"

"Later," Roz says, backing away from him. "I'm not getting dressed a second time."

Gage pouts.

"Go," Roz says, pointing to the hallway.

Gage stands and pulls her close. "Fine, but I am holding you to the 'later' promise."

Roz smiles. "Go, mister. We are going to be late if you stall any longer."

"Fine," Gage says, backing away with his hands raised. "Your loss."

"Good grief," Roz says, shaking her head. "I'll be in the truck."

Four minutes later, Gage hops up into the truck. "Where to?"

"Catricks," Roz says.

"We are meeting them in public?" Gage asks, pulling the truck around and starting down the driveway.

"Yes," Roz says. "Deanne and your aunt are meeting us there."

"Wow! Is the press coming too?"

"Well—"

"I was joking," Gage says, looking over at Roz.

"We are going to discuss this over breakfast," Roz says.

Gage nods and taps the steering wheel. "So about later?"

"Gage!"

He waggles his eyebrows and smirks.

"Just drive," Roz says, scooting away from him.

38

Baxton pulls out a chair for Silvey.

"Thanks," Silvey says. "I am starving."

"I don't think I've ever seen this back room," Scott says, looking around at the country décor on the walls.

"Well," Andrea says, sitting down next to Scott. "This group can't fit in a booth and the old ears up front don't need to hear our discussion."

"You invited my mother," Silvey says, rolling her eyes. "Give it an hour after were done here."

"Silvey Lynn!" Evelyn says from the end of the table.

"Oh, hi mom," Silvey says, smiling and waving. "I didn't see you there."

"Sure," Evelyn says, shaking her head.

"Get that stick out," Buzz says, scooting by Evelyn.

"What did you say to me?" Evelyn scowls.

Andrea stands. "Buzz, take a seat next to Silvey and Evelyn sit down next to Scott. I expect you two can remain civil for the next hour. Otherwise, leave now."

Evelyn frowns, but Buzz smiles and dances over to the chair next to Silvey.

"Dad," Silvey whispers. "Don't poke the fire until after she's had coffee."

Buzz elbows Silvey in the side. "It's just too much fun." He looks around the table. "Who are we waiting on?"

"Baxton's mom and aunt are coming," Silvey says. "Gage and Rozanne should be pulling up any second."

"And my godmother, Myra," Scott says, nodding to the entryway. "I'm glad you could make it."

Darryl stands and holds out his hand for Myra. "Thanks again for your help."

Myra nods and shakes his hand. "Just happy to see you're all here and in one piece."

Silvey looks up at Baxton. He grins, but she frowns.

"What is it?" Baxton whispers.

"The scratch from the branch is healed," Silvey says, gently touching his cheek.

Baxton runs his hand over his smooth cheek. "Odd. I could feel the cut last night in my sleep and there was some dried blood on the pillowcase this morning."

"Why are you frowning?" Evelyn asks.

"Baxton had a scratch on his cheek last night," Silvey says.

Captain Wilson winks at Silvey. "We heal fast, remember."

"Oh," Silvey says, widening her eyes.

Baxton audibly gulps.

"What are you talking about?" Gage asks, waving from the end of the table.

"Hey," Baxton says. "I'll explain later."

Gage lifts an eyebrow.

"Where's Roz?" Baxton asks.

"Our mothers were waiting outside in the car," Gage says. "She's letting them know it's safe to come inside."

"Why are they concerned with safety?" Evelyn asks. "It's Lawson."

"We had a threat delivered to our doorstep," Silvey says, glaring at her mother.

Evelyn sighs. "Well, you don't have to be smart about it."

"Sure," Silvey says.

Buzz nudges Silvey in the side. "No poking the fire."

Silvey lets her long blonde hair cover her face to hide her smile.

Gage pats Baxton on the back and pulls out a chair for his mom, aunt, and Roz.

"Alright," Andrea says, holding up a menu. "We'll put in our order first. Then talk."

"Thank goodness," Silvey says, rubbing her stomach.

Andrea laughs. "Do we need to warn the cook that you're starving?"

"Nah," Silvey says. "I'm tiny and only nibble at my food."

Buzz rocks back in his chair with a full belly laugh. "Ha, ha, ha."

"Knock it off," Evelyn says, waving her menu at Buzz, which only makes him laugh harder.

"Did I hear you're ready to order?" Tiff asks from the entryway.

Buzz wipes the tears streaming down his face and covers his mouth to quiet his laughter. "Come on over. Silvey's starving."

"Oh, Rick's on the grill today," Tiff says. "I'll be sure to warn him."

Buzz and Andrea burst into another round of laughter.

Silvey meets her mother's menacing glare. "Not my fault."

Tiff grins. "Silvey, what will it be?"

Silvey and the others order. Tiff brings back their drinks as they finish a round of introductions.

Darryl stands.

"First things first," Darryl says. "To the parents at this table. Thank you for raising smart, brave, and amazing kids. I would be neck deep in some lab without their help." He tips his head to Myra. "And thanks for helping a total stranger out."

Myra nods.

242

"I believe that we can trust this group with the information we are about to share." Darryl makes eye contact with each person. They nod in return.

"Great," Darryl says. "I'll start with how and when I first met Silvey. And we can run through the events that led to our meeting here today. How does that sound?"

"Terrifying," Evelyn whispers.

Darryl nods. "Some parts were very tense."

Andrea raises a finger. "We'll answer questions, but can we hold them until the person speaking has shared their perspective of the event?"

The group nods.

Darryl pauses his retelling of his first encounter with Silvey and the owners of Greening Up when the food is delivered to the table.

Tiff tops off the drinks and leaves the group alone again.

"We'll eat and then continue," Darryl says, picking up a fork.

"Can I ask one question?" Buzz asks.

"Sure," Darryl says.

"Any chance I can get a spin in the fancy chamber to fix my ticker?" Buzz pats his chest.

"We'll see what they've left at the base."

"That's a maybe," Buzz says, sprinkling copious amounts of salt all over his biscuits and gravy.

"Easy dad," Silvey says, cutting into her pancakes.

Buzz scoops up a large bite. "Mind your business."

Silvey sticks out her tongue and crinkles her nose.

"Seriously," Evelyn mutters.

Buzz and Silvey turn with matching grins towards Evelyn and tilt their heads to the left.

Andrea points her fork at Buzz and Silvey. "Play nice and eat your food."

Buzz smirks. "Yes, ma'am."

Evelyn rolls her eyes.

They eat peacefully for another fifteen minutes.

Darryl folds his napkin and places it over his empty plate. "I will continue with how I managed to flee the base and how I ended up in Elmira." He spends a few more minutes explaining his escape, and hitchhiking, but takes a moment. He points to Baxton.

"I believe before Myra and Silvey tell their bit we need to hear what happened at your place."

Baxton wipes his mouth and takes a sip of water. He recounts the drone, abduction, interview with the former FBI agents, the facility escape, and recapture with a few add-ins from Gage and Rozanne.

"The picture that showed up on our doorstep was taken from that drone?" Evelyn asks.

"I haven't seen it," Baxton says, "but from the description it sounds very likely."

"And that is why and how I ended up at Myra's place," Silvey says. "And where she found Darryl walking her property."

Myra explains the helicopters flying low over her house and her four-wheeler baited distraction to draw the agents away from Silvey and Darryl.

"How did they know Darryl was out in Elmira?" Evelyn asks.

Myra smirks. "Small town. People talk."

Darryl nods. "Especially when you hitch a ride with a few locals."

"True," Myra says. "I did some digging on the Department of Science and Technology. They've got a lengthy history of theft of private property taken under the guise that it used a government patent and in many cases of wrongful search or unlawful detainment. Those were mostly all settled and sealed, but there is one from the early nineties that made its way to a jury trial. The DOST was found guilty on several counts of theft of private property, harassment, and fined millions. The person who sued the department and won went missing less than six months later. And guess what their field of expertise included?"

Scott drum rolls his fingers on the table.

Myra laughs. "Biotechnology nanoparticles."

"Wow," Silvey says. "They've been after tech like this for years and the holy grail has been here for decades. Oh, the irony that it took mother nature to pull back the curtain."

"Doo da—doo da—doo—doo," Buzz sings.

Silvey laughs. "It is a little wicked witchy."

244

"Is the person still missing?" Andrea asks.

"The family gave up on the search and they were presumed dead in 2002."

"That's so sad," Deanne says.

Myra nods.

Tiff returns to the table. She tops off some coffee and collects the finished plates. "Can I put anything else in for you?"

"Half order of biscuits and gravy," Silvey says.

"You got it," Tiff says, walking back to the kitchen.

"How are you not three hundred pounds?" Andrea asks, shaking her head.

"She's got great genes," Buzz says, putting his arm around Silvey's shoulders.

"From me!" Evelyn says.

Buzz laughs and pats his belly. "You think?"

Andrea holds up her hands. "Ok, time out. We should get back on track. We left off with Silvey and Darryl hiding out at Myra's place."

They spend the next fifteen minutes rehashing the last forty-eight hours and how they ended up in a bunker in the middle of the woods.

"Good grief," Deanne says. "You kids have been through the ringer."

Buzz nods. "A bunker in the middle of the woods sounds pretty safe. What happened?"

"We received a get out now message on the ham radio from the caretakers," Silvey says. "And we got out before the agents arrived and scrambled through the woods in the rain to an old barn where we met our fourth savior of the day."

Darryl nods. "Retired Sheriff Obi and his lovely wife, Marge, took us in overnight and assured us they had the county deputies running the agents off who were trespassing on private property."

"Wild," Buzz says.

"Obi and I worked together on a chop shop case way back in the day," Myra says. "He's the best person to have on our side and the press loved him."

"He's agreed to give a statement about the agents trespassing," Darryl says. "And promised their unlawful search of his and their neighbors' properties will not go unchecked by the Caldwell county prosecutors."

"And I received a call this morning that the base is cleared of all previous government vehicles," Buzz says. "So, his deputies got them out of our county as well."

Bax's mom clears her throat. "Are they going to come after my boy again?"

"We aren't sure," Bax says, reaching for his mom's hand. "We hope our next steps will clarify this question."

"What do you mean?" Bax's mom asks.

"Bax and I have agreed to a sit-down interview and do a full tell-all segment with Heather," Silvey says. "We will be calling for an immediate ceasefire with the DOST."

"Whoa!" Myra says, shaking her head.

"We know it's risky," Silvey says. "But we have some insurance." She checks the entryway is clear before she continues. "I was given the schematics for the suspension chamber. Plus, I have a few particles we can show and send off to get tested to prove that we aren't lying about everything that has transpired."

"Between yesterday's segments, their interview, and the FBI agents confessions," Roz says, nodding. "They will be held to the court of public opinion and forced to the table."

"That is the fruit we are dangling over the DOST," Silvey says. "If they refuse to tell the public the truth—we will."

Tiff walks back in with Silvey's biscuits and gravy and pauses mid stride. She takes in the slack jaws of most of the people in the room. "Whoa! It looks like you just dropped a major bomb in this room."

39

Silvey nervously paces the green room.

"Sit down," Andrea says. "You are making me nervous, and I am not going on air."

"I can't do this!" Silvey says, shaking her hands out.

"Just take a breath," Andrea says.

Silvey lifts her arms out away from her body. "I'm sweating and feel like I might puke."

"It's normal to feel a little anxiety," Andrea says.

"Normal or not, I still want to puke."

"Well, maybe you should have thought that through before eating that fifth or sixth donut on the way here."

Silvey stops pacing. "Why is five the cut off?"

Andrea laughs. "I'm just saying you're on a sugar high and about to validate the truth that was buried for sixty years."

"Right, pile on the pressure."

"Sorry," Andrea says, holding up her hands. "You'll do great."

Knock knock

"Oh, it's happening," Silvey whispers.

"Come in," Andrea says.

"We're ready for you Ms. Rhoades," the production assistant says.

Silvey gulps. "Has anyone puked on air?"

The production assistant looks from Silvey to Andrea.

"Maybe have a trash can nearby just in case," Andrea says.

Silvey shrugs. "Not a bad idea."

The production assistant nods. "Follow me."

"Good luck," Andrea says, hugging Silvey.

"I'll need it."

Silvey follows them down the hall and spots Baxton's head over the camera. He turns, smiles and meets her eyes at the same time.

"Are you nervous?" Baxton whispers.

"Definitely."

Baxton takes her hand and squeezes it twice. "We can survive a tornado. We can survive the media."

They are mic'd up and directed to two chairs opposite of Heather Sanders.

Heather stands and shakes hands with Baxton and then Silvey.

"It's nice to finally meet the infamous Silvey," Heather says. "Ready?"

"No," Silvey says. "But we want to move on."

"Thirty seconds," a director yells.

"Have a seat," Heather says.

Silvey's vision goes a little spotty.

"And we are back," Heather says, smiling at the camera. "We are live with Silvey Rhoades and Baxton Auburn."

Silvey blinks and sucks in a breath.

Thirty minutes later, Baxton kneels in front of Silvey's chair. "Are you ok?"

"Is it over?" Silvey asks.

Baxton smiles and cocks his head to the side. "Yes."

248

"I think I blacked out," Silvey says.

"You were brilliant," Baxton says, standing and offering his hand to her.

Silvey takes his hand and stands. Her knees wobble under her weight.

"You good?" Baxton asks.

"I think I just need some air," Silvey says, squeezing his hand. "And maybe a burger."

Baxton laughs. "I think we can do both."

Andrea meets Silvey in the hallway. "You could seriously consider a career change with that performance."

"I don't remember a single moment," Silvey says, hugging Andrea.

"Fooled me," Andrea says, falling into step with them. "Scott's getting the car. He said he would pick us up out front."

"Ms. Rhoades!" a woman shouts.

Silvey stops and turns around. A middle-aged woman is walking as fast as she can towards them. She hands Silvey a phone. "For you."

Silvey hesitantly puts the phone up to her ear. "Hello?"

"Ms. Rhoades, my name is Director Gia."

"With the DOST?" Silvey asks.

"Yes, ma'am," Director Gia says. "I'm sorry we have not been formally introduced."

"I'm not," Silvey says. "What do you want?"

"That list is very long, but I'll start with an apology on behalf of the agents and my department. Our actions were extreme."

"Understatement of the century," Silvey says. "I have nothing to say to you until you provide a full account and transparent report to the public." She disconnects the call and hands the phone to the woman. "If she calls back, we're no longer here."

The woman nods. "Have a good day."

Baxton holds the door open for Silvey and Andrea.

Silvey squints. "Remind me to add sunglasses to the list of items lost."

Andrea nods and points to the car approaching. "There's Scott."

"Since we are downtown," Baxton says. "How does Town Topic sound?"

"Amazing!" Silvey says.

"You two are really meant for each other," Andrea says, bypassing the front passenger door. "Ride up front."

Bax smiles. "Sure, thanks."

Silvey slides in the back ahead of Andrea.

Scott checks the rearview mirror. "Hey Silvey, you've got a little something all over your face."

Silvey sticks out her tongue.

"I think she looks lovely," Andrea says, patting Silvey's overly blushed cheek. "But it's a little much for natural light and maybe even for my standards."

"Dre!" Silvey says, stretching her neck to look at the extreme makeup painted over her face in the mirror. "Oh, my god. I look like a clown."

Baxton looks over his shoulder and winks. "Hottest clown I've ever laid eyes on."

Silvey rolls her eyes. "That makeup artist is going on my naughty list this year."

Scott pulls on to Broadway and drives a few blocks. He slows and turns. "Never seen it this empty." He parks in the nearly empty lot.

"Good," Silvey says. "I can minimize my humiliation before I wash this crap off."

"It's not that bad," Andrea says, getting out of the car.

"Order me a double cheeseburger, chili fries with extra cheese, and a vanilla shake," Silvey says before bee lining to the bathroom.

The men's bathroom door opens and a man with thick bushy eyebrows steps into the narrow passage in front of Silvey.

"Sorry," he says, looking Silvey up and down. "Oh, you're…"

"Nobody," Silvey says, brushing by the man. She pushes open the door and stares at the rose red cheeks, heavy foundation hiding her freckles and dark lined eyes. "Unbelievable."

She scrubs her face until it is a new shade of pink and freckles. She dries her hands and turns towards the door to find Andrea standing in the doorway.

250

"Silvey," Andrea whispers. "We need to go."

"Why?" Silvey asks.

"That man you passed on the way to the bathroom was Neil Carlton," Andrea says.

"Are you kidding?"

"No."

Baxton and the jerk are outside shouting in the parking lot.

Silvey rushes by Andrea and runs outside.

"You have some nerve even asking!" Baxton shouts and points down at Neil.

"Whoa!" Silvey says, pushing between them. She turns her back to Baxton and points to Neil. "You can go straight to hell!"

"I'm trying to apologize," Neil says, folding his hands together.

"Scott, start the car," Silvey says. "We're leaving."

"Please!" Neil exclaims, stepping towards Silvey.

Baxton pivots and steps within inches of Neil to block Silvey. "Lay a finger on her and I will break them."

Neil takes a step back.

"Let's go," Andrea says, walking by them and to the car.

A waiter rushes out. "I've got your order almost ready."

"I'll get the food," Andrea says. "You two can wait in the car with Scott." She glares at Neil. "You're done talking to them or us. Take a hike!"

Baxton takes Silvey's hand and walks her to the car.

Neil backs up and walks back towards the restaurant.

The waiter stands in the entrance with their arms crossed. "Oh, no you don't. You've been permanently banned. Never show your face here again."

"Seriously?" Neil asks. "My meals on the table."

"No, it's in the trash," the waiter says. "You start stuff here, we finish it!" They hold the door open for Andrea.

"Thank you," Andrea says.

"No problem," the waiter says. "That guy never tips more than a dollar. No loss, honey."

"Order up," a woman shouts from the kitchen.

"Give me a minute to bag it up," the waiter says.

"No problem," Andrea says, watching Neil walk away and up the hill towards the financial district.

A young woman gets up from a table and walks up to Andrea. "Hi." She holds up her phone. "I recorded the whole thing while I was doing a live."

"A live?" Andrea asks.

"I have a food channel on TikTok and was reviewing the burgers," the woman says. "I can take it down if you want, but it's the highest numbers I've had in months."

Andrea sighs. "Just leave it."

"Really?" the young woman asks, rocking up on her toes. "Thank you!"

"But you better leave a stellar review for this place!" Andrea says.

The young woman smiles. "That's a given! I loved everything."

"Here you go," the waiter says, handing Andrea the bag of food and a drink carrier.

"Thanks," Andrea says. "I need to settle the bill."

"Nah, that's on the house," the waiter says, pointing to the manager. "She recognized your friend from the news." They gesture to a large TV in the corner.

Andrea smiles and lifts the bag. "Thank you."

The manager nods. "Have a good day."

Scott hops out and helps Andrea to the car with the food and drinks. "We're going to the memorial to eat it."

Andrea nods and gets in beside Silvey. "Good news that prick was on foot and walking to the financial district so he should be long gone. And they permanently banned him from the restaurant. Oh, and you're famous."

"What?" Silvey asks, frowning.

"The manager said the food was on the house because they watched you on the news."

Silvey's frown deepens. "Maybe a public park isn't a great idea."

"It will be fine," Andrea says. "Oh, there was a girl live streaming during the encounter with Neil. She asked if she could keep it up or if she should take it down."

Silvey nods. "Down."

"Right?" Baxton asks.

252

"Um," Andrea says.

"Dre!" Silvey says.

"It really only made Neil look bad," Andrea says.

"I told the man to go to hell," Silvey says.

"She only filmed the incident inside," Andrea says, opening the bag and handing Silvey a few fries. "Eat."

"But…" Silvey says, pouting.

Andrea lifts an eyebrow.

"Fine." Silvey eats the fries.

Scott's phone buzzes as he turns into the park. "Silvey, it's from your dad."

Silvey takes the phone and opens the message. *Tell Silvey the local Dodge dealership called and has offered her and Baxton new trucks.*

Silvey gasps and hands the phone to Baxton. "Read that!"

"What is it?" Andrea asks, craning her neck to read the message.

"No way," Baxton says. "The local Dodge dealership is offering Silvey and I new trucks."

"See you're famous," Andrea says, nudging Silvey in the side.

"Ha," Silvey says, looking around the park as Scott drives into the parking lot. "Maybe we should get them to throw one in for Darryl, too."

Baxton snaps. "I promised we'd call him after the interview."

"I still can't believe he agreed to stay with Myra," Scott says.

"Why?" Andrea asks.

"I thought he would want to be closer to his wife in St. Joseph," Scott says, parking the car.

"Maybe once the dust is settled," Silvey says, hopping out. "I don't think we'll feel safe until we know if they took the bait."

Scott hands out the drinks and they walk to an open picnic table.

"The Kansas City skyline is really pretty from up here," Andrea says, setting down the bag of food.

Silvey nods and helps Andrea pass out the food. "I'm just glad it's not packed." She nods to a few empty tables and a few people laid out on blankets.

"You can eat in peace," Andrea says.

"Good," Silvey says, looking at Baxton's food. "That's it?"

"It's a triple cheeseburger," Baxton says, shaking his cup. "And I've got a chocolate malt."

Silvey looks down at her chili cheese fries and double cheeseburger. "I might share a few fries."

"Ha," Andrea says. "Don't count on it."

They enjoy the food and the moment of peace for only a few minutes when a frisbee whizzes over and smacks Scott in the back of the head.

"Sorry!" a girl shouts.

A man dressed in the tiniest shorts imaginable sprints over. "Sorry mate. She's new at this."

Scott turns and waves. "All good."

The tiny shorts man snaps and points to Scott then to Andrea. "You're Scott and Andrea, right?"

Silvey drops her fry. "Who are you?"

"Nate, I did a bid for their roof."

Silvey tilts her head to the side. "Are you part of the Stanberry crew?"

"No," Nate says. "I'm a new contractor in the northland."

Silvey nods. "And you just remembered their faces?"

"Silvey," Andrea says. "I remember meeting with him."

"Oh, good," Silvey says, smiling. "Sorry, we've had a few trying days with strangers."

"No problem," Nate says. "Sorry again about the head shot."

"All good," Scott says.

Nate waves and jogs back over to the girl.

"Silvey Lynn," Andrea says.

"What?" Silvey asks over a full mouth.

"You can't possibly know every contractor in the area."

"I know," Silvey says, wiping the corner of her mouth and holding up her hand. "But did you see the size of those shorts?" She holds her fingers an inch apart. "No contractors I know would be caught dead in tiny shorts in public."

Baxton chokes on a bite and laughs. "They were pretty tiny."

Scott feels the back of his head. "I think he got one neighbor down the street to sign. You can go and inspect his work."

Silvey looks around Scott to the two playing with the frisbee. "Maybe."

254

"Are you always suspicious?" Baxton asks, lifting an eyebrow.

"Call it a post trauma response," Silvey says.

Andrea attempts to snag a fry from Silvey and is swatted away. "Hey."

"Ask first."

"Silvey, may I please have a fry?"

"No," Silvey says.

Scott and Baxton laugh and point at Andrea's mouth hanging open.

"Just playing," Silvey says. "Go ahead."

"Rude!" Andrea says, snagging a few fries.

"I know," Silvey says, winking at Baxton. "How do you like my true colors?"

Baxton's cheeks reddened. "I am pretty sure you could still be in clown mode, and I would still be over the moon."

40

General Hall stands at attention in front of Admiral Tyson.

"At ease," Admiral Tyson says. "Sit down."

General Hall sits in the chair across the desk from Admiral Tyson.

"We've reviewed the latest reports from your lab," Admiral Tyson says, tapping the folder in front of her. "It's truly unbelievable."

"Trust me," General Hall says, nodding. "I made them run the test several times before I could wrap my head around it."

"Although, the nanoparticles delivery system is finite," Admiral Tyson says.

"Yes, but they are testing silica and polymeric nanoparticles to replicate the material lost during use."

"Hmm," Admiral Tyson says, leaning back. "I believe that theory was tested in the early nineties and failed."

"Yes, but with the samples collected our lead bioengineer believes we have a chance of reproduction."

"Belief and fact are two far ends of the spectrum. Especially now, with every major pharmaceutical and biotech company aware that this technology exists. The race to find an answer may expand beyond your team."

"You can't," General Hall says.

"Excuse me?"

"I mean, ma'am, this technology belongs to the US government. We can't release any specs to outside vendors."

"It's a little late," Admiral Tyson says. "The data breach your department suffered leaked enough information to prompt nine highly funded research labs into a bidding war for a single particle that the civilians dangled like a cherry during the live interview."

"They wouldn't dare," General Hall says.

"They didn't," Admiral Tyson says. "Our intel says it came from inside your team."

"What are you saying?" General Hall asks.

"A consultant at the base took and sold a particle to a team in Zurich."

General stands. "Who! That's treason!"

"They did," Admiral Tyson says. "They hand delivered it an hour ago."

"They who?"

"Jimmy Ladvig."

"The hacker?"

"You let a hacker near the base?" Admiral Tyson asks.

"He was there when I landed!" General Hall says.

"Your team, your head on the block."

"Admiral."

"General Hall," Admiral Tyson says. "You are on leave pending further review."

"You're serious?" General Hall asks.

Admiral Tyson nods. "We've scheduled a closed session to review Captain Darryl Wilson's service and involvement with Project Rainbow. You'll be subpoenaed to testify. Expect that soon."

"Ma'am," General Hall says, holding up a hand. "Wait."

"You're dismissed."

"But—" General Hall says.

Admiral Tyson stands. "You're dismissed."

General Hall frowns.

Admiral Tyson raises an eyebrow.

General Hall turns and marches out of the office. He dials Director Gia.

"General," Director Gia answers.

"Did you know?"

"I received a call about thirty minutes ago," Director Gia says. "I've been told to cut communications with you until after you've been reinstated."

"Oh, no you don't," General Hall says.

"I have orders, sir. Have a good day."

General Hall looks at his phone. "She hung up on me?"

"Sir," a man says. "I've been asked to escort you off property."

General Hall looks the young man up and down. "I don't need an escort, Officer Thorne."

"Just following orders," Officer Thorne says, gesturing to the elevator. "Are you parked below or out front?"

"Below," General Hall says.

They step onto the elevator, and Officer Thorne presses the parking level button. As the doors begin to close Agent Vickers waves to General Hall from just outside Admiral Tyson's office.

"Son of a …" General Hall mutters, throwing his arm out to stop the door.

"What are you doing?" Officer Thorne asks.

General Hall charges towards Agent Vickers just as Admiral Tyson's door opens. General Hall stops immediately.

"What is she doing here?" General Hall asks, pointing at Agent Vickers.

"That is none of your business," Admiral Tyson says, nodding to Officer Thorne. "Take him to his car."

"You two were in on this?" General Hall points from her and to Admiral Tyson.

Agent Vickers smiles. "Bye."

258

41

"Mom," Silvey says, closing the front door. "Are you home?"

"Upstairs," Evelyn says. "What's going on?"

"I need to grab a few things before I head back to Baxton's place."

Evelyn comes to the top of the stairs. "So, this is actually happening?"

"What do you mean?" Silvey asks, stopping on the second to last step.

"You and Baxton are officially moving in together?"

"Yes," Silvey says, moving past her mom to her nearly empty bedroom. "We've been over this."

"But it's only been a few months."

"It's been over a year," Silvey says, holding up her left hand. "And we are engaged."

"Then why do you keep calling it Baxton's place and not our place?"

"Because our place isn't ours for another week," Silvey says, throwing a few items from the dresser into a bag. She looks up. "I thought you liked Baxton."

"I do. It just happened so quickly after…"

"After dad passing?" Silvey asks.

Evelyn nods.

"He gave Baxton his blessing."

"I know," Evelyn whispers.

"Even more reason to not wait," Silvey says. "Life is too short."

Evelyn forces a smile.

"Plus, now you can bring your dates back to your place."

Evelyn swats Silvey on the arm. "Stop that. You know I am single and happy."

"The first part, sure. The last part, debatable."

Evelyn rolls her eyes.

"Please, just try to be happy for me. I love him and the life we are building together. And his family is amazing."

Evelyn nods. "You're all the family I have left."

"And I am fifteen minutes away." Silvey hugs her mom.

"I know." Evelyn sighs and squeezes Silvey. "You've got a stack of mail on the table in the kitchen."

"Thanks, mom."

Silvey releases her. "Have you heard when they are going to set dad's stone?"

"They said it would be another week."

"Let me know," Silvey says, checking the remaining drawers. "I think I've got everything essential from the house."

Evelyn's phone rings from the other room. "Don't forget your mail."

"I won't. Love you."

"Love you too."

Silvey looks around her bare bedroom with only a mattress and box spring pushed to the corner of the room. She lifts the mattress and finds an envelope with familiar handwriting. *Open on your wedding day.*

"Oh dad," Silvey says, holding the envelope to her chest. "I promised I wouldn't cry today." She wipes a single tear and jogs downstairs to the kitchen. "That's a giant pile of mail."

Silvey sorts through the pile and chucks the political and sales ads. She stuffs the rest in her bag.

"Bye mom!" Silvey shouts on her way back out to her blue truck.

The dealership came through on their offers of a new truck, including a new ride for the captain.

Darryl about fell over when he saw the sticker price and the taxes involved. But the government owned up to their abandonment after months of back and forth in a closed session with pentagon officials and a few members of congress. He was awarded back pay with interest for the sixty years of service and a post-retirement promotion to General. This decision sent General Hall over the edge during the session and got him demoted.

Silvey tosses her bag up and in the cab. She grabs the door handle and hops in.

The evening sun hits her ring, and a halo of light dances around the cab. She grins.

Baxton surprised her three months ago with a trip to Florida. Silvey met Baxton's dad and new wife before they sailed away on a chartered sailboat. It was their second night on board when he popped the question and he nearly dropped the ring in the ocean.

Silvey knew it was coming because Andrea made her get a manicure with a threat to not screw them up before the trip. It was a success. Silvey's nails looked great in the engagement shots that the captain took on board.

Silvey checks the time and does the mental math before dialing Andrea's number.

"It's late," Andrea answers. "Are you ok?"

"It's eleven there, right?" Silvey asks.

"Almost midnight in Austria."

"Sorry, but I got another Buzz bomb."

Andrea clears her throat. "You found another note?"

"Under my mattress at mom's."

"Dang. Did you open it?"

"No, it said do not open until my wedding day."

"Oh," Andrea whispers.

"Right," Silvey says.

"He was clever," Andrea says. "Are you going to wait?"

"Yes," Silvey says. "I don't want his spirit haunting me for not following his instructions."

"You know he was high on morphine when he threatened that, right?"

"Yes," Silvey says, turning. "But I don't need that energy in the new place."

"Still closing next week?"

"Yes," Silvey says. "I still can't believe I can add homeowner to my list of accomplishments."

Andrea laughs. "You literally bought the farm."

"Hey, now. We got a hell of a deal on the old Clevenger farm. Plus, Roz and Gage are just on the other side of the creek."

"Jealous," Andrea says. "Did you convince Baxton to start from scratch?"

"We compromised," Silvey says. "We are going to rebuild on the foundation, but we are keeping a few of the beams and doors that were still in great condition."

Andrea yawns. "We've got flights scheduled in a month. Do you need me to come sooner?"

"No," Silvey says. "You've just moved. Settle in and enjoy the expat life."

"Ha," Andrea says. "With me, myself, and I. Scott is too busy to explore much. His work partners have dinner plans to introduce their spouses. Fingers crossed, I can find at least one that is up for a little mischief and mayhem."

"Hey now," Silvey says. "There is no way you can replace me my friend."

"Tell that to Roz," Andrea says.

Silvey laughs. "You know I just might. We are having margaritas tonight."

"Ugh. Hanging up now. Good night."

"Night," Silvey says, pulling up to Baxton's place and parking next to his black truck. She grabs her bag and hops out.

Baxton opens the front door. "We've got mail." He holds up an envelope.

"I've got an entire stack to go through from my mom's. Is it addressed to both of us?"

"No, but I would bet a few million that you have an identical one in the stack."

Silvey's eyes widen.

"Yep," Baxton says, grinning from ear to ear.

Silvey hurries inside and unzips the bag. She sets the stack of mail on the coffee table. "What am I looking for?"

He shows her the envelope he received.

She digs through the pile until she finds one that matches. "Open now?"

"Yes!"

Baxton and Silvey open the envelopes and pull out their final settlement with a copy of a check.

"I still can't believe it," Silvey says. "Eighteen million dollars."

"Each," Baxton says.

"It's crazy," Silvey says. "The price for two vials of blood every year for ninety years."

"All for the sake of science," Baxton says, sticking his chin out.

Silvey rolls her eyes. "Right, science."

Baxton scoops her up and swings her around before crashing on the couch.

Silvey squeals and snuggles against him. "You know I am not a little doll?"

Baxton chuckles. "I know...just my tiny firecracker of mayhem."

Silvey leans away from him. "Were you listening to my call with Andrea?"

Baxton frowns. "No. Why?"

Silvey shakes her head. "Tiny coincidence."

Acknowledgements

To my readers, thank you for your patience. This book was a new challenge for me as a writer. The setting for this book, like Who Is Maggie and Twisting Hercules, included many familiar landmarks in or near my hometown. I enjoyed the walk down memory lane and was happy to include a few more local spots. But the challenge was the ending. How did I do? Scratch that. Maybe don't tell me.

And thank you to my husband, Arti. He's the first to read and one of my toughest critics, but also my biggest fan. He's also agreed to sit and record the male characters for the audiobook. A challenge we'll endure together. He's becoming quite the pro.

About the Author

Kim Malaj lives on a vineyard and homestead in northern Albania with her husband, Arti, author of Northern Albanian Folk Tales, Myths and Legends. Although she is a Show Me State (Missouri) lady at heart, she loves her daily life at Homestead Albania.

When she's not writing, she's got a camera in her hands, shooting the garden, orchard, vineyard, and livestock. She's also been known to brew up batches of raki and wine, and other sweet and savory treats made from the fruits and veggies picked fresh from the garden. She is an avid photographer, an active blogger about the homestead, and a hobbyist drone pilot, learning the art of aerial photography and filming.

Visit her blog: www.HomesteadAlbania.com
For the latest publishing news: www.KimMalaj.com